"A superb collection—full of ___ tun's superpower is to reliably conjure from a variety of elements something unexpected and unsettling. There is magic in these stories. She might be a witch; she's most definitely a writer. Hugely enjoyable and highly recommended."

KAREN JOY FOWLER, author of *Wit's End*

"Who can resist murderous garden gnomes on a sacrilegious crusade, or zombie tourism in L.A., or the troubled life of a sentient message? Not me! Emily Skaftun's collection of stories is a delight, inspired zaniness with a knife hidden in the middle. Read it, and you will never view—as just one example—Teddy bears the same way again."

NANCY KRESS, author of *The Eleventh Gate* and *Sea Change*

"Each of the 18 disquieting pieces in Skaftun's debut collection twist reality into absurdity and are united in their exploration of death and the afterlife. Skaftun's stories set up everyday objects and events, and spin them into the realm of the surreal... thoughtful explorations of wildly unusual concepts will keep fans of literary chills hooked. Eerie, unsettling, and occasionally zany, this philosophically minded collection offers a delightful diversion."

PUBLISHERS WEEKLY

"Surreal dreaming on the fly. Killer garden gnomes, roller-derby, frozen heads, sex in the snow. Fresh, sinister, fey, punk. In a note on one literary, feelings-based story, Skaftun remarks, 'It needed dinosaurs.' She brings on the dinos and more. The most fun you'll have this year."

RUDY RUCKER, author of *The Ware Tetralogy*

LIVING FOREVER & OTHER TERRIBLE IDEAS

LIVING FOREVER & OTHER TERRIBLE IDEAS

Emily C. Skaftun

One apocalypse down,
? to go!

emily skaf—

FAIRWOOD PRESS · BONNEY LAKE, WASHINGTON

LIVING FOREVER & OTHER TERRIBLE IDEAS
A Fairwood Press Book
November 2020
Copyright © 2020 Emily C. Skaftun

FIRST EDITION

Fairwood Press
21528 104th Street Court East
Bonney Lake, WA 98391
www.fairwoodpress.com

COVER IMAGE:
Dance of Death from the *Nuremberg Chronicle*; public domain,
https://commons.wikimedia.org/w/index.php?curid=490534

COVER & BOOK DESIGN:
John D. Berry

ISBN: 978-1-933846-98-9
First Fairwood Press edition November 2020
Printed in the United States of Ameria

For Mom. If anyone could have made living forever a not-terrible idea, it was you.

Contents

Introduction | Tim Powers

THE TERM "Absurdist fiction" sounds forbiddingly academic, calling to mind Ionesco and Pinter and even Kafka, but science fiction has produced some lively examples of it, from the ironic but relatively shallow stories of Robert Sheckley to such genuinely affecting novels as Vonnegut's *Sirens of Titan* and Philip K. Dick's *Galactic Pot Healer.*

The best absurdist fiction doesn't just baffle and amuse—if it's *convincingly* absurd, it gets past the reader's surface attention and delivers an unexpected punch.

It seems oxymoronic, but one of the painful things about the characters in Emily C. Skaftun's stories is that they never lose hope! Even when crushed by overwhelming disasters, they see, or imagine they see, a chance. You admire their unbowed determination, even as you cringe for them.

Another thing her characters don't lose, amid their spectacular travails, is love and loyalty. Reincarnation is a reality in many of these stories, so even death isn't an insurmountable separation. And they do try with all their strength to surmount it, and then keep on trying. These are not fatalistic antiheroes.

Skaftun deals in the stuff of nightmares. As in real nightmares, the situations in her stories are often preposterous — animate toys and lawn decorations, jocular talking fish, invading aliens with wheels for feet who are captivated by the phenomenon of roller derby — but the earnestly striving humanity of her characters, even the non-human ones, forbids you to dismiss them with a laugh or an impatient shake of the head. Skaftun knows no more science than Ray Bradbury did, but, as with Bradbury, the sheer unrelenting force of her imagination makes that irrelevant, and reminds the reader that the strength of science fiction is to give characters problems—often literally shattering problems!—that comparatively merciful reality spares us.

In spite of all that, I don't mean to give the impression that her stories are gloomy! As with Vonnegut and Dick, there's generally a bright vein of deadpan wit sustaining her characters. And it's earned wit, not gratuitous quips and wisecracks—it's gallows humor in the shadow of the gallows.

The one trick any story has to do is convince the reader that the events are really happening, in real places, to real people—or to real sentient creatures, anyway. This is difficult enough even in mainstream fiction, but in science fiction and fantasy it's especially challenging. And in stories like "Diary of a Pod Person," "Frozen Head #2,390," and "Oneirotoxicity"—to choose three examples almost at random—Skaftun takes one impossibility and then mercilessly extrapolates the consequences of it, with the sort of logical peripheral details that let a reader vicariously experience the events of the story, rather than just note them. You wind up believing, for the duration of the story, at least, some awfully outlandish things, and caring about the characters enmeshed in them.

You'll come away from these stories with some odd new furniture in your subconscious—and you'll find that it definitely livens up the décor.

LIVING FOREVER & OTHER TERRIBLE IDEAS

Melt With You

EVEN AFTER BEING REINCARNATED as a plastic lawn flamingo, Irma still insisted that the scruffy panhandler on the I-95 off-ramp near our house had been Jesus. "We missed him," she'd say, painted beak opening to reveal a mouth that did not lead to a windpipe or vocal chords or lungs. "We mistreated Jesus again and now we're doomed." Sometimes she got so agitated she'd gallop around on her two skinny metal legs until she fell over and it took both of us pushing and pulling with our beaks to right her.

And then I'd shake my long plastic neck and sigh. It was useless trying to explain to her that *Jesus* and *reincarnation* were from mutually exclusive religions. And anyway she was right about the second part: we were definitely doomed.

The gnomes were coming.

A little bird told me about it. His name was Jay and before the apocalypses he'd been our mailman. Now he was a blue jay. I shit you not, and not only because I am now made of plastic and incapable of shitting. But no matter how much we all giggled about it, Jay the blue jay had the last laugh, because he'd been reincarnated into a living being. Cindee, a one-time yoga instructor who was now a stone Buddha, said Jay must have been better than all of us in his last life. He was alive. Alive and able to fly.

And on a recent flight Jay had spotted an army of garden gnomes cutting a swath through what used to be an affluent Florida neighborhood, burning houses with cities' worth of toys and action figures inside, spreading poison for the remaining rats and birds and insects, smashing anything smashable that might have a soul in it, and generally making a mess of things. Their advance was slow, but they were relentless. Some of them even had weapons, axes and other tools they'd been carrying when they were inanimate lawn decoration, or improvised slingshots and flamethrowers made of cast-off barbecue lighters and aerosol solvents.

Not only could Irma and I not fly away on our pink plastic wings—they barely peeled away from our bodies—I could hardly even hop. The body that God or Buddha or Cthulhu or whoever had seen fit to shove my soul into had only one skinny metal leg.

Jay warned us as he flew by, ducking into the broken windows of all the houses to warn the souls inside. And then he was gone, a blue dot against the always-cloudy sky, and those of us in the yard looked at each other with as much panic as our various inhuman faces could convey, which wasn't much. But we felt it.

After a beat Chip the ceramic frog started hopping away. His legs worked better than I thought they had a right to, considering how useless my wings were, and he made decent time through the jungle of overgrown grass that had been a lawn. "He's right!" another frog said, and most of the other amphibians and small mammals hopped and lurched after him.

"No," twittered a weather-worn bird. "We should hide. They'll never find us all."

Some of the small critters paused then, a painted stone squirrel looking between factions much like a live one would have. It occurred to me, not for the first time, what a tacky neighborhood this had been. Even with some of the lawn art broken beyond repair, we were quite the menagerie.

Irma looked to me for an answer, just as she had in life. I tried to shrug, before remembering I didn't have the shoulders for it.

"You should run," I said to her, twining my neck around hers by way of goodbye. "You have two legs, sort of; I think you've got a chance. As for me, I can't outrun the gnomes, and I sure as a pink flamingo can't hide from them. I guess I'm gonna fight."

But Irma shook her head, which with that new neck of hers was quite the maneuver. "I'll stay with you, Bubby. We fight."

———

As it turned out, we only had about half an hour to prepare. We managed to contact some of the inhabitants of the house, about a million precious little ceramic figurines and human- and animal-shaped candles that had probably been the pride of the house's owner. Most of them were so small it would take them all day to cross a room, but there were a few stuffed animals that were pretty mobile, and they helped us get the supplies we needed to mount a defense of the property. They also sent an envoy into the attic, where a taxidermied jackalope stood watch for us.

A great many of the fleeter of us did choose to flee, but when the jackalope cried its shrill rabbit's wail, the rest of us took up arms.

The battle was bloodless. Many were killed.

Despite being made of concrete or whatever, gnome axes cut right through other stone beings. I watched as friends shattered, cleaved by those weapons or hit with slingshotted debris. A few pebbles hit me hard enough to dent, but they only knocked me over. I started to feel guilty about leading the menagerie into battle, when I was so much more shatterproof than most of the rest.

Our side gave as well as we got, for a while. We'd made very decent slingshots by staking fallen tree branches into the ground and stringing rubber bands between them. Irma and I even turned our own selves into a slingshot: she flipped over so her two metal legs were in the air and I used my beak to fire projectiles at the invading gnomes. We had pretty good aim, if I do say so, shattering quite a few gnomes with high-velocity nuts and bolts. The teddy bears from the house helped by shoving whatever heavy and seemingly inanimate things they could lift out the windows onto the gnomes' pointy heads.

It was tough selecting projectiles in this new world, and we'd gone back and forth a lot about whether it was right to use bolts, or throw lamps and heavy tomes. One of the bears thought that everything had a soul now, anthropomorphic or not, and that to use anything was wrong. I tended to disagree. Once again, Cindee had settled it, saying that without a face there was no soul. She was Buddha, so we had to believe her.

So I was crouching on my one stupid leg, holding a lugnut in my plastic beak and tugging against the rubber band, sighting through Irma's legs trying not to imagine how obscene her pose would be if she were still human, thinking the battle was going pretty well.

And then the flamethrowers came out. A big gnome with a cross painted on his red pointed cap came at us. "In Jesus' name!" he shouted, and with the click of a big lighter unleashed hell. Flames shot from a nozzle in every direction, catching the grass and weeds on fire. The stone and ceramic animals rallied, trying to stomp out the spreading fire. A cherubic angel that had once held a birdbath had some success, being the largest. But Irma and me, we started to feel a little droopy.

"Come on!" I shouted, dropping the lugnut. I wished I had arms, hands, anything to reach out to her with. She struggled to right herself, flailing her metal legs in the air. I'd dropped the rubber band, but it was still stuck around her legs, and her neck seemed to be caught under her. I nipped at her with my plastic beak, but couldn't get ahold of anything. And then, stomping through the flames and the high grass like an action hero, the cross-headed gnome came at me. I was staring down the nozzle of a WD-40 can, with the meanest face you ever saw glaring at me over it.

I ran. Or rather, I hopped, as fast as my one spindly leg would take me, feeling the heat at my tail.

Flames roared as the house caught, and all I could hear over it as I fled were the thousand tiny screams of melting candles, and then the jackalope's anguished cry.

———

At some point, after the gnomes had moved on and the fires died down, while the remains of the house shuddered and smoked, I hopped sheepishly back toward the yard I'd lived in since the apocalypses.

It was a wasteland. What had been overgrown grass was now blackened. The trees were singed, and the house was rubble. All around were shards of friends and foes, chips of cement and ceramic that had broken apart. The cherub's huge water dish lay upside-down atop a pair of cracked red gnome feet that stuck out from the thing like ruby slippers beneath a fallen house.

"Irma!" I shouted, knowing it was hopeless. No one was going back to Kansas.

Cindee hobbled out from behind a singed tree. Because she was a seated Buddha she had no feet. "She's gone," she said. Cindee led me in her limping gait to the last place I'd seen Irma. Amid the char and ash was a dirty pink puddle with two metal spires sticking up out of it like an old-fashioned TV antenna.

If I'd had knees, I'd have fallen onto them. Cindee put one stone hand on my flank. "You mustn't weep for her; she's in a new form now."

"If the gnomes are right she's dead."

"The gnomes are *not* right. Her soul is free now."

I looked up at her and the serenity on her ever-smiling face bugged the hell out of me. "You know you're not really Buddha, right?" I snapped. "You're not even Buddh*ist*, are you? Not anymore than off-ramp guy was Jesus or I'm the pope."

"Aren't you Jewish?" Cindee asked mildly.

And then I was laughing. "I haven't been to temple since my Bar Mitzvah. Irma and I went to Unitarian church a few times."

A pair of singed teddy bears sidled up behind me. "Would you like to bury her?"

I nodded my long neck, almost laying it on the ground. Out of the corner of my eye I saw the cherub searching dead gnomes, and before long he came up with a shovel. He was kind enough to dig the hole for me, and when it was done Cindee said a few words about the soul's eternal nature. After that the survivors milled around for a bit, unsure what to do. There were only a handful of us: the two teddy bears, Rocky and Rowan; a few of the tiny figurines from the house; a tailless stone squirrel; and about half of a plastic barn owl that had been wired to the roof. The fire had freed her, but also melted her legs. She hobbled around using her wings like a pair of too-short crutches. Most of the dead were in so many pieces that burial seemed a futile task. But I was glad everyone had helped me with Irma's remains.

For the first time since the apocalypses, I felt really adrift. Part of me hoped the gnomes, in their insane religious crusade, *were* right. If our souls could be killed, then maybe we could all finally go to heaven.

I said one more prayer over Irma's grave: "Jesus, Shiva, Allah, Flying Spaghetti Monster, Yahweh, whoever's out there. Give Irma's spirit peace, and let us one day meet again."

We found Rowan the next morning, cut to shreds.

We'd been adrift that night, each seeking a reason to go on and a place to go on in. Being inanimate, we didn't need food or water or shelter. We didn't sleep, so the nights were long. That one, without Irma, was the longest of my life or my afterlife. I'd hopped to the very edge of the lawn, where the cracked pavement began, and stood there looking into the scorched neighborhood for a long time. Standing on pavement was really hard for me, but I thought about trying to leave, crawling if I had to, to find a new home.

In the end I didn't. I hopped back toward the house but stopped dead when I saw Rowan. It was an explosion of stuffing that dotted our charred lawn like snow. Strips of his brown faux fur were mixed in, and I stood there wondering what sort of animal could have done this—most of them had died along with the humans—when I found his head. Half of it anyway, the left side of his face from nose to ear. The stuffing was still attached, but the eyeball wasn't. In its place, stabbed all the way through the head, was a long, sharp shard of ceramic. I leaned my long neck toward it and when I saw what it was I screamed like the jackalope.

The shard was a broken gnome leg.

My screams drew the attention of the others, who scrambled over as fast as their various locomotion would carry them. Rocky wailed when he saw, beating the blackened ground with furry fists. It struck me once again how the reincarnation machine had grouped us together, me and Irma, Rocky and Rowan. We hadn't known them well before the apocalypses, but they'd lived in the neighborhood. We all had. So where had the gnomes come from? They were united by their psychotic belief in the true Christian apocalypse, the crusade they'd undertaken to kill everyone on earth to bring it about. I'm not sure what made them think the souls whose unusual bodies they eliminated didn't just come back as someone else.

We burned the rest of Rowan's body on a pyre made of broken house. While smoke still curled into the air I saw a blue speck that grew and resolved into Jay the blue jay. He circled the house and yard slowly before alighting on top of the overturned bird-bath with the crushed gnome underneath. Still looking around in his new, flighty way, Jay whistled. But it wasn't birdsong, it was one of those long "look how messed up this shit is" whistles.

I glared at him. I couldn't help it. The little bastard could've helped us, but he'd flown.

"You broke a lot of gnomes," he said.

It was true. Pieces of gnomes were scattered all around us, from shards barely visible to whole hands or feet. "Yes," I said, feeling a little defensive. "We fought them." After I said it I re-membered that my fighting had been less than courageous, and if I hadn't been bright pink already I swear even my plastic self would have blushed.

No one seemed to notice. Jay continued: "They seem mad about it."

"What are you talking about?" Cindee asked, squinting her serene face.

In response, Jay flew up in the air a few feet. When he dropped back down he landed on the cherub's head and immediately pooped on it. He gestured all around us with one wing. "They left you a message."

The cherub stopped swatting at his head and looked around. He was by far the tallest of us, and I could tell from the look on his face he'd seen what Jay was talking about. He was made of bleached concrete, but the way his fat cheeks slackened made him look even paler. "It's a cross," he said.

"The pieces *moved?*" asked Rocky, perking up from his mourning. His black eyes looked wider than usual.

"They can't move," Cindee said. "They're dead. Their souls have moved on into new hosts."

I was standing as high as I could on my one leg — actually, everyone was trying to stretch upward — to try to see the effect Jay and the cherub had. I couldn't really make it out, so I hopped to the nearest piece of gnome and peered at it with one eye at a time. "Actually it's worse than that," I said. "Obviously the gnomes have come back. The survivors, I mean."

"Oh god," Rocky said. "We're all gonna die."

I thought he was probably right. But we'd all died before, and it hadn't been so bad.

I hopped down the length of the cross, following a trail of gnome bits. There was no pattern to it that I could see. A foot here, a chunk of torso there, a scrap of pointed hat. It was creepy as hell, looking at all those body parts. The eyes seemed to follow me.

Then I got to one fragment of gnome head that contained the thing's whole mouth. It wasn't much more than that — a half-inch-thick slab of face and chin with a pair of lips painted on. I wouldn't have even noticed it, really.

Until it started talking. "Your end is at hand," it said, lips moving. Another fragment a few inches away blinked its eye, pupil swiveling toward me. The eyes really *were* following me.

I jerked my head away from it as quickly as I could. The other survivors reacted predictably, with panic and frantic movement. They ran and hopped and scooted, but not knowing which way the danger was coming from they largely went in circles.

I scanned the horizon for colorful pointy hats, but I didn't see anything.

"In the name of the father!" the mouth shouted, and I backed away so fast I fell right on my tail. I was scrambling away using my stupid metal leg and my stumpy wings, and not getting very far at all, when the gnome pieces began to rise. I don't know how they did it, since even if they were still imbued with spirit, most of the chunks had no physical way of moving, but they came together into a sort of Frankenstein's monster of pottery. Maybe it really was god's will.

Before I knew it there were many of them, surrounding me. I had nothing to use as a weapon, nowhere to run. I couldn't even get up on my foot, as it were.

I wish I could say the last thing I remember was the gnome's club coming toward my head, the beast's self-righteous, seamed grimace. But I remember the whole thing. I had no brain to concuss, no lights to go out. And whatever was creating my consciousness, it wasn't going to let me off that easily.

On the other hand, it didn't really hurt either, with no nerves. The first blow squished my head, and I guess it must have wiped the paint off my right eye, because after that I couldn't see out of it. The gnome pounded me until I felt as flat as roadkill. And all the while, out of my left eye, I watched friends shatter.

Some time after the gnomes left I picked myself up and looked around. It wasn't easy. The gnomes had pulled out my metal leg and used it to skewer Rocky. They'd also dented me all over, and part of my neck was so thin that the weight of my plastic head made it droop.

But I saw right away that I was the only one left. The others had been brittle; they had broken. Rocky the teddy bear had gone the way of Rowan. I couldn't see the plastic half barn owl at all.

The worst part was the secret the gnomes had taught me: the fact of eternal life. It horrified me to think that the shards of my friends might still have consciousness, trapped in whatever powerless form they had left. The thought of Irma tormented me. She'd been melted into a shapeless blob of plastic with no eyes, no ears, no limbs, no mouth to scream. And then I'd buried her.

The gnomes' behavior didn't make any sense, in light of their ability to re-form and keep on going. If they knew that these forms we now inhabited were deathless, then why had they tried to kill us? I could only hope that they really had been divinely animated, and that my friends and family wouldn't be. But in order to believe in that I had to believe in god, and those days were long, long behind me.

It took me a damn long time, broken as I was. First I had to gather the things I'd need, and they were hard to find in the wasteland the property had become. Then I needed to dig up my Irma. The gnome's shovel was still where we'd dropped it, but it was hell to wield it without any hands. In the end I gave up and dug with my pathetic wings, one scraping millimeter at a time. But what did I have but time? I didn't need to stop for food or sleep; I didn't have muscles to fatigue. So I didn't rest until I'd uncovered my love.

She was at the bottom of a shallow hole, a dingy pink puddle of plastic with two metal legs still sticking out at odd angles. God, I hoped she wasn't in there. But if she was, it was where I wanted to be. I dropped my own mangled body on top of hers, then doused us both with the little bottle of lighter fluid I'd found.

"I'm coming, Irma," I said.

And then I lit a match.

STORY NOTES:

Garden gnomes have been following me since I wrote this story in 2013.

It was originally written for an anthology I was asked to submit to called *Yard Gnomes of the Apocalypse*, a prompt that I clearly took very literally. The story poured out of me in just a couple days, in a frenzy of sacrilege and giggling, and when I ran it past my writing group they told me it deserved to be published in a market with a larger readership, so I sent it to *Clarkesworld*.

But I still wanted to submit something to the anthology, so I wrote *another* creepy gnome story. My writing group started to make fun of me, so I swore I would write gnome more forever.

(The anthology never ended up being published, and that second story still hasn't seen the light of day. It wasn't as good as this one.)

But in 2014, I took a job as editor of a Norwegian newspaper, and guess who its mascot was? Nils Anders Wik, a century-old nisse who'd been enchanted by an evil cabinet-maker. He was a mostly benign sort of gnome. Mostly.

Diary of a Pod Person

THE FIRST BODY to slide out on one of Lab-14-H's morgue slabs was a chimp, and seeing its slack and frozen face startled me more than anything had since the accident. I jumped, and my new heart dropped a beat like a person stumbling off a curb. It was a giddily familiar sensation, so as soon as the shock wore off I smiled with genuine happiness—I'd been scared, physically scared. I acknowledged the feeling with joy.

I pushed the chimp back into the fridge, and opened the next drawer more gingerly. After a few more chimps—failed Kokos, I assumed—I found the corpse I was looking for.

If you've never looked at your own dead body on a slab, nothing I say about it can fully convey the feeling. I looked at the body for a long time without moving, without thinking, without feeling. I refused to think of it as *my* body.

The woman in the drawer had suffered a trauma; that much was obvious. Her long black hair was matted on the left against a skull dented out of round. Blood had been cleaned out of the abrasions and lacerations on her face, and they hung whitely open like dead mouths. But it wasn't just the violence that rendered the woman's countenance eerie.

"There's identical, and then there's *identical*," one of the other techs had told me on my first day at ExtraLives. "So we make chimps, and they look like Koko, right? But all chimps look the same, pretty much, anyway. So how can we tell?"

The body I was in now was printed from the same blueprint as this woman's, using the same DNA. But there's identical and there's *identical*. The blueprint was more of a sketch, with the details left to the builder. I'd noticed it immediately, of course. My new muscles hadn't been jogging for twenty years, so though the incubator had toned them to almost the right level, these legs tripped just walking down the hall. This body hadn't indulged in sea-salt potato chips a little too often; it was skinny. The lines on these fingers weren't the same as hers, were in fact barely lines at all, and these new retinas held divergent patterns. I'd had to convince a passing colleague to let me into this room, since the security door no longer recognized those signatures. Even our irises looked different: the color was the same, but the specific interplay of dark and light varied.

I spent what felt like hours with the other body, measuring and comparing and tallying up the differences. Some were quantifiable, like a half-inch difference in our heights, and my almost freakishly long pinky toes. Most were more subjective: both faces looked uncanny to me, the new and the old. But I knew enough about perception and mirror images to let that go.

There's identical, and then there's identical.

There was also the disturbing fact of the other woman's injuries. In addition to the skull fracture, there was a broken leg, a shoulder that would never again fit into its socket, and a number of smaller wounds. One bruise, on her back, looked almost like a handprint. It was hard to tell through the pooled blood under her skin. Overall she appeared as though she'd tumbled down a rocky slope, or fallen under a bus.

Or been pushed.

It occurred to me, not for the first time, that I'd been murdered. But the thought held no terror, not even anger. If I felt anything it was relief that the other me was actually dead. I didn't want two of us running around, and though I acknowledged that she had the better claim on our life, my loyalty was to me.

I am still not sure how to feel about that. I'm pretty sure the old me would be horrified.

My personal effects were in a pouch in the back of the drawer. The clothes were trash, but my shoes were okay and my purse was just as I remembered it. Keys, credit cards, sunglasses. Phone, with seven voice messages, thirty-one texts, and eighty-eight emails. Obviously ExtraLives hadn't told my family anything. They must be frantic with worry.

I tried to slip on the shoes, but they didn't fit anymore. My new feet were bigger in every dimension.

The only other thing was the necklace I'd been wearing, a plastic pendant with a tiny dried flower inside. A gift from Lucy. It felt smooth in my fingers; I would have recognized the object, even with these new fingers and their new lines, by touch alone. I tied it around my neck and the pendant hung in the same place against my sternum, and I remembered that my fingers used to find their way here all the time, an unconscious gesture that I supposed must have given me comfort. But it didn't anymore. I dropped my fingers and they hung at my side, purposeless.

———

A few months back, my Wellness Director had told me I'd smother Lucy if I didn't go back to work. I'd laughed, a little too fast, and joked about the situation. "You mean metaphorically, right?" I'd clutched the pendant that I always wore, a tiny pressed flower in plastic resin that Lucy had made in arts and crafts group.

I *remember* joking. I even remember what I felt then: anxiety and frustration and a kind of aimlessness that, if I'd been a word lover, I might have described as *ennui*.

The woman had scads of pictures up on her walls. Two children, two parents, dozens of perfect white smiles so huge they seemed unreal. White-water rafting trips and tropical vistas and artistic family portraits. Each one looked normal enough, but their sheer volume pointed toward some inner madness. I believed her without hesitation.

But I'd cashed in my workforce rotation when I had Lucy, and there was a long wait list for work. Even under Wellness Director's orders, and with my degree in animal behavior, my hopes were slim. You couldn't even volunteer at a soup kitchen more than once a week without using up your work vouchers, and I couldn't chance losing benefits.

I was watching Lucy run like a crazy monkey around a playground when ExtraLives called me. My daughter wore star-shaped sunglasses even though it was cloudy, and her hair was a tangled mess, and with every step I was sure she'd trip and there'd be blood and tears. Despite everything I know about cognitive development and learned helplessness, my fingers twitched toward her all the time. I wanted to keep her safe. I wanted to hold her to me, and comfort her and ohmygod, I was going to smother her. I *remember* that.

So I didn't hesitate when ExtraLives offered me an interview and then a position. I didn't even ask what ExtraLives did. I just called my mother and Lucy's father and my best friend and my brother and arranged a care schedule for Lucy. I just dusted off my old lab coat and went to work.

Not wanting to seem crazy, I decorated my desk with only one photograph of Lucy, a shot of her splashing her big red boots in gentle ocean waves. Against a backdrop of water and seagulls, she peers intently into the foam, poised with one foot ready to stomp.

On my first day at ExtraLives, after signing about a million documents I barely skimmed, I met Koko. Koko was a chimpanzee named by someone who was both uncreative and apparently unaware that the original Koko had been a gorilla. Like the original, though, Koko was a whiz at American Sign Language. Better than I was. Since Lucy had learned to speak, I'd been letting my ASL rust, and when I met Koko I told her so, haltingly. "You talk okay," she told me, and we shook hands. I longed to bring Lucy in to meet Koko; I wondered what they'd talk about and how they'd play. I could just imagine the two of them signing back and forth, both in star-shaped sunglasses. My hand fluttered to the pendant at my throat. I still *remember* it all.

Koko lived in a lab that looked like a nursery, along with her pet cat, a big black tomcat with white paws that Koko had named Feet. Koko was mellow for a chimp, but I was warned not to mess with Feet, not even to touch him if possible, lest I incur her wrath. The place smelled a little like cat and monkey, and two entire walls were one-way mirror, but overall it was a homey room, filled with toys and gadgets for Koko to play with.

There were many more like it, furnished but empty of primate and feline life.

After introducing me to Koko, my supervisor, Caleb, took me down a long dark hallway lined with nondescript doors. Each had a stenciled-on number and a door lock with a keypad, thumbprint sensor, and retinal scanner. My credentials had been established that morning, in a baffling ordeal of scans and medical procedures. But before Caleb let me try them out on Lab 14-C, he stopped me. He was grinning like a new dad on Christmas morning, like someone who's in on a fabulous secret.

"Are you ready to see what's behind the curtain? Are you ready for the red pill? And also do you remember that you signed an NDA?"

"Which one was the red pill?" I asked, as Caleb stepped aside.

I punched in my code, pressed my thumb to the plate above the keypad, and, pushing my glasses up into my hair, ducked down slightly to stare into the retinal scanner. A red flash stunned my left eye and then the door clicked and I hurried to paw the handle. I'd always been bad at opening those hotel doors with the credit-card-type keys, but this door swung right open, revealing a room full of machinery and tubes and vats and computer screens. In the center of the space was a raised platform with what looked like a large but shallow aquarium. It was empty now, and I could see that the sides were made to come apart and fold down. It also had a lid that could be lowered onto it but which currently hung suspended from the ceiling. All the tubes and wires and hoses terminated in that lid.

Caleb was right beside me, watching my confusion. I guess I wasn't seeing the lab's potential, because his face fell. I admit, I was slow. My first thought had been to wonder what they were doing to fish.

"I guess you really do have to see it in action to understand. Come on, I'll show you on one of our smaller models."

He led me down the hall to Lab 6-A, where the whole setup was repeated with an aquarium the size of a shoebox on a counter-height table. He went to a console and keyed in a series of commands too quick to follow. The machines whirred to life, LED lights blinking on and off. Coiled tubes jumped as something flowed through them into the little glass box. Soon it was filled with a thick clear liquid, and then I watched in awe as needles inside the box started moving like the jets of a printer and structures appeared.

It was a skeleton. A rodent, by the looks of it, and I guessed rat.

When its skull was only half built, another set of tiny fingers went to work laying down brain and eyes seemingly one cell at a time. This part took longer than any other step.

And then the skeleton was obscured by muscle and tendon and blood vessels and a thin layer of fat and then skin. It was definitely a rat, hairless and motionless, floating in the tank's goop.

"You made a rat," I said, intelligently.

The lid pulled away from the tank with a loud unclamping sound, and cables pulled it out of the way. Caleb stepped toward the tank and pulled the naked rodent out. He wore thick rubbery gloves, the type my mother had once worn to do dishes. And he was grinning from ear to ear. "*Copied* a rat, actually. Her name is Stella, and if this has gone right she's an exact copy of the original Stella, complete with the memories up to her last upload."

I remember the physical sensations of my stunned reaction. My pulse felt loud; my mouth went dry.

The rat hadn't so much as twitched a whisker. Or rather, twitched its nose. It had only the barest of stubble for whiskers. Caleb took it over to a small incubator box, where it was swaddled in circuit-printed canvas. "Is it alive?" I asked. My mind was boggling already, working out the implications and designing mazes to run Stella through.

"Sort of," he responded, setting some dials on the incubator and closing the door.

ExtraLives already had hundreds of clients who had signed up for immortal life. I could understand the appeal. To have a backup, to know that I'd always be around to love my Lucy; that was a powerful pull.

Caleb told me that the company had perfected the upload process. It was simple, non-intrusive, and accurate: an implant no bigger than the RFID chips in everyone's pets and children. Whenever the chip neared its base station, a tiny device that most people kept under their pillows, it sent the data to ExtraLives' storage facility. Clients uploaded themselves every night, in case they died in their sleep.

Of course, if they did die in their sleep that night, they were probably going to stay dead. The process of putting a person into his or her shiny new body hadn't been tested. The memory files couldn't even be verified; without a brain to read them the data were meaningless.

"Obviously human trials are a legal issue," Caleb said, eyes flicking in the general direction of a bowling trophy he kept on his desk. "The process hasn't yet been tested on anything more human-like than a cat." But that was where I came in.

I spent a few weeks getting to know Koko. Dr. Kim, the trainer I was replacing, had exhaustively catalogued Koko's vocabulary. There were endless hours of video documenting conversations they'd had and every other aspect of Koko's life: how she played with her toys, the way she petted Feet, how she laughed when tickled, when and where she usually slept.

Dr. Kim had also kept a kind of journal, which I was only partially able to decipher. It seemed to cover experiments she'd overseen, but parts of it were in a shorthand that reminded me of one of those vowel-hating Eastern European languages. More than once I wished I could call her up and ask about it, but Caleb made it clear she was not going to return. I couldn't even contact her on my own; her name was too common to google.

Copying Koko felt anti-climactic after all the buildup. We printed her in the first lab I'd visited, then she was swaddled by a large incubator for a few days while it toned her muscles, and then she was deposited, stubbly and a bit dazed, into one of the identical Koko habitats.

My job was to determine, in my expert opinion, whether the new Koko was identical to the first.

She was different in some trivial aspects: her hair and claws were still growing in, and her teeth were bright white. At first she was clumsy, but that wore off within a week.

She was the same in more ways than I could count. When introduced to her quarters she gave everything a solid sniffing but otherwise reacted to it with familiarity. She knew my name. I tested her over the following weeks and found that her vocabulary was intact, and seemingly so were her memories. I pestered her with questions about her life until she grew bored with me, and she knew the answer to every one. When she tired of these sessions, she puffed out her lips and lolled her head just like the first Koko had done.

This was good enough for Caleb and the rest of ExtraLives' executives. By the time Koko2's fur had fully grown in, they were uncorking champagne. No one but me was troubled by the fact that the new Koko hadn't so much as asked about Feet the cat. Curious what would happen, I snuck him away from Koko1 while she slept and brought him into Koko2's enclosure. She groomed him and stroked his head once, twice, just the same as the other Koko. Feet sniffed her in return, and then seemed to decide that all was well. Koko2 turned away and poked listlessly at the goofy felt teeth of a stuffed shark, and at Koko1's insistence I returned

Feet to her room. She snuggled him for an hour straight, him purring all the while. Koko2 didn't seem to mind his absence. Certainly, there was no wrath.

ExtraLives rewarded my success with a week's vacation on a tropical island I'd never heard of, at a resort with a three-year waiting list. Lucy and I spent every minute on the beach, all bare feet and sunglasses. I jogged each morning on the wet sand. She brought me every shell and ocean-smooth pebble for inspection, and even splashed around in the shallow reef with a snorkel, frightening off all the pretty fish with her childish enthusiasm. We walked in tide pools and I rambled about barnacles and starfish and hermit crabs. She loved the idea of a crab changing clothes, and collected all the shells she could find into a chic crustacean boutique. I tried to tell her it was more like an RV dealership than a shopping mall, but she didn't care. She just shook her head and squealed and lined up more shells.

I remember the feeling of the sun on my skin and the smell of water and wind and suntan lotion. I know that I was happy then, that I was full up with love and satisfaction.

Even though I knew better, I let Lucy bring a pocketful of beach findings home with her. On my first day back to work she pressed a pearl-pink shell into my hand and told me my office needed it, "so you can have a home with you." I put the shell next to her picture on my desk and smiled whenever I saw it, feeling at home with that little piece of her.

I do not remember the accident.

I woke in a hospital bed feeling weak and disoriented. The light stung my eyes, but the first thing I noticed as I stared up at the acoustic-tiled ceiling was how clear it seemed. I raised one hand to my face, but my glasses weren't on. My hand felt heavy.

Feeling too weak to sit up and get a better look around, I stared at my hand. My fingernails were shorter than I remembered, and the tan I'd earned on vacation had faded to a pasty shade that seemed paler than ever. *How long have I been asleep?* I wondered. But I wasn't afraid. In fact, I felt calm and little more than mildly curious.

Presently a doctor came in to check on me, and I managed to sit up in the bed. I could see him clearly from across the room. "What happened?" I asked. I looked down at my body, clad in its hospital gown, and it finally occurred to me to look for injuries. I turned my arms over and didn't see anything. Both my legs moved under the blanket.

"You've been in an accident," the doctor said.

And yet no part of me felt particularly painful. But perhaps I was heavily medicated. I felt my face again, and then up to my head.

I froze, realization setting in. Where my long hair had been there was only peach fuzz, perhaps a quarter-inch long.

"Have I?" I looked at my arms again, my hands. And this time I realized what had seemed off before: there was nothing there. The long white scar where I'd caught my arm on a jagged screen door, gone. The bumpy red knuckle I'd mangled with a cheese grater, smooth as a baby's. The half-brown, half-pink mole that had been just above my left elbow, gone. I still had a few moles on my arms, but like looking at the night sky on an alien planet, these constellations were unfamiliar.

"What happened to my body — my other body?" I asked, still feeling remarkably calm. It occurred to me that I ought to be upset. My heart should be racing. The little hairs that had barely grown in on my arms should be standing up in recognition of the eerie thing that had happened.

"I'm not sure I understand what you're saying," the doctor said. He babbled a lot of medical jargon and injected something into my IV. It made me sleepy, but after he left and before I drifted off I pulled up my hospital gown to check the skin of my new belly. As I suspected, I had no belly button. But what struck me even more was the absence of the pearly pink curves of my stretch-marks, leaving my skin clean and featureless as a beach under a receding wave.

I knew this loss should've hit me like a punch to the chest. I wanted to weep for it, but my new tear ducts wouldn't comply.

———

As it turned out, I wasn't in a hospital at all. My hospital-like room was in a wing of ExtraLives that hadn't been on the tour.

As soon as the doctor cleared me to go, I went straight to Caleb's office. My clothes and purse weren't with me, but some-one dug me up a pair of crisp blue scrubs to wear and I padded up and down hallways in my bare feet. I half expected to find my shoes and other effects in Caleb's office. I half expected to find my whole self waiting there, or working at my little desk.

But it was just him. "You know, you could have taken the rest of the day off. You're still recovering from your accident."

"I can't remember the accident," I told him. "Can you tell me what happened?" He'd lied to me, he'd violated my privacy in about twenty different ways, and maybe he'd even killed me, the first me. I tried to put some anger into my voice. "What sort of accident can erase all a person's scars, fix her myopia, and not involve any actual physical injury?"

Caleb's mouth performed a complicated dance of smile and smirk and guilt.

"Seriously, though. What happened to me? To the original me."

He climbed around his big desk, laden with trinkets and trophies, and found a spot on the front of it to lean on. His face was very close to mine now, but I saw no reason to back away. The excited look had returned, only now he wasn't a dad on Christmas morning; he was a kid. "What's the last thing you *do* remember?"

I sighed. "I remember sitting at my desk working on a report."

"Yes." He nodded, still staring at me creepily. "That's where your base station was set up. My god, you really do look just the same. Better, maybe."

"You must be very proud," I said. Was I being sarcastic? It *sounded* sarcastic, but I felt no venom, only annoyance with the way Caleb was staring at me. I looked past him, around the room, and noticed for the first time his bare walls. They were sponge-painted in red and gold, but held no art, no photographs. No photos on his desk either, only a menagerie of crystal and metal objects that all looked like they'd make terrific blunt weapons.

Caleb was still looking at me like a lab specimen. I swatted at his face, and he took the hint and backed up a bit. "You never told me you were uploading me. I didn't agree to it, and I don't remember getting an implant."

He shrugged. "You should have read your paperwork more carefully."

All the papers he'd shoved in front of me on my first day, when I was so grateful for employment that I would have signed anything. The intrusive scans they'd done ostensibly to get my retina and other biometrics on file. I still didn't remember being injected with anything, but the implants *were* very small.

What I did remember, suddenly, was that I'd taken this job so I could be a better mother to Lucy. Lucy, who I hadn't seen in — how long? That was the moment I recognized that something had gone wrong. I thought of Koko2's indifference to Feet, and saw it paralleled in my own new self's behavior. I knew I should want to rush home and wrap Lucy in my arms. But I felt no urgency. Sure, I wondered if she was all right. I hoped she was. I thought I would be sad if anything had happened to her.

"Where is my body?" I asked.

Caleb sighed. "Lab 14-H. I'll go with you." He stood to lead me from the room, but I waved him off.

"I'll go myself, thank you."

But I ended up needing help after all; my thumbprint and retina didn't match the ones on file and wouldn't open the door.

I stood staring at my dead body for a long while, my brain running through a complicated and somewhat recursive chain of thoughts. I was dead. I had possibly been murdered. But I was alive; I'd been copied. I was a copy, but I felt real. But I didn't *feel* with the intensity I had before.

I thought I should feel angry at Caleb for murdering me, but I really didn't. I guess it's hard to be upset about your own murder when you're alive. Or anyway, part of me figured that. The other part worried I was missing something, the same something as Koko2, the loss of which made me less than I'd been. But even my worried side wasn't too concerned. There was no urgency to the feeling of loss; in fact there was no *feeling* to it. I didn't feel wrong, but that was just more evidence that I was wrong, because I was unable to feel it.

I tried to think of all the things that had been important to me before. It was a short list, with Lucy at the top. So I asked myself if I still loved Lucy. I wanted to say that of course I did; it was like a reflex. But I wasn't sure. The only thing for it was to go right home and find out.

I got all the way there before realizing Lucy wasn't *at* my home. None of her other caretakers would have left her there alone. It had become springtime while I slept (for that is how I thought of it, despite knowing the more complicated truth), so I agreed to meet my Mom at Sunlight Beach Park to get Lucy from her. Mom was relieved to hear from me, but not as relieved as I expected. "I was so worried when I couldn't reach you last night," she said.

Last night? I thought. It had been almost three weeks since the last day I could remember.

"Yeah, I'm sorry," I replied. Because I still wasn't sure how to explain my absence, or my new shaved-head look, I offered no excuse. I just put on a sunhat and headed for the beach.

Mom and Lucy were sitting side-by-side on a beach blanket when I arrived. Mom stared straight out over the water, running sand through her fingers absently. Lucy was nominally building a sandcastle — she held her little shovel in one hand, with the pail set next to it — but she seemed preoccupied and kept looking around her. Still, she didn't see me until I was almost on top of them. I blame the sunhat.

When she did notice me, Lucy jumped right through her sandcastle and hugged me around the thighs as hard as her little arms could. I didn't even have time to kneel down to hug her properly. I settled for placing one hand on her head. Her hair was warm from the sun, but tangled and a little crunchy, as if she'd wet it with seawater and let it dry. My hand didn't linger.

Mom rose more slowly, and hugged me awkwardly over Lucy's head. "Where were you? I've been trying to reach you since Tuesday." And then she seemed to actually *see* me, and her eyes widened. "What happened to your hair?"

Lucy let me go and I stumbled. A breeze caught my stupid sunhat and tilted it back, revealing more of my baldness. "OMG!" Lucy exclaimed. "What *did* happen to your hair? Mommy? Where were you? I missed you!" And on and on in a sort of mantra of hyperactive need.

"Um," I began, more to Mom than Lucy. "Can we just call it an accident? They had to shave my head."

Mom leaned in close to look at it, humphed, and, still looking questioningly into my eyes, shrugged. I guessed we'd talk later.

Meanwhile, Lucy's excitement continued unabated. Now it was, "Mommy, look! Look what I learned in school today!" in-between flailing maneuvers that I guessed were cartwheels. The soft sand seemed to trip her, and she fell more often than not. Sand clung to her cheeks and elbows and curly, matting hair. I thought of the time I'd spend bathing her, combing out her tresses, and sweeping up the whole apartment after the sand got everywhere, and it all seemed like a chore. She did a cartwheel she was particularly proud of, then looked up at me, beaming, from a sandy crouch. "Mommy! Did you see?"

"Mmmm," I said.

And Lucy, who'd always been a sensitive child, tried for a moment to pretend she wasn't hurt. She wiped a lock of hair away from her forehead with her arm, turned toward the water — and started bawling. Her cheeks scrunched up and reddened, she wailed, and big hot tears welled up in her eyes. They streaked down her face, washing sand away with them like tiny flash floods.

"Oh, Lucy," I said. I knelt beside her and placed a hand on her back, but she squirmed away and kept crying. I sat next to Mom on the blanket, brushing sand away.

"What's wrong with you?" she hissed at me, then Mom knee-walked toward Lucy. Lucy turned to her and collapsed into a hug, burying her weeping face in her Gramma's shoulder. "It's okay," she told Lucy, until the girl seemed to believe it.

Finally her crying subsided into breathless gulps and she sat between us on the blanket, underneath the glares Mom was throwing me. I could sense Lucy's ambivalence toward me, as clear as day. When she remembered that I'd made her cry, that she was mad at me, she leaned toward Gramma. But the rest of the time she seemed pulled to me like a plant to sunlight. I knew she wanted my attention. I also knew that she'd never had to beg for it before. Wasn't this Lucy, the love of my life? Wasn't this little creature the reason I woke in the mornings and most of what I thought of in-between? Why hadn't I run to her like a cheetah after prey, swept her up and hugged her, spinning, with all my might? That's what the old me would have done. I knew it, because I *remembered* it.

I just didn't feel it.

I knew I should be bothered by that lack of feeling. Feeling had been important to me before. But now that it was gone, it wasn't. Sort of by definition, I guess.

What I did feel was the warmth of the sun on my shoulders and the softness of fine sand between my toes. The water was sparkly, and though too bright for my new eyes — my old sunglasses were prescription, which meant they now blurred my vision — it was a beautiful view. I knew my mom and daughter were irked with me, but that didn't really upset me. I felt glad to be alive. Content.

Well, not completely. It bothered me a little that I'd made Lucy sad. I turned to her, putting a smile on my face that I hoped didn't look too awkward. "What do you say we get some ice cream?" I asked.

Lucy's smile was immediate.

And you know what? The ice cream tasted amazing. When I thought that the battered body in Lab 14-H could have been the only me, I felt nothing but gratitude to ExtraLives for giving me a second chance.

———

"How do you like the new you?" Caleb asked. Ever since I'd first stumbled into his office, he'd been looking at me the way all the techs looked at Koko2, with an evaluating, appraising eye. I understood that I had replaced chimpanzees as the company's primary object of study. I'd been through a seemingly endless battery of physicals, during which all the differences I'd noted, plus more, were discovered and measured. And just like Koko2, I'd been grilled on my own life history to check for holes in my memory. ExtraLives wanted to go public with what they'd done. But no matter how many doctors and psychologists declared the experiment a success, they still needed my endorsement.

Caleb waited until the MDs and PsyDs had finished with me. For the first time in over a month, I returned to my office, sat down, and logged into my computer. I was mindful of the fact that—assuming they had re-implanted me with a recorder chip, which seemed probable—I was now being uploaded. But I didn't have time to dwell on it before he came bursting in without knocking.

"Well?"

"It's weird," I answered. My new body was in almost all ways superior to the original. Though I wasn't quite as strong as I'd been, and my hair would take a year or two to grow all the way back out, every cell in my body was new and healthy. I was flexible and thin and my skin was unlined. "People will love getting a new body," I told him, for all the obvious reasons. "Especially people who were sick or injured. It truly is a fresh start."

Caleb beamed. I could see him writing marketing copy in his head.

"But it's still weird. All my scars are gone."

"Isn't that good?" he asked.

I shrugged. "I remember being fond of some of them. But overall..." I trailed off, because my eyes drifted to the photograph on my desk. Lucy in her big red boots. Lucy against the waves. The seashell she'd given me sat in front of it, and these were the only decorations in my office. That felt significant, but although I *understood* that these were treasures, I couldn't comprehend why. The seashell looked dull and out of place, an ordinary trinket from the sea, and I felt keenly that I was missing something, something that had once made it seem to shine. And that was enough to give me pause.

"Overall..." Caleb prompted, looking at me with a scary level of expectation.

"Overall it's great," I told him. "Way better than being dead."

He laughed. "Is that all?"

"I wish I'd known," I said.

It was clearly an unfinished statement, but Caleb didn't ask me to elaborate. "No one knows when they're going to die, Reva."

I nodded, and he seemed satisfied—in a "for now" kind of way—and drifted out of my office. I turned back to my computer, switching it on.

A second later it prompted me for a password, a thing it had never done before. I stared at the screen for a moment, wondering if I should call Caleb back and get the password from him. But there was a password hint button, so I clicked it just to see.

At my last workplace, the password and the hint had been the same.

It read *Same as your bank pin, dummy*, so I punched in the numbers and my desktop faded into view. And right in the center of it was a new Word file called "WelcomeBackReva." Of course I opened it.

Unless you're a total moron — and god, I hope you're not — you've realized by now that you're not the original. I mean, hello? No belly button?

I don't know exactly when your memory stops, because I don't know exactly when Caleb started building you. Do you remember deciphering any of Dr. Kim's notes? We started on it shortly after coming back from vacation, when it was clear to everyone but us that Koko2 had been a complete success.

I did remember beginning on it. With nothing left to do in an official capacity, I'd turned to word games, seeking a cipher that would turn Dr. Kim's gobbledegook into useful information. I hadn't gotten very far. But I guess I'd eventually got further than I remembered.

Well, we did it. Those files are on this computer too, all decrypted for you. But here's the summary: Koko2 is really Koko14. This technology didn't come out of the box working perfectly, and by the time Koko13 rolled off the assembly line Dr. Kim was deeply troubled. She'd been saying since Koko3 just twitched and twitched that the project needed to slow down, but Caleb would have none of it.

One day Dr. Kim walked in on Caleb in his office, changing his shirt. He tugged it down immediately, turning away from the door, but Dr. Kim still saw his belly. With no belly button. At this point Dr. Kim's notes, though still coded, verge on hysterical, with rantings about pod people.

She became frightened of him.

Koko13? She was almost perfect. Just like your Koko2. I don't know what became of her because Dr. Kim never knew. I hope she's in a zoo or another lab, and isn't one of the chimps in 14-H. The last pages of Dr. Kim's notes are musings about quitting and going public. But she didn't get to. I found her in the freezer. Two of her. One is waif-thin and pale, scrawny but otherwise perfect-looking, except for the bruises around her throat. The other is Dr. Kim, a real body with a life behind it. That one looked like it put up a fight.

So I went a few doors down, and I was only a little surprised to see a body growing in the aquarium there. It was just bones and a little muscle, but I felt sure it was me. That was a few days ago already. I'm afraid of what I'd see if I looked now.

I'm afraid, Reva of the future. I think the technology will work this time, and you'll be effectively me. And so I will continue, sort of. But I will die. I don't know when or where or how, but once Caleb is satisfied that it worked, he'll kill me.

So I'm not waiting around for it to happen. After I say goodbye to Kokos 1 and 14 I'm leaving, and I'm taking Lucy with me. I hope that that leaves a hole in your life. If it doesn't, it will mean that you're not really me after all. If it does, well, I guess I'll see you again.

Sitting in my little office, I felt the old Reva's presence strongly. I looked again at the framed photo that I knew used to mean the world to me. Big red boots on little feet. Waves. Rocks. A pearl-pink seashell. It didn't mean anything now.

But I put it in my pocket anyway.

———

When I walked into the lab adjoining Koko's habitat, my colleagues almost jumped out of their skins. I hadn't been down there since my re-birth, and I guess they weren't expecting me to come back. But after a moment of shock they crowded around me, mouths agape as they studied me like a specimen, throwing questions faster than I could answer. Behind the one-way glass, Koko shrieked.

"It's nice to see you too," I said, forcing a casual laugh. "If you like my face, you'll love this." And I pulled my shirt up, exposing my alien belly. *Just like Caleb's,* I thought. I was dying to know how long Caleb had been a pod person, but since I'd never observed a change in him — and since Dr. Kim had discovered his secret — he must have died well before hiring me. I wondered what he'd been like before. Could this explain his almost psychopathic behavior? Could this explain why he'd murdered me and Dr. Kim? For I was now certain that he had.

The gathered techs seemed shamed by my mild exhibitionism, backing off sheepishly. "I'm here to visit Koko2," I said.

And now all eyes were on me again, but it was silent. Even Koko had calmed down. A young tech named Scott broke the spell first. "Of course she doesn't know," he all but exclaimed, as if solving a riddle. Immediately he clamped a knuckly hand over his mouth, but it was too late.

"I don't know what?" I asked.

They exchanged nervous, almost guilty looks, before seeming to elect Maria, a soft-spoken graduate student, to break it to me. "Koko2 is dead," she began, using a tone reserved for the very worst of news. I almost laughed then, amused that they thought I'd be heartbroken over a chimp. But then she went on. "We had to put her down after she ... killed, um, you."

And if I'd hypothesized that this body was incapable of feeling emotions, my reaction then provided significant counterevidence. My legs went wobbly and my heartbeat jumped, and I almost sat down right on the lab's cold floor. I'd never felt that way hearing news before, always thought asking people to sit for shocking news was silly.

Still, it only took me a moment to pull myself together. I'm not sure the techs even noticed my near-swoon.

It took them longer to try, vainly, to prevent me from pulling up the footage and watching myself die.

The chimp lounges on a cushion, arm around a stuffed shark. She ignores Reva as she enters the enclosure, pretending to sleep. So Reva kneels next to the cushion and lightly tickles the chimp's foot. But instead of laughing like the first chimp, this one just pulls her foot away.

Reva signs to her, trying to say goodbye, trying to wish her luck, using concepts that she must know are too advanced to do the chimp any good. Still, she tries to get the chimp's attention. She reaches for the stuffed shark, and as soon as she touches it the chimp springs into furious action, pummeling Reva with her fists and anything else she can grab. Anything but the shark. In between blows, her hands form quick signs.

It goes on and on.

Even looking at the footage in slow motion I couldn't make out what Koko2 had tried to tell me. The techs all avoided me while I watched the footage, but I pulled Scott in when he walked behind me on his way somewhere else. "What's she saying?"

He shook his head. "We think she's saying 'teeth.' The words, 'no,' 'hurt,' 'touch,' and 'teeth' come up a lot. Our best guess is that it was the shark. She got wicked pissed that you — she — touched her shark."

And I laughed then, hysterically. I laughed like I remembered laughing at things that were genuinely funny. I laughed until tears leaked out of my new eyes and Scott scurried off, probably afraid I'd go berserk like Koko14 and murder him. Which only made it funnier.

I didn't even care right then that Koko14 had killed me.

Koko14 had *cared*.

———

I was so excited about Koko14's emotions that it took me a while to realize the other important factor: Caleb hadn't murdered me. Sure, he'd copied me without my consent, but the first Reva would still be alive if it hadn't been for a chimp's love of her stuffed shark.

If Caleb wasn't my killer, maybe he didn't kill Dr. Kim either.

On my way out of the lab I cornered Maria. "What happened to Dr. Kim?"

She stuttered, then started to tell me that the woman had left.

"No, Maria. What *really* happened to her." Behind her, I could see the other techs slinking about and eyeing me. I raised my voice. "Is there footage of *her* death? I know she was scared. I know she knew about —"

"Dr. Kim quit," Scott said, his booming voice drowning out the name on my lips. "Now get out of here and stop harassing the interns." But as he came toward me as if to muscle me out of the lab, I saw something conspiratorial in his eyes. I let him guide me into the hallway.

Instead of angling toward the exit, Scott led me to his office. "You know there are cameras everywhere, right?" he said under his breath. "I don't *think* they pick up audio, but you can't be too careful."

Scott rummaged around in a drawer and eventually pulled out something that looked like a thumb drive. "A backup?" I asked. "Your backup?"

He rolled his eyes, clearly exasperated with me. "Dr. Kim was a friend of mine. I wish I could see her again." He pressed the backup into my hand, and as I realized what it was, I tried hard not to let my face show anything for the cameras.

I left the office after that, but I didn't have anywhere to go, so I just walked and walked for at least an hour. Caleb called me several times, but I ignored his calls. At best, he wanted to pressure me some more about going public. At worst, he saw my breakdown in the lab and wanted to "talk" about it.

I ended up collecting Lucy from her father's apartment. It was his day to have her, but he didn't protest when I suggested a trip to the park, and soon my walking was livened up by her excited prattle as we headed for the playground she thought was her favorite, the one with the biggest play structures and the zipline I'd never let her ride. The park wasn't really her favorite, because she left in tears almost every time. We had a pattern going, in which she'd start out all excited to climb the big monkey bars, then she'd trip over her own feet before we even got to the playground, then I wouldn't let her do any of the dangerous things she wanted to try, then she'd throw a tantrum and we'd leave.

We started out true to form. Lucy wanted to show me more of her cartwheels, and face-planted into the grass on maybe the fourth one. But she sprang right up, blades of grass stuck to her forehead, and thrust her arms up and pelvis forward just like every gymnast ever saluting the judges. I laughed, then gave her a round of applause. "A perfect ten," I told her.

A blade of grass peeled off her face and drifted to the ground like a leaf. "Momma, can I go play?"

"Of course," I said. "But stay low, okay?"

She rocketed off toward the play structure and I watched after her, wondering what Reval would be feeling. A love that made her chest tight, I thought. I didn't feel that.

My phone buzzed, this time with a text message from Caleb. I still hadn't listened to any of his voicemails. *Press conference tomorrow, 10:00 a.m.*, it read. *You're the star.*

The fingers of the hand not holding the phone curled into a fist and my heart beat faster. I felt rage, real physical anger. Without even thinking, I unflexed my fist and typed a reply: *I never agreed to that.*

But I remembered a thing or two about anger, so I paused before hitting "send" and took a deep breath. I looked around.

Over at the huge play structure, Lucy had her foot on the bar that I'd long ago set as her upper limit. She looked toward me as she did it, like a guilty kitten, testing to see if I'd let her get away with it. I knew the old Reva would have shaken her head, no. I knew because her old nightmare scenarios ran through my mind: Lucy's foot slipping off the rung, her face slamming into a bar, teeth cutting through her lip, blood running down her chin, her wailing through broken teeth. But then I kept the what-if going. We'd go to the hospital, she'd get a few stitches. Her adult teeth would grow in fine, and her scar would fade with time. And she'd be okay.

I shook my head, but only to clear it.

Encountering no resistance from me, Lucy climbed tentatively higher. Another girl, much bigger than Lucy, approached her and they conversed with some gesticulating and the occasional sound shrill enough to carry to where I was. The other girl ran off, and Lucy ran toward me, obviously on a layover between the play structure and her next destination.

"MommycanIridethezipline?" She asked what she obviously considered a futile and perfunctory question as fast as she could, poised to explode either with joy or temper tantrum. I'd denied this request many times.

But today I really looked at the zipline, watching the kids play. It was a rubber swing dangling from a cable stretched between two posts. At the high end, kids had to pull the swing up onto a platform, then the bigger ones pulled it back as far as they could, running and jumping on at the last minute to collect as much momentum as possible. They zoomed down to the other end, where there was a stop in the cable, and the swing arced up before turning to its return journey. A kid could fall off, I figured. But the thing wasn't very high, and it ran over a wide sand pit that looked soft enough. If a kid flew off the end, she might go some distance, but if she didn't hit the well-padded end post she'd land in the sand. The most dangerous spot seemed to be the wooden platform at the high end. Some of the kids came back to it at a fairly high speed, and its edges had only minimal, crumbling padding. But, I told myself, I could stand watch at that end. I could catch Lucy if she came in too fast.

I looked down into her face, which was looking up at mine with so much hope it made me laugh out loud. "Okay," I said, and before she could completely dissolve into hysterical happiness I hastened to add, "But hold on really, really tight, okay?"

Her head moved up and down at an incredible rate.

We went over to the zipline and waited in line while some other kids took their turns. None of them hit their heads on the platform and died, so I was somewhat comforted. But still I whispered in Lucy's ear, "Are you scared? It's not too late to change your mind."

She squirmed a little, and I realized that she *was* scared. I patted her back. "You'll be fine. Just don't let go."

She was too small to pull the swing back while climbing onto the platform, so I held it for her. She stared it down for a while before wiggling her butt onto the seat. "Are you sure it's safe?" she asked, her face pale. I felt a pang then, not of doubt, but of guilt for how thoroughly I—the old me—had conditioned fear into this child.

"I'm sure," I said.

Lucy gripped the chains with white knuckles. When she was secure, I pulled it a little farther back and let her go. She seemed to drop away from the platform fast, but when the swing came to the stop at the end it only made a gentle swoop before coming back. I needn't have worried about the platform; Lucy barely made it halfway back before the swing started to head the other way again. It rocked a few times before coming to rest about three-quarters of the way down, and I jumped off the platform and lifted Lucy out of the swing.

"Can I go again?" she asked, before I'd even set her feet in the sand.

We took half a dozen more turns on the zipline—I even went a couple of times, to the surprise of the other kids, and it was fun! —so it was a while before I got back to my phone and Caleb's text message. I deleted my angry reply unsent. *I'll be there*, I replied instead, *on one condition*. The backup drive in my pocket felt like leverage: if Caleb wanted my endorsement, Scott would see his friend again.

But all that could wait. For the moment, I walked my ecstatic daughter home from her favorite park.

Lucy grabbed one of my hands and I shoved the other in my pocket. I was feeling for the thumb drive, but instead it brushed against something hard and round. I pulled it out: the seashell.

"Why do you have that?" Lucy asked.

I looked between the shell and my daughter, wondering the same thing myself. I knew I was supposed to feel something, but the shell still just seemed empty. I knelt in front of her, seashell in hand. "Do you remember what I told you about hermit crabs?"

She nodded. "They live in shells like pretty dresses."

Close enough. "Well, I think we should take this back to the beach and throw it in the water. I think we should put it where someone like a hermit crab can use it for a home. Or a dress. What do you think?"

Lucy's face fell, but only a little. "But I gave it to you," she whined.

"I know you did, but it's too small for me." I mimed like I was trying to climb into the shell, and she giggled.

"Momma, you're silly!" When she smiled, I felt something like happiness.

And you know what? That was good enough for me.

STORY NOTES:

Some tropes are used so often and so unthinkingly in genre fiction that they are taken as a given. Putting a person into a new body is one of them. But surely things wouldn't be as simple as all that.

One of the things that sparked this story was reading an article about how fingerprints are formed in utero. A body reproduced from DNA would never be exactly the same as the original, whether it's a calico cat with new markings or a human with moles in new places.

How a person in a new body would feel is, of course, entirely my speculation.

Last of the Monsters

SCALING TARP-COVERED HURRICANE FENCE, I survey the landscape. A guard sleeps below, rhythmic snoring barely audible in the breeze. I drop to the ground, quiet as a myth.

In the moonlight, one stone looks like another. Any ruin, any boulder-strewn field. A desolate spot, but not without its beauty.

Could it really be my sister's grave?

I laughed when the gods died out. One by one, they crawled off like dogs to die alone, and I danced on their unmarked graves. It was difficult for me to control my eyes in those days; the rage and bitterness within me was still fresh, white-hot like a spearhead fresh from the forge.

The only grave I could never find was Athena's, that bright-eyed bitch. But if I understand the news bites and rumors that have found their way to me, a Texas rancher seems to have stumbled upon the goddess's final resting place — and her gorgon-emblazoned shield — and paid a terrible price.

I imagine poor Tex's wife: he goes out onto the land one day, like any day, except that tonight he doesn't come home. She waits, she worries, but he has stayed out late before. In the morning she makes phone calls, friends come in, parties go out to search the hills and fields. But she is the one who finds the statue. The corner of the ranch in which it crouches is remote, but the place is not unknown to Tex and wife. The statue must be new. Some sort of joke, perhaps?

It looks just like him.

It is before me now, a stone figure, bent over like a boulder in the field. A boulder with a cowboy hat. He stretches his hand out as if to brush dirt from something embedded in the earth. The moonlight makes his cold flesh eerie; it glows like marble. The folds of his shirt sparkle with glints of quartz. There are certainly uglier ways to die.

Mythology remembers my sister as a monster. Her sheer ugliness would freeze you where you stood, or so the legend goes. And yes, she turned a few people to stone. But it was rage, not ugliness, that turned my sister's gaze to killing beams. Raped, vilified, and hunted like a beast. Can you blame her for being angry?

Stheno was no monster either, the poor sweet thing. After Medusa's murder, she sheared the writhing mass of hair from her head, plucked out her eyes, and stumbled into town to find and marry a boy she admired. She didn't know that doing so would render her mortal. She didn't know either that he would find her repulsive, bald and blind, and reject her. She never petrified anyone. By the time she wanted to, she'd traded in her power.

I do not know what word best describes me. I have lived and searched for centuries now, and some days I think that that alone makes me monstrous. Yet I blend in now more than ever. The snakes of my hair lie still at my command; they tuck their faces into the ends of the dreads that cocoon them. Thousands, perhaps millions of mortals have looked upon me in my long life, and only a few—mostly deserving—have paid with their lives.

The man in front of me didn't deserve his fate, but then it isn't my sister's fault anymore. Murder was in her eyes when her life was ended, and there it remains. And maybe that's why I hesitate, studying the stone rancher, the moonlight, the oddly lunar landscape roughly bounded with temporary fencing—anything but the patch of dirt where I expect to find Athena's shield, and embedded in it my sister's severed head. Maybe I am afraid.

Stepping around the statue, I crouch to look into his frozen face. His eyes are nothing more than pebbles now, but in them I see the fear, the shock, the sadness. I can almost hear him whispering to me: *Go on; what are you waiting for?*

I nod, wishing I had a hat to tip. I close my eyes as I turn to follow the cowboy's hand with my own. The stone is softer under my fingers than I expect, as is the dirt. Blindly, I probe the earth, feeling cool sand and rocks — and nothing else. I dig like a dog after a bone, but I find nothing. The shield is gone.

I sit down heavily on the ground, opening my eyes. "Where is it?" I ask aloud, but Tex doesn't answer me.

It's then I hear the crunching of footsteps toward me. A flashlight clicks on, startlingly close. I flinch, frightened, but a monster doesn't run. The light soon finds me. The glare makes it impossible to make out who carries the light (or *what*, I think, before remembering that I'm the last of the monsters). The guard? The wife?

It doesn't matter who. Someone else has put the pieces together and recovered the deadly treasure I sought. I was foolish to think I'd do it first.

When the light goes out I am struck by the illusion that it's *her* standing over me. Her snakes look so lifelike, animated by the moonlight. Her eyes look so wild, surprised and hurt and molten with rage.

I cannot bring myself to look away, though I know I should. Bring the rage to my own eyes; dispatch the shield-bearer, whoever it may be; destroy my sister's image so she can never kill again.

I feel a coldness creeping into me. I feel stiff and solid and old, old, old. I know I should look away.

But oh, Sister, it's good to see your face again.

STORY NOTES:

Gorgons get a bad rap, undeservedly so in my opinion. Some men are simply begging to be petrified by women's eyes, if only more of us had the ability. Be careful who you tell to smile.

Frozen Head #2,390

MY LIFE AS A HUMAN wasn't my first, but it was in a very real way the start of my journey, a life that would leave an outsized mark on all subsequent lives.

Humans have this thing where they're born really stupid and it takes years before they're aware enough to store memories. Things happen to them in that time, but most of them bounce off like raindrops on duckfeathers. It's a mercy, really, because who wants to remember sucking on the dog's squeaky toy or waking up in a bag of their own feces?

And yet, a few early memories are formed, and they hold an outsized, mythical importance.

Being a human was like that.

Humans at the time had a lot of really strange beliefs and customs. They were picking up any old concept they could find and sticking it in their mouths. They had thousands of religions, all to explain what happened after death, because they feared it like a toddler fears naptime.

We feared it. My sister and I.

Humans are usually born in clutches of one, but ours was two. Kathleen and I had split from a single genetic source and grown up parallel. We looked the same—more even than most humans do—and we were raised doing the same things—attending the same schooling, playing the same sports, learning the same musical instruments. We joked that our parents were raising us for maximum redundancy and invented elaborate theories on what role we—or one of us anyway—were being groomed to fill. Astronaut? Politician? Spy? If it had been any of those, our parents failed. Kathleen went into neuroscience and I worked on artificial intelligence.

When Kathleen got sick it was like a cosmic joke. Good thing there was a spare, huh?

Remember all those religious beliefs humans had at the time? Kathleen and I held none of them. So there was nothing to give us comfort when we learned that she was dying. We thought of ourselves as scientists, rational, and there was no evidence of a life beyond death. We scoffed at the idea of heaven or hell, and derided reincarnation as a mathematical impossibility that failed to account for the geometric increase in sentient beings on our planet.

"I'm going to freeze my head," Kathleen told me.

"Are you insane?" I answered. A worry about metastatic brain tumors floated through *my* head, though her particular cancer didn't usually spread that way.

"I'm perfectly rational," she wheezed. Her cancer *did* spread to the lungs, filling them with tumors and fluid. "I want to live on, and this is the best chance available."

"But the tech isn't ready," I argued. "The freezing damages cells. You don't want to come back all . . . freezer-burnt. Do you?"

"Of course not. But they're not going to unfreeze me until they can fix it."

"And give you a new body to go along with it?"

"Yes," she said, perking up. "Exactly. The company I've booked with promises to store me as long as it takes."

"But . . ." I stammered. I felt deep misgivings about this that I couldn't put my finger on. "Look, I've read about this a little bit and I don't think it makes sense. Even if they can fix the cell damage or recreate the structure of the brain down to the tiniest synapses, it's no given that your memories will be intact. You might not really be *you* anymore."

"Shelby," Kathleen said, that long-suffering tone creeping into her voice. I ignored it as usual.

"Plus, why would they even bother to store you that long? Making a new human body is still far-future science fiction. Hundreds of years. Maybe more. Assuming they decide to store you that long, and the facility never has a power failure—"

"They use liquid nitrogen."

"Even *if* your head is still there in the far-distant future, what makes you think they'll actually do what they promised? There's no way whatever you could pay them will be enough. And—"

"Shel," she said, this time with cold urgency. "Look at me."

I looked at her. At her head, which no longer looked exactly like mine. Her face was thinner, her hair gone. Her eyes were full of fear and pain. But then so were mine.

"I'm not stupid. I know there's only a slim chance that this will work. But I will take a slim chance over no chance. That's just simple math."

And I couldn't argue with that.

"I paid for yours too," she said. "Promise me you'll use it?"

I couldn't think of anything to say to that.

"Not for a long time, I hope. I want you to live a full, long life first. For both of us, just like we talked about."

And then I was crying too hard to say anything. So when she asked me again to promise, I just nodded.

A few weeks later, the company came to collect her head.

And I felt as though a part of me had died too, as if we hadn't been two beings all along but one, incomplete without the other.

One of the most logically insane yet deeply held beliefs humans of that time held was in a "soulmate," one other human, usually a romantic partner, who was "meant" for the other. This, despite the impossibility of finding one soul among some eight billion humans alive at the time! Despite total lack of evidence for souls in the first place, let alone deficient souls in need of another to complement and complete them.

But if there *were* soulmates, surely identical twins were each other's. I thought I'd die without her, and spent months, a year, longer, in mourning her.

There was another human cliché about time healing all wounds (though clearly not cancer!), and that one turned out to be pretty true. Somehow my life went on. I lived and worked for decades. I partnered with a human who was certainly not my soulmate and we produced offspring and *they* produced offspring and I died an old woman, still afraid of the permanent blackout I assumed death would be, but more or less at peace with it.

I did not have my head frozen.

———

On Roptrango-B, a sunny little oceanic planet, I spent most of a 200-year life as a star drive mechanic, wielding tools with my twelve skinny tentacles. As a hobby, I restored ancient reef-houses, singing to the coral in the traditional manner. My partner was a poet from Roptrango-M and our offspring ended up living on three different planets, so we spent our blue-water years traveling between the system's planets.

If sometimes I felt an ache like another phantom tentacle had been ripped off and never regenerated, I didn't think much of it.

———

I only lived for four cycles in the Katlas System before a rogue asteroid took out my whole station, but that was enough. Cybians were hybrid organic computers and clocked the world so fast it felt like centuries. Before my last upload I'd simulated dozens of parallel lives.

———

As a Ferguloid my whole lifetime was spent at war with a race of giant feathery lizards that looked like Earth dinosaurs. I remembered dinosaurs very clearly, but no one else in my platoon had spent any lifetimes on Earth and they all flapped their mandibles at me in exasperation when I joked about T-Rex arms. I died young in that life, as we all did, when our transport was blown out of the sky. We literally never knew what hit us.

———

And there were more, many more. Each life filled me with memories, pressing down upon the last like sedimentary layers of rock in the shifting, expanding geology of what I still thought of as a "soul." Previous lives receded like the gentle waves on Roptrango-B's few atolls, but some things remained.

On a planet much like Earth, with even more striking and diverse climates and landscapes, I retired for decades to a monastery in a valley of orange and violet blooms, devoting my life to the selective breeding of ever-more-potent hallucinogenic spores.

It was toward the end of this life that I first applied for membership in the Collective. The Collective is . . . well, to be honest I didn't entirely understand it. I guess it's similar to the old Earth concept of "heaven" or "nirvana," except that it's also a machine intelligence. It is ancient, and it is where souls go when they are ready to rest, and it is said to be a state of ineffable joy, incomprehensible to those on the outside.

I brought my crumbling body into the temple, past the rooms in which I'd worshipped or labored or studied, and interfaced for the first time with the uplink. The spores were kicking in, the strain we called "dusk," which each acolyte ingested only once, if ever. Figures danced through the candlelit room and my head spun. I sank to my foreknees.

I felt the pressure waves of giant wings beating, my flockmates from two lives back welcoming me home from school. I saw the bulbous bobbing heads of the river cephalopods I'd hunted as a refugee in the Sauran system in the life before that. My partner's tentacles from Roptrango-M wrapped around me, stinging for just one delicious instant before peeling away. And I heard a booming voice. The Collective?

Entry not permitted. Application incomplete.

I tried to stand, but four of my six legs had gone numb and I only stumbled before falling back to the stone floor. "What do you mean?"

The words flickered in time with the candles. Was their light dimming?

Soul incomplete.

"How can that be?" I croaked. My throat was dry.

You were one but now are two.

Leave it to the interface of a mystical computer afterlife to be cryptic. But I didn't have time to ask any more questions; the spores had done their work and dusk had turned to night for that lifetime.

In the lives following my human one, I rarely thought of my one-time sister. I never saw her again, but that wasn't unusual—it was a big damn universe, after all, and in eons of study no one had solved the equations governing reincarnation. No one—save perhaps the Collective—knew why souls took the paths they did, why rebirth was always immediate, or why young sentient species usually did not perceive the fact of reincarnation.

If I'd thought of Kathleen at all, I assumed we'd only missed each other. I assumed her head-freezing scheme had failed and she'd been reborn, just like me, only on the other side of the galaxy. Oh well, maybe I'd see her in my next life.

The Collective's riddle led me back to her.

In my next life, once I'd matured enough to recall it, I pondered the meaning of *you were one but now are two* until I was no longer blue in the face (just kidding; my face was blue that whole life, despite multiple moltings). I retraced my steps looking for a time my soul might have fractured. That time I tried to stop a geneplague and ended up starting one, and a billion Yusofors were mutated? When I died on Rokos Nine without completing my fourth metamorphosis? What caused a soul to split, anyway?

I worked my way back through lives as methodically as I could. Had I been a cybian *before* or *after* the Sauran war? These things got fuzzy. But the furthest back I could recall was my human life —before that all was tooth and claw, flashes of non-sentient existence that it almost *hurt* to try to remember. And in that human life, there had been two of us. Two twins—but maybe with one soul?

If that were true, did it mean I could never join the Collective? Or, did it mean that Kathleen's soul had never been given the chance to rejoin mine?

By the time I got that far, it was a whole 'nother life, and not a particularly philosophical one. But in the darkness between stars, over fermented tradzu root, I spilled it all to my ship's engineer, a Roptralian named Astrill. I had a fondness for zir not only because ze was the best star-drive wizard on this side of the galaxy, but because we'd been three of the same species at one time or another. During the 1600s or 1700s—as near as we could figure—he'd been a sailor in the British Navy. Give Astrill enough distilled Kranellian snapps and ze told swashbuckling tales of conquest and cannonballs. And dysentery.

Astrill had been through more lives than me, but never even thought about joining the Collective. "Sounds boring," ze'd said. "But I bet you a case of snapps you'll find your clutchmate's head still frozen on Earth."

"And pigs can fly," I replied. "Even if it wasn't a scam in the first place, there's no way humans kept a thing like that safe all this time."

"No? You got another explanation for your soul staying split?" I didn't.

"With the proper application of thrust, anything can fly," ze went on. "Pigs, frozen heads, even this rust bucket." Astrill patted the ship's hull lovingly with one tentacle.

I fluttered my tail in my best approximation of dismissive Roptralian body language.

"Find the head, destroy it, free ol' Kath's soul, then you can join the snooze fest next time you die," Astrill said, performing a complicated twining gesture with three of zir twelve tentacles. "Couldn't be simpler!"

Simple? It seemed impossible. And yet, I had no better answer. Plus, a case of snapps was on the line.

So that's how I finally returned to Earth: on a crazy bet slash mystical quest slash legitimate interstellar trading visit to the just-opening Solar system. A couple millennia had passed since my human lifetime, and against all expectations humans were still there, slowly maturing. The quarantine of their Solar system was just beginning to be peeled back.

Humans were still struggling with their fears of aliens, so I was lucky to be in a bipedal, mammalian, air-breathing body this time around. Chirrlings, despite being fur-covered with big bushy tails reminiscent of those of Earth squirrels, had been deemed humanoid enough not to scare the locals. A great many of the things I'd been since I'd been Shelby wouldn't be allowed to visit Earth for at least another century, give or take a few generations.

Earth had been through a lot since I'd been there, I learned, as my ship's computer sucked historical documents from Earth's archives and distilled a summary for me. Planet-wide ecological catastrophes that reduced the human population by a quarter, then by a half; nearly being wiped out by the artificial intelligences they created (whoops); treaties with those same beings, arbitrated by genetically modified ravens; expansion into neighboring planets and the asteroid belt; impressive restoration of the home planet's biological diversity.

One thing they hadn't done yet was the one thing my ancient sister had been counting on: unfreezing of people's cryogenically stored heads.

As soon as we'd finished offloading the tech gadgets, stasis-preserved fruit, and alcohol that constituted our cargo, I put in a request to visit the planet itself.

When Kathleen died—and as late as when *I* died—her head had been stored in Scottsdale, Arizona, United States, in the southern part of a mid-sized continent in the northern hemisphere of the planet. As we orbited the blue and brown planet, I tried to spot the place, but my memories of its geography were thousands of years old. Old for a memory, short for a planet. Yet nothing looked quite how I thought it should, as if someone had blurred all the shorelines. Hadn't that mid-sized northern continent had a prominent peninsula in the southeast corner before?

While I waited to hear about my shore leave, the ship's computer searched for records of Kathleen. As it did, I flashed back to one of the many arguments we'd had about cryogenic freezing. "Why wouldn't they just throw you away once they have your money?" I'd asked. Well, they hadn't.

"What makes you think the company will even last that long?" It had, almost. Apparently she'd been right about the power of compounding interest, if nothing else.

"What are the odds of any location surviving into the distant future?" The company had moved, I learned, a few decades after Kathleen's death. The desert they'd originally chosen had become too hot for aboveground human habitation, and the water supply had dried up. One batch of heads was lost when climate rioters overturned a tanker of liquid nitrogen on its way there, but my sister's wasn't one of them. By then almost no new heads were being frozen, so the company moved first to the planet's southern ice cap, where they manufactured their own liquid nitrogen, and then they sensibly relocated the whole operation into a hollowed-out asteroid once those became cost-competitive.

"Why would people of the future want to revive you?" They didn't.

The heads' final move had been back to Earth, after the supposedly eternal board of the company had called it quits and made off with the last of the money. When a mining crew discovered 3,289 frozen heads inside an asteroid that had been marked for extraction, it kicked off an ethical and legal debate that was still simmering on one of the Solar system's political backburners, and the heads were back on metaphorical ice, having been farmed out to any museum, research facility, or university that would take them.

A shuttle planetside, six hours of quarantine, and two hyperloop rides later, I strolled through Washington, DC, with a 48-hour visitor chip.

Somewhere in the Solar system's governmental bureaucracy, citizens might be petitioning officials to revive the 3,289 frozen heads — though I doubted it — but wherever such politics happened, it was no longer this place. DC had become a city of museums, broken up by placid pools and genetically engineered ever-blooming cherry trees, all sheltered by a massive seawall whose presence was betrayed by an uncanny shimmer as its camouflage tech tried to keep up with a changing sky.

All that remained of the capital of the nation-state Kathleen and I had lived in as Earthlings were memorials of white marble piled one on top of another, centuries of memories clamoring for dominance. I knew how that felt.

I swiped my ID chip for entry to the Museum of Religion, an architectural mélange that — my translation chip helpfully read for me off a plaque — incorporated the aesthetics of dozens of religions and sects (without achieving the gracefulness of any of them). It had bell towers and minuets, stupas and stained glass. It had statues in way, way, way too many styles. And that was just the exterior.

Past databases' worth of informational plaques, upsetting renderings of violence, and armies of statues of men nailed to things was a small section with the title "Science Attempts to Address the Afterlife." And there, through a window into a very thick boxy enclosure fed by pipes, I saw my sister's face for the first time in centuries.

———

She didn't look good. The window distorted my view somewhat, but even so, I could see that she was as pale as the marble that formed this city of monuments. Her eyes had been taped shut during the freezing process, and the indentations on her eyelids remained. Her head, which had already been bald from the primitive medical treatments that failed to save her life, now had two small holes drilled into it, like reverse devil horns. He mouth was slackly open, making her look dumb.

And yet.

The memory of her hit me with a pain I had not expected. She looked so *lonely*.

I placed a hand against the glass, the nano-dissembler tucked between two fingers, armed and ready to chew through window and pipes and frozen flesh alike at my command.

Do you think there'll be aliens? Kathleen's voice in my memory is shaky and weak. *In the future, when we both get unfrozen. Do you think there'll be uplifted chimpanzees and aliens?*

I hadn't thought either one very likely. *Of course,* I'd said, already 80% sure I wasn't going to join her in the icebox. *And lunar colonies and wormhole travel to other star systems. Once we get unfrozen, we'll go everywhere together.*

My fingers twitched, their tawny fur looking extra bright against her ice-white hairlessness. It was too much. I took a step back, then another, then whirled around looking for a place to sit before collapsing to the floor, wrapping my tail around me like a child's blanket and purring to still my racing heart.

The few times since our life together that I'd thought of Kathleen and her quest for immortality, I'd laughed about it. Because obviously we were living the real immortality: we'd dismissed reincarnation because we'd been thinking too small, believing our planet had the only souls—if souls existed at all. What fools we'd been! What a big, marvelous universe it had turned out to be, even wilder than the distant future she'd believed in.

On the floor of the Museum of Religion my eyes were leaking and my heartbeat throbbed into my fingers and ears. Because while I'd been out living it, up she'd been *here* the whole time.

I didn't know much about the science of the soul — no one really did, not even the so-called "soul scientists" — but I *felt* that the immortal part of Kathleen hadn't been freed with her death.

When I could look my sister in the face again, the plaque under her grotesque bloodless head answered it for me: "The process of what was then called *vitrification*," it read, "was initiated in the moments between the subject's heart stopping and brain death several minutes later."

I could free her soul with the nano-dissembler, and if Astrill was right she'd be sucked back into me when I died. But I found I couldn't go through with it. She deserved better than that.

The legal battle to acquire Kathleen's head was brief but ridiculous. In the end I had the Chirrling ambassador to the Solar system pull rank for me. Did the humans *really* want to risk an interstellar diplomatic incident over one frozen head? They didn't.

Once we'd loaded up the cargo hold with Earth handicrafts, salt, stasis-preserved pigeons, and one frozen head, we set a course for the Brontolli system, where the pigeons would net us a tidy profit (and no, I didn't know what the Brontolli wanted them for; an interstellar trader learns quickly not to ask about such things).

"I can't help but notice that your sister is in the freezer," Astrill trilled, suctioning toward me up what our hard burn out of the Solar system had turned into a vertical shaft.

A twitch of the tail was all the response I gave.

"I thought you were going to destroy the head."

"I am," I said, not turning from the ship's controls. "Today, tomorrow, in a hundred cycles. It's all the same to her, so what's *your* hurry?"

Ze let out the wheezy cough that Roptralians made when they laughed outside water. "Fair enough. No skin off my soul. Can't see the profit in hauling a frozen chimp head all over the galaxy, though."

"Don't talk about my sister that way," I mumbled, finishing my fine-tuning of the cargo bay's scanner. "Computer, can you read the matrix now?" Its happy chirp told me it could.

"Then run program 'Kathleen Carson.'"

I imagined the miracle that was about to happen in great detail. I'd argued with Kathleen about this, but the vanishingly slim chance she'd bet her immortal soul on had worked, and now here she was! I pictured her waking up, calling my name, and feeling as though only a minute had passed while she slept.

With no fanfare whatsoever, Kathleen appeared in my ship's cockpit. Well, not the real Kathleen, not even the real Kathleen's consciousness, but a full holographic simulation of her based on the scan of her brain. She was a little grainy around the edges, and she'd been generated in the body position her stopped brain last remembered, lying on a bed. Since there weren't any beds in the cockpit, she hovered in mid-air, torso awkwardly bisecting the pilot's empty chair and feet somewhere inside the control panel.

But she snapped instantly upright, pulling her ghostly limbs inward, clutching a blanket that wasn't there. "I'm not ready!" she shouted, the sound coming from the nearest speaker on the ship's console. Kathleen looked around wildly as the computer subtly adjusted her position until it appeared she was sitting in the chair. Her image was still wearing a hospital gown, though oddly it also had hair.

I don't know what she thought of the two of us, Astrill hanging from a handhold by two tentacles and me leaning toward her worrying my bushy tail between my hands. But it was enough to render her speechless as her eyes darted between us. The computer was feeding her visual information from as close to her position as possible, but I imagined the input felt pretty uncanny. She finally managed to squeak out, "Where am I?"

"You're..." I started, my language download letting me use period-correct American English. "It's a long story. Where do you think you are? What's the last place you remember being?"

"The hospital. Oh fuck, I'm dying. It's not how I thought it would be. No white light like in the NDE reports. And if I was wrong about heaven, then where's the harp music? Plus, no offense, but you two *really* don't look like angels."

"I was an angel once," Astrill interjected, unhelpfully, probably referring to zir life as a Terrawk, a humanoid race with giant feathery wings. I gave zir the signal to go back belowdecks and ze replied with a crisp, mocking salute before letting go with both tentacles and dropping down the shaft.

"You're not dying, Kathleen." She looked like she wanted to interject with a *how do you know my name*, but I barreled on. "It worked. We had your head frozen just like you wanted, and it's the mid-43rd century as you reckon time, and here you are! Yes, there are aliens, and so many more things too."

Kathleen's hologram shook its head violently. "Not head freezing again! This must be a nightmare. Maybe it's the drugs." She ran her hand nervously through her hair, just like old times, then startled and brought some of the long black strands to her face to examine. Then she reached out to touch the ship's console and her hand went right through it. This seemed to calm her down.

"Oh good, it's not real. What a weird dream." She looked me up and down from my fuzzy ears to my sneaker-clad feet.

I was just about to try to tell her it wasn't a dream when she went on, seemingly to herself.

"I hope to medical science I wake up from this one. Can't let Shelby actually go through with that crazy head-freezing scheme."

I let my tail drop and it hung limply off the back of my chair. "You can't... what?"

Kathleen laughed. "When in Rome," she muttered, then went on: "Okay, crazy space dream squirrel, since you asked. Back in the real world I'm dying of cancer, and my sister just cannot let go and insists I get my head vitrified. I actually said I'd allow it to make her happy, but I've never wanted to."

I stared at her, openmouthed, as all my memories from our conversations ran through my head. They'd been so clear. "No," I finally managed. "I ne—your sister never wanted to do it. It was your idea."

"Hardly!" Kathleen snorted. "I know the science on brain freezing. Hell, I'm a *neuroscientist*. Waste of resources at best, disastrous at worst. I mean, I'm still 99.9% sure there's no such thing as a soul, but some promising studies suggest that a small amount of energy leaves the body at brain death. Who knows what that might turn out to be? It's got to be better than a frozen lump of meat in a jar. I just hope I wake up from this dream in time to put my foot down about it." She turned her holographic head toward the front of the ship and its field of stars.

"I—that's just not how it happened. This simulation must have errors, or the freezing process scrambled your—"

"What would you know about it, space squirrel?"

My heart was beating in my throat and my tail swished furiously. "I'm . . . I'm her. Your sister." Kathleen turned toward me, a dreamlike look on her face. The only way I could get it all out was to rush through it, so rush I did. "It's true. You did die, or not really die because your head was preserved. But surprise! It turns out there's reincarnation and I've lived a couple dozen lives since I was Shelby, but I *am* her and I remember. I *remember* trying to talk you out of your insane head-freezing plan! But anyway it worked."

"This is the wildest dream ever," Kathleen said to herself, but I could tell she was starting to worry it wasn't. "That's not how it happened. I told her a thousand times that the idea was ridiculous. And let's just say that if you *were* Shelby and you *had* let that mad scientist shit happen to me, well, you better be glad I can't seem to interact with matter in this fucked-up cancer- and pain-drug-fueled nightmare."

Her holographic hands were bunched into fists. "Okay," she said, screaming now, though the computer limited the volume to a dull roar. "I'm ready to wake up now!"

"Computer, end program," I whispered, and she was gone.

All that remained was her unsettling recollection of the way our conversations had played out. I went over them again and again, but I just couldn't believe that I'd argued the other position. It was, as Kathleen had just said, ridiculous!

I sat in the cockpit for I don't know how long, just staring into space — staring into literal space, a field of stars like glittering sand out the window — running the ancient argument over again and again in my brain searching for clues to which of us was remembering properly.

The computer terminal in front of me dinged: a message from Astrill. It was a digitized file from ancient Earth, a payment record for the vitrification of head #742, one Kathleen Carson. And guess whose signature was at the bottom? One Shelby Carson.

"Astrill, you eavesdropping octopus!" I yelled. Ze couldn't help it, though. Sound waves vibrated through the metal of the ship and right into zir tentacles.

Another ping. *I told you to destroy it*, this one said.

And don't call me octopus.

———

For a long time I just refused to deal with the problem. And I mean a really long time. I left Kathleen in her chiller unit in the cargo hold, cutting into my profits for dozens, hundreds, thousands of trading runs. No matter where in the galaxy we were, her head was there weighing on me like a second conscience.

I'd cost her lifetimes of experience—of discovery, growth, adventure, mistakes, and love. I could do the "merciful" thing and free her, but even that would only bond her back to my own soul, and my soul felt weary at the thought of going on. I'd done my share of living and yearned for whatever enlightenment the Collective offered.

Even if Kathleen's half of our soul forgave mine—could a part of a soul remain angry with the rest?—would her half also bring mine a new sense of curiosity to carry us both forward through dozens more lives? Or would my soul's age weigh hers down and dull whatever joy she might have had? Would our halves even be able to merge back into one when mine had grown so much since the time of our shared life, while hers remained unchanged?

I couldn't cope with what I'd done and I couldn't decide what to do about it, so I did nothing. For almost a whole lifetime.

Kathleen's head was there when Astrill finally got sick of me and transferred to a more profitable ship. The head was there when, on a run back to the home planet, I met a fantastic piece of tail who would become my wife. It was there when we settled down on a killer piece of creekside property, necessitating regular deliveries of liquid nitrogen to maintain the status quo of my guilty indecision.

The head was still there when my wife got sick, her now-silver fur thinning from treatments that only postponed the inevitable. The day she passed away I looked in the mirror and saw with a shock how gray my own fur had gotten. It was time to, as Astrill had been so fond of saying, "shit or get out of the pot."

I went out to the shed housing Kathleen's chiller unit and brushed a thick layer of dust off her enclosure's window. There she was, same as she'd been for centuries, her slack face judging me.

"What should I do?" I asked her, not for the first time. She didn't answer.

Keeping her frozen wasn't a good solution. For Gravity's sake, it wasn't even a *possible* solution: the only choices I could see were to destroy her head on purpose, or wait until I died and the liquid nitrogen deliveries stopped, to let her die from my cowardly neglect.

Staring at the tank, I realized I was again choosing my sister's fate for her. I was making the same mistake all over again, even after all those lifetimes of experience.

And that thought made me realize the one true and fair option I did have.

A colony of cybians in the Sauran asteroid belt owed me a favor, which I cashed in for two things.

———

Kathleen floated in a wing of cold steel hallway in an honest-to-Clarke space station. At least that's where the robots and disembodied AI voices calling themselves cybians had told her she was. The space station had no windows.

Yet she found herself staring through a thick portal at the frozen head of a giant rodent claiming to be her sister. Well, not exactly a rodent. The thing had an almost-human—though furry —face with tufty ears on top. Kathleen wished she could see its eyes, but they were frozen shut.

All told, it wasn't the kind of family reunion she'd expected. Not that she'd expected one at all.

"I can't believe you were right," Kathleen said finally, flexing her right hand and studying it. Her left hand had a death grip on one of the hallway's many handholds. "Your crazy head-freezing scheme actually worked."

The frozen head remained still, silent. Its expression was something between a smile and a smirk. There was something very *Shelby* about that look.

"My teeth feel weird," she went on. "It's the little things, right? They chew fine, but I can tell they're not *mine*. I wonder if I'll get used to them, like you do after having your wisdom teeth out, or if they'll always feel wrong, a constant reminder of what you did to me . . ."

The head, of course, refused to answer.

Kathleen sighed, digging in a zippered pocket for the holo-cube the cybians had given her, after explaining where — and when—she was, and putting her through a series of tests to make sure her brain was sound and had accepted the body.

"Run program 'space squirrel,'" she told it, and a life-sized hologram appeared in the hallway, floating next to Kathleen: a monster squirrel sitting in what looked like the inside of a high-end RV. It spoke:

Hey sis, it said. It wasn't Shelby's voice, not at all, but something in the tone was familiar. *I assume the cybians explained everything to you. Hopefully by now you've accepted that it's not a dream or a dying hallucination.*

The squirrel-Shelby hologram paused, ears twitching. Kathleen wasn't sure how to read the hologram's body language, but the squirrel seemed to know *her* well—she was only moderately convinced this was really happening, and only because she'd experienced linear time for longer than typical in a dream.

I know it's a lot to take in, and maybe you won't ever believe during your human life that there will be a next one. But as long as my head stays on ice, for you there will be next lives. Use as many as you want; I'll wait. She—was it a she? how could you tell?—gave a strange giggle, like nerves, or maybe hysteria.

I've paid the cybians to store me for a little over three millennia while you live your lives. If you don't forgive me by then, I deserve . . . The squirrel absently grabbed its bushy gray tail in both hands, looking over Kathleen's shoulder. The hologram was pre-recorded, but Kathleen found it hard to shake the feeling that it was staring right at its own frozen head.

Anyway, it went on with a twitch. *I've left you my accounts, and my ship in the docking bay, all yours and user-friendly; you shouldn't have much trouble figuring it out. I've asked my old friend Astrill to come show you the ropes anyway. Don't let zir try to collect on a case of snapps ze thinks I owe, 'cause I already . . . that's not important.*

Another pause, this one longer. Kathleen might have thought the program had frozen if the squirrel's oddly human hands hadn't been in constant motion.

I can't change what I did to you. Heck, I can hardly even believe I did it! But I can give you the chance to enjoy what I did and see a little of the universe. As you once told me, I want you to live a full, long life. For both of us.

I hope you remember me in your next lives. Not just as Shelby, the short-sighted human sister who betrayed you, and not even as the "space squirrel" I now seem to be, but as a part of you. Someday, if you choose it, we can become one again.

I leave it up to you.

Maybe Kathleen was projecting, but she thought the squirrel was crying.

I love you, Kat. Whatever choice you make, you'll always be my soulmate.

The hologram blinked out like an old tube television. Kathleen's vision was blurry and when she brought one hand to her eyes she discovered tears. From sadness or love or anger, she couldn't quite say. A swipe of her hand dislodged them, and she watched in awe as the droplets spun off into the hall, coalescing into perfect little spheres in this zero-g part of the space station.

Everything here was so alien.

Pulling against the handhold, Kathleen swiveled to face the furry alien her sister had become.

"Oh, Shel," she said, placing one hand gently against the viewing port. "What in the great wide galaxy am I supposed to do now?"

The frozen head just kept on smiling. Maybe it was wishful thinking, but Kathleen thought it looked peaceful.

STORY NOTES:

This story was sparked by a brunch conversation in which one person insisted that the slim chance at prolonging her life through cryogenics was worth the risk, weighed against the certainty of death, while the rest of us threw every pragmatic argument in this story—and probably many more—at her.

We did *not* talk about potential afterlives, but afterward I jotted down the story idea as "frozen head v. reincarnation."

The idea of reincarnation has only ever made sense to me if it stretches beyond our little planet, where the number of souls that would be required continues to increase. After that, I just had way too much fun creating aliens and other lives.

10 Things To Do in Los Angeles After You Die

1) Forest Lawn Memorial Park, Hollywood Hills

Breaking out of your grave will be the hardest part. Remember not to panic; you're already dead. Once you punch and kick and claw your way to the surface, enjoy the serenity of Forest Lawn's rolling hills. Don't bother looking for *her*; she wouldn't visit your grave if she could. Do check in on your famous neighbors like Lucille Ball, Liberace, and Buster Keaton. They'll be home. Only some newly dead celebrities shamble over the hills to feast on the brains of star-struck tourists. Though small, these brains are highly prized by Los Angeles area living dead.

2) Hollywood Sign

You took her to this iconic spot for your first date, but you weren't looking at the fifty-foot letters then. You're not looking at them now; you're remembering how, even years before the change, she loved to bite. Gaze down at Los Angeles spread before you. A carpet of lights twinkles through smog and thin columns of smoke. For now.

3) Grauman's Chinese Theatre

If you still have shoes, see how they compare to Steven Spielberg's prints in the forecourt. Imagine your life as one of his films: would you be happily ever after, or spattered with unnecessarily red blood? Be careful comparing hand prints; if your fingers get stuck in too-small spaces, they're likely to fall off. While in Hollywood, enjoy a fine foreign meal. Even a shambler can catch the sight-seers gawking at costumed cretins in front of the dramatic theatre. They'll see you coming, but they'll only be amazed by your costume, posing for a picture with you while you gnaw on their ears.

4) Venice Beach

She used to perform here. You used to watch her, you and the other men, as she twirled and danced in her short shorts and tall skates. You used to taste her skin down on the hot sand, feel her teeth tickling yours. Go there now, moaning and shuffling along the concrete paths. With so many garish street performers, body builders, and ragged homeless, no one will notice the grave dirt and blood that streak your face. Wander the canals where feral alligators choke on the occasional floating body, and realize how far from the real Venice you are. You will never go there now, and neither will she. You will never have a tenth anniversary.

5) Disneyland

If you need a pick-me-up, try the Happiest Place on Earth. Zombies get in free; simply chew your way past ticket-takers with pith helmets and fake-looking elephant guns. Try to hit weekends and school breaks, when the park is mobbed with children and their smug, fat parents. Kids make excellent snacks, and it's fun to watch Disney security in cartoonish riot gear scramble bodies off-site even while parents wail and rend their clothes, becoming a kind of zombie themselves. There is no death here, or so the guards say. Stand under the Matterhorn (you will never see the real Matterhorn) and remember the feel of that ring in your fingers as you held it up to her. Remember how her *yes* sounded like a *maybe*.

6) Watts Towers

In life, you were afraid to go there, though she loved the place. *The neighborhood is too rough*, you said. Look up now at Simon Rodia's bizarre masterpiece, see the spires like antennas broadcasting to an absent god. Walk among arches and touch the bits of tile and broken glass and garbage so lovingly arranged. But be attentive: the neighborhood is rougher now than ever before, fortified against your kind with sawed-off shotguns and machetes. If you are spotted, run. If you lose a rotting limb in your flight, leave it where it falls. As you run, imagine what a lovely wedding site it would have been.

7) The Queen Mary

Some love it for its history, some for its grandeur. Some are drawn to this stately ocean liner by rumors of hauntings. You thought it would be the perfect place to wed, but now you'd like to torpedo the whole thing, sink it finally beneath the placid harbor. Go ahead and rampage; bite and tear. Knock drinks from elegant hands and swab the decks with blood.

8) Farmers Market

Fresh, organic food is the name of this game. Ironic that the rotting scourge caught her here, among the snobs and foodies. She wasn't one of them when you met, nor when you married. *He* was the one who got her interested in cooking. *He* was the one who dragged her here. And the biting — well, you can't say that was entirely his fault. She always did have an inviting mouth, a generous, promiscuous, wandering mouth.

9) Union Station

This Art Deco classic was the last place you saw her, leaving you. The zombie rage was starting to take her over, but your rage was entirely human. To leave you? With *him?* On a *train?* Their laughter had more than a hint of the groaning sickness, but still it echoed lightly in the great hall. You confronted. They attacked. And the next thing you knew you woke up in a grave.

10) LaBrea Tar Pits

Or was there one more chapter between the train tracks and the graveyard? Recall the last of her yellow hair as it sank into oily mud beside plastic mammoths tethered to the shore. Remember the blood on your hands. Your wounds were deep, but you thought you'd survive. You were wrong. Watch now as bubbles of gas blub up from the stinking, shimmering pit. If you stumble into it, no one will question your motives. After all, zombies do not think. Driven by demonic hunger and rage, they are clumsy beasts.

Think on this as you fall.

STORY NOTES:

You know all those clickbaity travel articles with headlines like "28 Places to See Before You Die"? Doesn't the "Before You Die" part seem kind of redundant?

I set out to write a short, funny piece about posthumous tourism, but it turned sadder than I meant it to. Oh well.

This piece also needs a thank you to singer-songwriter-accordionist Jason Webley. The phrase "between the train tracks and the graveyard" was lifted from his song "Goodbye Forever Once Again."

Only the Messenger

DOZENS OF LIVES I've lived now, as all manner of things that swim, run, slither, and fly, and it's the same damn story every time. You may think you've found love of a profound and time-less nature, but that love will still swim away from you when the current is right. If you're very, very lucky, it won't happen until you die and get reincarnated on opposite sides of the galaxy.

I'd give three tentacles to be that lucky, just once.

Zaraell is the closest thing I've ever found to a soulmate, and the last holo message from Roptrango-A makes it clear that that's over. Holo messages are slow. She recorded that one almost a full Trango year ago, which means that the ranch-style coral home we sang into shape together has already been dismantled, the seeds divided among our offspring. I can barely think about what must remain, my portion left sick and sinking into the shifting sand leeward of West Volcano Spaceport.

Better to think of happier times: our first launch together; the day our first clutch of offspring hatched and the pride we felt in the survivor of the post-natal melee; the last time we mated, Zaraell's sinuous tentacles twined in mine until neither of us knew where ours ended and the other's began— Actually, thinking of happier times isn't helping either. My third stomach churns with sick bile. *I can't live with your choices anymore,* Zaraell's holo had said, grainy image of zir head softly shuddering. *Or is it that I can't live without them?*

I can't live without zir.

So what am I doing on this heap of an interstellar trader

speeding faster-than-light away from my truest love? I've been thinking about that a lot since I watched Zaraell's latest message, and I still don't know. All I know are three true things:

1) Illegal cargo is lucrative cargo. We're going to make a cloaca-load on this trade, bringing lab-grown meat to the Tro'o, if we can steer clear of the Intra-Stellar Trade Organization (ISTO).

2) The universe is stupidly, laughably big. Even with the hummingest star drive, it would take lifetimes to get from one end to the other (assuming there *are* ends — I have a vague memory of an edge, a starless pool of nothingness I may once have seen, many lives ago, but you can't really trust memories from toddler lives, so who knows?)

3) There is no such thing as a soulmate.

And yet...

The InstaComm pings, reminding me that I'm lost in the space of my own head. Words scroll out on the console's screen — a return message from the Tro'o, acknowledging our new ETA and providing new coordinates for the exchange. A moment later, a fresh sphere rolls out of the chute.

A shiny, rubbery sphere where a second ago there was nothing.

This new InstaCom unit has me baffled, and I'm the best engineer in this arm of the galaxy, if I do say so myself. To instantly — and I mean *instantly*, not at light speed or even faster-than-light, but right exactly *now* — send a message anywhere in the universe, you just type up a message, pop in a sphere, the machine does its thing, and the flattened disc that was the sphere comes out for disposal. When a message comes back, the machine spits out the message along with a fresh sphere to "fuel" your reply. It's not any kind of matter transfer I ever learned in school, and I'm itching to take the thing apart and uncover its secrets. But there is a *very* serious warning label on the sucker, and if even half the rumors about InstaComm are true, it's no idle threat.

Besides, these things are expensive. I've only been on two ships could afford one, and the captain'd have my beak if I broke this one poking about. So I shove off toward the stasis chamber to get the fresh sphere tucked away until we need it. You won't believe what the rumor mill says could happen to us if I don't.

———

Living on a little trading jumper like this one is tough for us Roptralians. I can hear *everything* that happens, whether I want to or not, vibrating through the hull and inner bulkheads and even the air.

So I know that Captain KrunZo, gruff and scaly in person, sings Kranellian arias in his grooming pod. I know that our pilot, Jorusz, wakes regularly from nightmares about his last life, in which he was an indentured guard for his species' royal family, a great humorless flying thing who was kept chained at night and eventually fed to a clutch of royal fledgelings. All through his sleep cycles his shoulderblades twitch, phantom escape attempts from muscles where in this life wings do not attach. I try to make allowances for his recent trauma when he (frequently) lashes out. I know that Quonka's calm and cheerful façade isn't phony—that she dances to the happy tunes in her head anytime gravity allows, humming along with them even while performing surgery and scrubbing out infected wounds.

But the same overly sensitive tentacles that make crewmate overshares a certainty also make Roptralians great stardrive mechanics, so what are you going to do? I tune out what I can and I ignore the rest. When gravity allows, I spend as much time as I can floating in a ball; not touching anything really helps reduce the noise.

But it leaves me alone with my thoughts, which are presently mired in contemplation of the size of the galaxy versus the size of this growing unease in my hearts.

From our present location, if we turned around and burned hard, our little ship could make it "home" to the Trango System in about 1.3 Trango years. Not that KrunZo would do such a thing with a payday on the line. If I really want to get back, my best bet would be to jump ship at the Tro'o rendezvous. Who knows? Maybe I could get hired on by something faster, make it back home in less than a year.

Home. Is it still home if you don't live there, and your partner has left you, your house un-sung and surrendered to the seas?

How did I let it get this far?

One cargo at a time, that's how. One better payday than the last; one more puzzle to solve, carrying me a little farther along, then a little farther, then a little farther still.

I feel so small, a speck in the vast uncaring universe, going the wrong direction.

And then I hear a knock at the door.

It's a testament to my preoccupation that I barely register the oddity of a knock on my hatch — the crew knows to leave me alone when I'm in my bunk — before I realize the knock isn't at my *hatch*. I uncoil one tentacle, uncovering one eye, which happens to have a perfect view out my porthole.

I gasp involuntarily, tentacles splaying, air bladders inflating. There is a face peering in the window. A cute little mammal face, with white fur and whiskers not even frozen by the vacuum of space. So I'm hallucinating. But then the knock comes yet again, and then an adorable fluffy paw waves at me, pointing one digit toward starboard. Toward the nearest airlock.

This is how those scary holos always begin, I think. But I swivel toward the hatch anyway.

In case we are about to be murdered by the Thing From Outside, I swing past the captain on the way to the airlock. KrunZo is a FranKoporp, another species you'd think would want to avoid the spacefaring life at all costs. Mostly round, covered in thick scales with stubby limbs and a thick, thick head, KrunZo maneuvers in low-g like a bowling ball propelled by anger. Planet-like gravity makes the ship even worse for him, turning it into a mountain of ladders too big for those poor little limbs to climb easily. KrunZo stays on the bridge most of the time, or in his quarters, and uses Captain's Prerogative to make the rest of us do his running about for him.

"Come quickly!" I say to him as I swim past his perch—a little running joke he rewards with the usual frown. "There's someone at the airlock."

"Funny," he says. But his tone suggests he doesn't think it's funny.

"Permission to let zir aboard?"

"Of course," KrunZo says with a barely perceptible wave of a forelimb. "It's bad luck to ignore impossible things that cannot be happening."

I choose to perceive only the permission and ignore the sarcasm. The airlock cycles, and in floats... something. It's small for a sapient, a little smaller than me and maybe a third the size of the other crew members. It looks like a mammal, one of those fluffy little pets from Earth that are all the rage? A kitty? Except. It's been a while since I was near Earth, but I'm pretty sure kitties don't have eight legs. And I also suspect they can't survive in vacuum. And their eyes aren't vast purple oceans of intelligence and love.

Those eyes spark something in me I haven't felt in lifetimes. Something I've been missing.

"What are you?" I blurt out, like some kind of mollusk who's never left the shell. "And *how* are you? I mean, how did you get here?"

The ship AI's security and medical protocols finish scanning the airlock's contents, various scanner beams and decontamination flashers causing a rippling blue-green light show to dance across white fur and ocean-gray walls, almost like a sunset back home. Then the inner airlock door hisses open.

The octo-cat doesn't say a word, just rams zir head right into me and nuzzles, purring softly. I feel like I could almost understand the purring, if the frequencies ze used were just slightly more... *cerulean?* But I don't need to understand it because I feel soothed by it, rocked in a gentle current that's almost like the warm waters of...

Without meaning to I reach one tentacle up to just stroke the creature's fur.

It's still cold.

"Now hold on a second," I say, pulling back and vibrating myself into a more alert state just as Quonka's shiny horn pops into view.

Technically Quonka is the ship's doctor, but her species' calming pheromone secretions make her a useful asset in brokering deals. She also tries to be around when we get boarded by ISTO, which is more and more frequently.

The creature visibly relaxes as Quonka enters. "Who is your new friend, Astrill?" she asks. Anyone else on the ship would be mocking, but Quonka sounds sincere.

"I am..." the kitty thing says, looking around as if searching for the answer. "... just a traveler."

"Um, no," Quonka says, horn glinting and hair tumbling as she shakes her pretty head. "One does not just bump into random travelers in the vastness of space. Especially not travelers without space suits or supplies. The odds are, well, astronomical. And if we had just bumped into you somehow, at these speeds, the impact would have turned you into a splat on the hull — or into shards of meaty ice, since you ought to be frozen solid."

The kitty thing backpedals in the air, all eight legs working, until zir tail touches the bulkhead and wraps itself around a handhold there. Prehensile tail. Do cats have those? The tail almost seems to lengthen as it grabs.

"At least tell us your name," I say.

But again the thing looks around like this is a really hard question, zir violet eyes flicking back and forth. "Call me . . . Ennesta," ze finally says.

"Okay, Ennesta," Quonka says, reaching one three-fingered hand out in greeting. "That is a start."

But Ennesta doesn't seem to like that gesture. Ze launches off the hatch and into my tentacles, sending us both spinning.

As we spin, I see another new visitor in the area outside the airlock room. Jorusz is here, and as always he brings his aura of cold-blooded menace. Jorusz is like an anti-chameleon; he always uses his metachrosis to clash as much as possible, and therefore right now he's an angry bright orange-red.

"Let me question it," says Jorusz. "It's probably from ISTO."

"Ennesta does not look like an Intra-Stellar Trade Organization agent," Quonka says, head tilted.

"And Ennesta isn't an 'it,'" I add, trying to prize Ennesta far enough away from me to look at zir. "Hey, are you —" Ennesta looks up, huge eyes wielded like a weapon. "Does your species have gender?"

Ennesta looks around at the three sapients in the small space like choosing from a menu. "Female?" she answers, but it sounds like a guess.

"That was convincing," Jorusz hisses, rolling one eye while keeping the other fixed on Ennesta.

In the end, the matter is settled by KrunZo, who apparently found the commotion interesting enough to leave the bridge. He comes barreling in and almost crushes me and Ennesta (by now three of her four pairs of limbs are wrapped around me), but Quonka catches one of KrunZo's forelimbs and swings him into a relatively stationary position.

"Are you a spy?" KrunZo demands.

Ennesta manages to squeak out a *no*.

"Then welcome aboard," the captain says. "And Jorusz? Pull yourself together. You really getting bent out of shape over this slip of fluff?"

Jorusz flushes an even more glaring orange, and for a moment I fear he's about to challenge the captain. But a moment later he skitters off, muttering so low that only I can hear him. "Slip of fluff that can live in space. That shit ain't right."

He's right, of course. So says my brain, at least, despite — or even because of — how the newcomer's purring tugs at the rest of me like a syzygetic tide.

———

Ennesta stays. The ship has empty cabins, but she commandeers mine, climbing into my hammock and leaving me to choose whether or not to join. I'm torn, so torn.

Her presence on the ship is suspicious. And it feels disloyal to Zaraell...

But the sting of Zaraell's last message and the stingless absence of zir tentacles are wounds that Ennesta's eight furry limbs staunch to a surprising degree. I give in, and, wrapped in her desperate embrace, I sleep better than I have in many lunar tides.

But Jorusz does not pull himself together. Well before my next shift, his vibrations cut through Ennesta's purring like a klaxon. *Astrill, report to the bridge*, Jorusz whispers. *Don't bring the hairball.*

Jorusz is a deceptively mellow mottled teal shade when I get there, strapped in to the comms chair rather than his normal pilot's station. He points to the screen as I arrive, then switches the display to holo. A life-sized Ennesta springs into the air, slowly rotating like a showroom model. "I found it," he says, slapping one hand through the holo image for emphasis.

"Found what?" I croak. It's too early for riddles.

"I found Ennesta's species. If that is her real name. She's a toyopop." He says it like a dirty word.

"So?"

"So," Jorusz says, rolling his bulbous eyes, "it took me forever to find this out, and it's a miracle I did at all, and you know why? Toyopops aren't sentients. They can't even talk. They're pets engineered by the Argotenkers for their deep space workers."

That wakes me up. A tingling chill rolls from my beak to my suckers like the ghost of a purr. "Wait, so . . . ?"

"So she's not what she appears."

And then, of course, because we are talking about her, there she is, a silent presence that we nonetheless notice right away. "Oh, hi," I say, waving a couple of tentacles feebly. I feel tossed like flotsam in a storm. All I really know about Ennesta is how comforting I find her. What if she really is a spy? What will Jorusz do to her if she is? What will he do to her to find out whether she is?

"I missed you," she says, but her eyes are glued to the larger-than-life holographic version of herself as it rotates slowly in the silence. Its ears are different than hers, longer and thinner, and its paws look different too, less fingery.

Ennesta—the real Ennesta—looks from the holo to me with a question in her eyes that borders on accusation.

The InstaComm chooses that moment to ding, a message from the Tro'o scrolling onto the screen. Ennesta screams for about a millisecond before turning it into a yelp, while something like a shudder roils down her long body, making her look for a moment less than fully solid, like a thing about to explode.

A fresh message sphere plops out into the net.

"We'll finish this conversation later," Jorusz hisses, turning to the screen. He grabs the sphere and spins it to me. "Make yourself useful and take this to stasis."

Ennesta is looking around the space in a sort of panic. One of her hands darts out toward the sphere as if to intercept it before it gets to me, but she pulls back.

"Aye-aye, captain," I say sarcastically—Jorusz, as pilot, does not outrank me—but I wrap a tentacle around the sphere anyway, grateful for any excuse to get out of there.

Ennesta's eyes burn into me as I grab the sphere, and her mouth opens as if to say something. I wait for a beat, but her words don't come, and the terror in her eyes mutates into something more like despair. "You got something to say to me?" I ask, harsher than I mean to.

Ennesta dips her furry chin.

Her big sad eyes follow me all the way down to the stasis chamber, and if I go back to my hammock they'll just follow me there, too. And then we'll have to talk, and after talking is when folks usually start leaving. And I'm not ready to be left, not so soon.

So I take the fresh sphere to the ship's smallest stasis chamber, open the door, and slot it into the new racks we installed in there, next to the scant half-dozen others we were able to buy. Then I head to the engine room to get an early start on the cycle's routine maintenance.

I see Ennesta lingering in front of the stasis chamber, her eyes darting shiftily between the chamber and myself.

We start burning to slow our way to the Tro'o rendezvous, so gravity returns to the ship. Jorusz and Quonka are relieved, and they start the usual chatter about stretching their bones—I don't really understand bones, but I guess gravity is good for them. KrunZo has bones *and* an exoskeleton, because evolution wasn't messing around on his home planet, but though he loves planetary gravity, he hates the ship's gravity more than anyone. I can hear his complaining loud and clear even over the roar of the decelerating star drive.

According to the info on toyopops that Jorusz dug up, Ennesta, as a standard-issue mammal, has bones too. But I have my doubts. Sometimes the way she curls up in my hammock makes her seem more sinuous than should be possible for something with a spine.

Despite almost constant togetherness, I still don't know much about our new passenger. Though I've found myself telling her all about Zaraell and my journey out into the black, she won't tell me where she came from, how she came to be floating in space, or how she *survived* floating in space. What she does do is listen, and purr, and on the rare occasion she speaks, it's with a surprising depth.

When Ennesta's not trying to weld herself to me—which I admit, I enjoy more and more—no one can find her.

I could find her, of course. I can feel and sort through every vibration on this ship when I wish. I don't look for her at first because, well, I didn't work as hard as I have for my whole damn career on politely ignoring my crewmates' vibrations to violate Ennesta's privacy.

Still. The computer logs Jorusz shows me are suspicious. Someone's been scouring the star charts. For what? We can't tell. But it's happening during the times when Ennesta's unaccounted for.

So okay, I listen for her. I pick up Quonka singing to herself in her cabin and KrunZo barking something to Jorusz, who's climbing his way to the bridge, ignoring the ladder in favor of just suckering up the wall. With all those sounds accounted for, and the hum of the ship's star drive, whatever's left must be Ennesta. There isn't anything left, not at first.

And then I hear a whispered voice command in one of the ship's unused cabins: *"One quadrant X-ward,"* it says. *"Systems with F2V stars."*

What is she looking for?

Ennesta is quiet, but I can be quieter still, even in the ship's increasing gravity. I slink up to the cabin's open door before she knows I'm there, and I see...

I'm not sure *what* I'm seeing. The creature using the computer terminal is clearly Ennesta. It's all covered in white fur, and it still has eight limbs—but none of them are right. The topmost pair has dexterous six-fingered hands instead of paws, and the middle two pairs have shrunk to nubs, while the bottom have elongated into wobbly-looking legs that boost Ennesta high enough to see the computer's screen.

A gasp escapes my beak.

Ennesta turns so fast her face looks blurry. She pulls her front hands off the controls even as they start morphing back into paws. She shrinks as her legs even out.

"What are you?"

Ennesta shakes her head.

"Well, you're clearly not a toyopop. You lied to us," I say, and it's all I can do not to say *You lied to* ME. The hurt I feel registers as an actual ache in my second heart. *Figures*, I think. You start to care about someone; you get hurt.

"No," Ennesta says. She walks toward me on her hind legs, unsteadily, other limbs wiggling awkwardly, and it occurs to me that not only is this the first time I've seen her navigate in gravity, it also looks like the first time she's ever tried it. Or at least the first time in her current form. "I just haven't told you things." All of her top six arms are held out placatingly.

"This whole body you're in is a lie. What do you even look like, really?"

"I . . . can't show you." Ennesta's face looks as sad as only a genetically engineered pet can look. Except there is real intelligence behind those eyes; intelligence and sorrow.

"Of course not," I say, tentacles fluttering in frustration. "Look, Jorusz thinks you're a spy for ISTO. I don't want to believe him, but. What is it you're looking for in our star charts? Why can't you—or *won't* you—tell us anything about yourself? Where you came from? What species you are? Anything?"

Ennesta is close enough to touch me, but she doesn't. She turns over some of her paws and looks at them as if for the first time, then flings them out in a gesture of raw hopelessness. "I don't know!"

"What do you mean, you don't know?"

Ennesta slumps onto the deck like a shipwreck hitting the ocean floor. "I don't know, not any of the answers. I don't know what I am or where I came from or what I'm supposed to look like. I've never seen one of me before—not after metamorphosis, anyway."

"Okay..." I say. "So you're a shapeshifter."

She nods.

"But you don't know what your natural form is."

"I've never seen it. I've always just been—"

"Been what?"

And she hesitates, then sighs and starts again. "I haven't ever lived long enough to find out what I am."

No kidding, I think, somewhat bitterly. Who has?

"I'd seen these toyopop things in previous lives, and everyone treated them with kindness. It seemed like a good thing to be..." She shrugs two sets of her fluffy arms. "I didn't realize they were pets."

I laugh, despite it all. "And the star charts? What's that about? Just what are you looking for?"

"Home."

That little word hits me hard, echoing through an empty place inside me: a coral house with no one home. Gravity, who *isn't* looking for a place to hang that word on?

"Okay," I say. "It'll be all right. Come on, let's tell the others. I bet Quonka will even help you look." I extend a tentacle to Ennesta, who places one paw in it and stands on two legs.

She takes a few wobbly steps, then lets go of me and drops to all eight legs. "Hold on," she says. She makes a couple circles on all eight, tripping herself a few times. Finally she bends her spine in a way that doesn't look anatomically possible and ambulates on six of the legs, leaving the top two to function as arms. "Oh, that's much better," she says.

It looks completely unnatural.

"How do real toyopops walk?" I ask.

"They use all eight," she admits. "But I can't get the hang of it, and since my cover is blown anyway..." She shrugs with the top two limbs.

"Do you need all of them? May as well drop the middle two pairs."

"Do you need all of yours?" She elongates a finger to gently stroke one of my tentacles, and then I can't speak, all I can do is wait for the electric thrill to pass through my whole body, from beak to cloaca. A shockingly erotic thrum lingers there, and in the sensitive inner curve of the tentacle where Ennesta's paw still explores.

This is madness. Am I really *attracted* to this creature in this false and somewhat ridiculous body, about whom I still know almost nothing?

Yes, I am.

"I can certainly use them all in interesting ways, if that's what you're asking," I say when my voice returns, only a little quaver in it. "But, see, I'm not a shapeshifter. Mine aren't optional."

Ennesta drops her finger, which is a true tragedy. She looks at her body, her limbs, as if for the first time, standing on the rear ones to hug herself around the middle with the second and third pairs. "I like them," she finally says. "They aren't very practical, but they feel like a part of me. Even if they do trip me up sometimes." She wiggles them suggestively. "Of course, I could be something else if you wanted."

Madness or not, I give in, standing on six tentacles to match limbs six for six with Ennesta's in a slow embrace. "I like you just how you are," I say, and we go from there, and before long neither of us can say how many limbs we have, only that we need all of them to properly explore and pleasure each other.

Afterward, Ennesta gets her limbs tangled on the ladder up to the bridge, and I can't help but chuckle when one of them slips off and bonks me lightly in the head. I use a spare two tentacles to guide her paw back to the ladder, and she pushes off my head up into the bridge with a little more force than is strictly necessary—a gentle poke.

"Well, if it isn't the stowaway," Jorusz says, scales throbbing between red and purple. "What do you want?"

"Ennesta's a shapeshifter," I blurt out. "She isn't sure what her species is supposed to look like. Tell them, Ennesta."

The InstaComm pings, and Jorusz mutters at the screen.

"Ennesta?"

She's left my side, running almost all the way up to Jorusz before seeming to remember she's afraid of him. Her eyes are wide and full of fear.

The InstaComm ejects a fresh message sphere, and Jorusz casually tosses it into a bag of them. Clearly the Tro'o are being their usual high-maintenance selves.

Ennesta's eyes are glued to the bag of message spheres. Or maybe it's the bag of flattened, used spheres she's eyeing, in stunned horror. Jorusz touch-types something into the Insta-Comm, head swiveled to look away from the screen toward us.

"Stop," Ennesta says. "Please!"

"Stop what?" KrunZo asks. He hits the blue button and the machine pings cheerily.

And Ennesta looks at him with such hurt and rage that I recoil from her.

The flattened message sphere pops out of the InstaComm console. Jorusz makes to toss it into the bag with the rest of them, but Ennesta holds out one trembling paw. Jorusz looks to

KrunZo, who grunts a confused assent.

Ennesta takes the oblong disc in one paw, then holds it in both before her, reverently, as though it's not just a bit of trash destined for the matter reclamator but something very precious. She holds it up to her face, looking closely, then sniffing, and after a moment during which none of us breathe, she takes a deep breath and releases it as a keening, piercing howl.

For a long while none of us move, shocked into inaction by Ennesta's uncharacteristic, unrelenting loudness. KrunZo, as befits a captain, is the first to recover. "What in Gravity's name are you doing?" he demands.

"She's mourning, you idiot," Quonka says mildly, climbing up into the cockpit. She kneels beside Ennesta, placing one hand on the place where Ennesta's back bends unnaturally upright. "There there, sweetie," she says. "You want to tell us why the message sphere makes you so sad?"

Ennesta quiets, nodding. "It's dead," she says. "Dead again and again and again."

———

The machine births me, as usual. The ping, as usual, is the first thing I remember. And then the words of a message, as they're squeezed from me. They slip away, leaving little behind. In larval stage, my senses are not sharp. I feel movement, textures against my exterior. I sense light, though I have no eyes.

Then a flash of cold, and nothing.

I wake back in the machine, again. Words are stabbed into me, a destination, the sharp-sweet-rotten smell, and then the crush, the pain. I expect the momentary nothing pause and then the ping of a new life. But the crushing goes only partway. I hear the ping, but it's a different one than before, and my senses are alive like never before, alive with pain.

I am grabbed. I am in a hand, and the voice attached to the hand is weary and grumbling, and I tumble into a bag with other refuse. For I realize that's what I am. They do not know I am alive. I am lucky garbage.

For a kilosecond or two I can't move. I am too young, too wounded. But we grow fast. I consume the other refuse and by the time they throw us all into space I am a fat sphere again, lucky garbage of lazy ship.

In larval stage, I have no need for air. I float, I tumble like asteroid.

I am lucky a third time, because you shoot through my space. I have just enough strength to end larval stage and choose a form and hold onto your ship. And here I am.

We stare at her, waiting for the punchline. Ennesta lifts the flattened sphere of the most recent message sent in one paw.

"This is what I should have been. The machine should have killed me; sent my soul to the other end to be birthed with the message."

After a moment of silence, Jorusz is the one to break it. "You're trying to tell us you're a damn *message sphere?*"

Ennesta shakes her head. "No. I'm trying to tell you that the message spheres are the same as me."

Jorusz's scales pulse brighter and brighter orange. "That's impossible! It's a damn machine. It doesn't *birth* any larvae."

"How do you know?" Quonka asks, still kneeling next to Ennesta.

In response, Jorusz only flashes a ripple of colors at her.

"It's a fair question," I say, the concrete puzzle of a mechanical question snapping my mind back into focus. "I've worked on just about every kind of machine there is, but never on an Insta-Comm. No one has. It's common knowledge that you just can't even think of opening one of those things up, but did you read the warning on the unit closely? *Punishable by memory wipe.* So for all we know it *does* birth larvae."

"That would explain a few things," Quonka says. "I've always wondered how the messages are transmitted so fast, faster than anything else in the known universe. If they do run on reincarnation..."

KrunZo, still as a mountain in his captain's chair, does his best to steeple his stubby arms. "Well, sure. Reincarnation is instant. But it's also random."

Ennesta looks alarmed. "It is?"

"Isn't it?" I ask.

"It isn't for me. For my people. The machine controls it, and now that I am free from the machine I could control it."

"Gronkshit," Jorusz grumbles. "There is no such thing as a species that can control its reincarnation. We'd've heard about it!"

"That's what you've been looking for, isn't it?" Quonka asks, ignoring Jorusz even though he's strobing between black and orange.

Ennesta blushes her furry face somehow—she must be changing the color of her fur. "I was born into the machine. I don't remember where home is."

"And you want to find it so you can die and be reborn there?" Quonka asks.

Ennesta nods.

And my third heart sinks like a stone. Of course. She's just waiting for the right current to swim away from me. Stupid of me to have thought otherwise, for even a nanosecond. "Now hold on," I begin, but—

"This is nonsense!" Jorusz interjects. "First of all, you're all listening to a wild yarn from a stowaway who's probably an ISTO spy. And second, if it *is* true, then we're probably all going to get disappeared for violating InstaComm's terms. I can't believe what a ship of fools I'm on."

"I can prove it," Ennesta says quietly, and it only takes following her gaze to the bag of fresh message spheres to figure out how. According to InstaComm, they must be put into stasis within four kiloseconds or one standard Galactic Hour. But what if they weren't?

"Let them grow up," she says.

"Astrill," KrunZo asks, "what's the penalty for that?"

It takes about another few days — as I reckon them — to reach the Tro'o rendezvous, a jungle moon of the system's third planet. Needless to say, we send no more InstaComm messages. Luckily, we're close enough by now that holos really will do just as well, even for the anxious Tro'o.

The gravity lovers — including KrunZo, who takes any opportunity he can to ambulate on flat land — shuttle the cargo down, while Ennesta and I tend to the brood of message spheres whose number increases with every transmission from the Tro'o. We've been feeding them table scraps and anything else otherwise headed for the matter reclamator that Ennesta deems suitable. It's unnerving how they absorb the food into themselves. The spheres are getting big; the first ones we freed from stasis are almost half the size of Ennesta, who, now that I think of it, also seems to be growing. She's about my size now, and I wonder if she'll end up towering over me the way the other crew members do. I'm sure even she has no idea how big she'll get.

Over the holo from down on the moon, the Tro'o are stomping around on their feathery hind legs, roaring at KrunZo and Jorusz and Quonka and waving their clawed hands. While most of the Tro'o take pride in their reasoning, the sect we most often deal with behaves like the monsters they resemble. It's only a matter of time before they demand not just lab-grown meat but *murdered* meat, and then live animals to hunt. I'd bet any quantity of the finest Kranellian snapps on it.

I mute the holo display. How am I supposed to know if negotiations are about to turn south, when the Tro'o bellow like that to say hello? I enlarge a scanner screen tracking nearby ships. None of them squawk ISTO, but then they wouldn't, would they? I scroll through the ships' actual images one at a time.

In the unused cabin we've turned into a message sphere nursery, holographic dinosaurs stomp and spaceships fly. And a non-holographic sphere wobbles, cracking open like an egg with no shell, stretching and unfolding tentatively. I'm breathless to see what Ennesta's species looks like, even more to see her finally see it too, but no. Limbs emerge (four of them); a head stretches into shape. A tail extrudes from what is now the creature's posterior, and proportions adjust to account for it. After a long moment the newly born... whatever Ennesta's species is called... claws zir way out of the bunk's netting and opens zir toothy mouth to roar. Congratulations, it's a Tro'o! Clearly this former sphere's choice of form was influenced by the holo.

We've done our best to research Ennesta's species, with no luck. There is no record in the libraries of either a shape-shifting species or one that can control its reincarnation — only legends of feats performed by acolytes of the Collective, none with provable results. My theory is that a species with that kind of control might never choose to leave their home system; perhaps none have ever been reborn as something else, somewhere else.

It sounds like paradise.

I've had more lives than anyone else on this crew, having bounced all over the universe since the days of the fifth Galactic Empire. I've ended up in regions so remote that there was no interstellar trade, even been planet-bound a couple of times. I've been mammalian, reptilian, avian, heptopod, and almost every other kind of thing there is, with no connecting thread that I can discern. Yeah, it's exciting. Variety is the spice of lives, right?

It's also lonely. I've never been reunited with any past loves. Or past friends. Or acquaintances. A person starts to feel like love is pointless at best, counterproductive even.

We've also been trying to research InstaComm. How was the miraculous technology developed? How does it work? All we've found are more legends and conspiracy theories. Was the Lost Generationship of the Pro'oco steered into a star because they knew too much? According to the lead-hat wearers, yes.

All official inquiries lead to the same result—a form allowing one to place a request to purchase a system or to request technical support. Don't call us; we'll call you.

—————

By the time the shuttle is back on board, three more of the spheres have hatched. One looks like a kind of bat-winged bird, one looks like a miniature Quonka, and the third can't seem to make up its mind, shifting between two legs and four and six, experimenting with skin and scales and fur.

Peering into the net they're incubating in, Ennesta's arms twined with my tentacles, I can't help but think of my own offspring, swimming the various seas of the Trango System. Each one was hatched from a clutch like this; each was the lone survivor of a brutal post-birth scrum. Ennesta assures me that these babies won't start murdering and devouring each other, but I'm not sure how she knows that.

Looking at them, each certainly possessed of a soul, I wonder for the first time about my offspring who didn't make it through the melee. Roptralian wisdom holds that they have no souls, that only the survivor is imbued with one. But what if we're wrong? What if each of them lived a brief, violent life? Born to die, never even named, mourned by none.

All of Ennesta's lives have been like that.

I stretch my tentacles to pull her closer to me, and she purrs. She's nothing like Zaraell, but we feel like new parents.

None of the "children" the memory spheres have become know what their species should look like or where the home planet is. Yet they have memories — or at least fragments of memories — dating back almost a terasecond. Tens of thousands of Roptralian years. Further back than the first life I can remember. Messages mundane and critical have passed through them to all parts of the galaxy — for those who can afford InstaComm's rates.

Zaraell is not one of those. Zir messages come as holos, bound by the universe's speed limits. One is here now, and the computer asks me if I want to view it. Why not? The meat deal is done and the crew is back on board. The dinosaurs have stopped stomping and turned to their cargo, presumably. At any rate, they're no longer my concern.

Zaraell's face appears much larger than life, and Ennesta momentarily starts, then goes back to chatting with the newly hatched message spheres and hovering over the younger ones, waiting.

Zaraell sits in a peach-colored coral house I've never seen before, that opens behind zir to a stunning vista of clear water and lovingly sculptured kelp gardens and the rolling hills of Roptrango-A's trendiest city. It's rendered in 2D, of course, but I still feel the punch I know Zaraell intended—why else spend the extra to render the background at all?

But despite the perfection of zir setting, the lines around zir beak betray worry. "I can't imagine why you haven't responded to my last message," ze begins, and I quake thinking about the distance that separates us. I *did* respond, though there wasn't much I could say about it, but we are just so far away that Zaraell won't get that holo for another dozen lunar tides—most of zir solar year. Ze's probably about to get one I sent five jobs back, before I ever heard ze wanted to split up, and I can't imagine what ze'll make of its sunny long-distance love platitudes now.

"I decided not to wait, as you can see. I moved. I really like my new apartment—there's even a sundeck on the top floor that's dry at low tide. You can see the stars. I still look at them at night and wonder which direction you're off in."

Zaraell's image sighs, bubbling out tiny, pretty spheres that I feel I could almost touch. Ennesta sidles up to me, nuzzling. Her eyes are as wide as oceans.

"Please message me back," Zaraell says. "I want to see your face." And the holo flickers off.

I slump to the cabin floor. We've started burning away from the Tro'o on to the next adventure, and gravity is as high on the ship as it ever is, but that's not what's weighing me down. A heavy lump sits on my second heart, and it's made of the distance from here to home.

"That was your home system?" Ennesta asks, with surprising intensity. Her six legs are all dancing like she has to pee.

I gesture *yes* with the roll of a couple tentacles.

"What is it called?"

"Trango," I say, and Ennesta yelps, covering her mouth with

her paws. "Zaraell lives on Roptrango-A, the first planet, but they all look pretty similar."

Ennesta squirms, looking anguished in a way that I'm pretty sure isn't jealousy. I don't know *what* it is, and that sinks me with worry.

"Why do you ask?"

Still, Ennesta stalls. "Is it really that beautiful there?"

I laugh. "Can you breathe in water? You probably can. Yeah, it's really that beautiful. But I'm biased, you know? It's home."

Ennesta is quiet.

"I guess you wouldn't know. Sorry. We'll find your homeworld someday."

There is a look dancing in her purple eyes that I cannot place.

"Why are you asking about Trango? You wanna go? I'll take you there, but it's far..."

"I can get there very fast," Ennesta says sadly. "I have to tell you something. I have horrible news."

Research Vessel H6Alpha to Trango System defense.

Disaster imminent! Misfired gravito-stellar beam on intercept course with Star Trango, ETA M141 K498 H122 S020. Trango System will be obliterated unless you build and deploy capture array by M133.4. Instructions for array follow.

The message is so brief—before devolving into schematic in-structions, that is—that I can barely understand it. It seems so clinical for something that will wipe out my entire solar system. I imagine a laser blast, shot into space, traveling forever at the speed of light. I imagine myself, behind it, trying to shield my family (because they *are* still family, Zaraell and the kids, despite everything) from something I can never get in front of, no mat-ter how hard I try.

How soon is M133.4? I've never been a natural with Universal Standard Time, so all I know is that it's *soon*. Sooner than we can get there. Is it sooner than a holo can get there? *Where's that conversion chart?*

"Is there still time?" I ask, when I can think enough to form words. *How long will it take to build the capture array?*

Ennesta shakes her head. "I don't know. I'm just the message."

I look at her, really look, deep into her sad purple eyes. "You're a lot more than that."

She shakes her head vehemently, pulling away from me even as I reach for her. "Am I? All I've ever been is a message. From here to there, life after life. Never a person."

"You're a person now. A person who I..."

"Who you what?" Ennesta is so still, not even breathing.

"Who I..." The words stick in my throat. "Am very glad to have met."

Ennesta sits, heavily, folding limbs in ways I suspect real toyo-pops can't. "I think I'm lucky garbage at best. Or maybe not-so-lucky garbage. If I'd stayed a message, your home would be safe."

It's true, isn't it? True in a way that nothing else about Ennesta is: from her name to her gender, to—I fear—her affection for me, she's making it all up as she goes along. So I find no reply I can make to comfort her.

Worse, a part of me wants to ask the unthinkable from her: for her to deliver the message after all. But stars, what would that mean? She'd have to die, and when she was reborn, it would be back into unending slavery, countless cycles of life and death that would take her Gravity-knows-where in the universe—and away from me forever. Not only can I not ask it, I'm not even sure I want it, even with every other thing I've ever loved in the universe on the line.

Ennesta doesn't offer.

M133.4 is only eight lunar tides from now. Less than half a Trango year. Not even a holo can get there that fast.

Thoughts whirl in my mind like fish darting through tidal eddies. Can the doom beam be stopped any other way? Sometimes I convince myself that it's no problem at all; surely the research station would have sent more than one message, right? Right? Even Zaraell sent more than one message to break up with me. Although, the second message wasn't sent until *after* going ahead and leaving me.

So maybe it's not safe to assume another message was sent.

I keep circling around the thought that since only an Insta-Comm message can get there in time, only Ennesta can save the Trango System. But that's not really true, is it? There are other former message spheres on board the ship, seven or ten or a dozen of them now, all matured out of their larval stage into whatever form struck their fancy. They've made themselves at home, filling the extra cabins and taking up almost all the computer's time on the star charts searching for home. They're piecing together their bits of knowledge, looking for a binary system, perhaps, or something with a nebula view. They're also plotting something that they think I don't know about: a plan to free the rest of their species from the evil machinations of InstaComm.

But the point, the one I don't want to admit, is that any of them could be used to send a message.

Or maybe not. They don't fit into the slot on the InstaComm anymore, so I'm not sure how we'd encode the message onto one of them, let alone the coordinates for rebirth. I've tried to get the information out of Ennesta, and all that her evasive answers seem to imply is that it *could* be done.

Of course, it would mean murdering a sentient being. But just one. One little life, to save Zaraell and the kids. One little life to save all the beaches, all the coral homes, all the clear waters and the schools of colorful fish and the gardens. One murder to save all of it, the star and the planets and the tides that whisper songs of home . . .

If it was *only* a murder, maybe I could do it. Death is not forever. One life ends and another begins. But the new life I would be sending that being into would be a life of slavery, again and again and again.

I can't do it, and not only because I don't know how. There's also Ennesta's big eyes that light up when she sees me coming through the nursery hatch, and her eight furry limbs that intertwine with my tentacles like they were engineered to do it, and her soft rumbling purr when I wake with her nestled asleep under my beak. And something else: a feeling that though the shifty tides of the universe brought us together, I can't let them pull us apart.

The InstaComm pings. Ennesta and I both jump almost out of our skins, and Jorusz rolls his bulbous eyes and flashes a lizardy green. When the fresh message sphere pops out into the cockpit he tosses it toward Ennesta, saying, "Here's another new friend for you."

Then he turns to the screen and fades a sicker shade of green. "Oh shitballs," he says. "ISTO."

Intra-Stellar Trade Organization. This means evasive maneuvers, maybe boarding, maybe a fine, confiscation of our current cargo, which is probably illegal. I've lost track. I just scoot toward the engine room, anticipating trouble from whatever crazy shit Jorusz is about to ask the star drive to do.

Ennesta follows, message sphere in one hand, and, despite the danger of ISTO and gravity suddenly slamming us both into the wall as Jorusz sends us hurtling through space, I have a thought. A terrible thought.

A fresh message sphere. One I can still use.

I know all the details of the message Ennesta carried. Sending it would be as simple as typing it into the InstaComm and pressing that blue button.

And getting the new sphere (which I am trying hard to think of as a thing, a tool, definitely not a sentient being with a soul) away from Ennesta.

And murdering zir—no, *it*—and returning it, and all its future reincarnations, to an eternity of slavery.

———

I try to focus on wringing power out of the ship's star drive so we can careen and duck through this system's asteroid belt and shake ISTO off our tail.

But during the cilia-raising escape, our scan detector sirens more than once, so even though we once again make it out with our lives (in time for dinner, even!), now ISTO knows exactly who and what we are. It's only a matter of time before they find us again, surround and board us, and then the best we can hope for is that their memory wipe leaves us with some of the things we hold most dear. *Zaraell*, I think, twisting three tentacles into a wishing pose. *Ennesta*.

Trango.

After fixing the minor damage Jorusz's evasive maneuvers did to my star drive, I climb into my hammock next to Ennesta —may as well call it *our* hammock by now—noting the small sphere maturing in a bit of netting beside us. It's visibly bigger than earlier already. But I think it'll still fit into the InstaComm's slot. If I act soon.

I wait until Ennesta's asleep, purring heavily with six of her limbs wrapped around me. I peel them off one at a time, once again, and creep out into the night. No one is stirring, not even Jorusz, who should be on watch after an ISTO sighting. Not a single one of the former message spheres. Not the one wrapped in two of my tentacles. It feels for all the world like a rubber ball. Maybe slightly warm. Maybe with the slow, almost imperceptible beating of an alien heart.

I get as far as the InstaComm console. I type in the message. I input the coordinates. I burble something like a prayer to the sphere cradled in one tentacle, pressing it up against the hole it's just slightly too large to slide easily into. I tell myself it's not much. Just a little push. Just a little more pressure. Then push the blue button. Then, ping! The death and eternal slavery of a sentient being. But just one. One little being for millions. Surely that's good math?

I have no idea how much time passes in that moment, in which all of my senses are directed inward, warring with myself. I'm so consumed that I don't even hear Ennesta approach. I don't notice her until a furry white hand comes into my view, delicately moving my tentacle away from the sphere stuck halfway into the slot. She pries it free, cupping it in a pair of hands, while other hands wrap around me. I turn into those arms, weeping without tears, a coughing, rasping wail that pulls up from the depths of my third heart only to be lost in Ennesta's furry embrace.

"There there, sweetie," she says. "It's okay. I knew you couldn't go through with it."

I weep, shuddering in her many arms.

"It's okay," she repeats. "Let's go back to bed."

"I can't," I say, pulling away. "I may not be able to kill anyone, but I can't live with letting Trango die either."

I guess I can't live at all, then. The idea hits me like the jolt of an electric eel. I wrap my tentacles around Ennesta's wrists, gripping hard.

"Teach me," I say. "I'll deliver the message. Just teach me how."

———

Ennesta resists for days, as doom races toward Trango.

"What if it can't be taught? What if it only works for my species?"

It's a risk I'm willing to take. "Worst-case scenario, I end up reborn somewhere else. That's what happens."

"Do your people mature fast enough for you to remember the message in time?"

Honestly, no. Even if Roptralian lore is correct and only one offspring has a soul (and that would be me, right, by default?), it takes time to prevail against one's soulless clutchmates. And that's if I could even bring myself to devour them this time around, and if I didn't have the hearts to go through with it, they'd surely make short work of me. And even if I did make it through the melee, it takes time to grow enough to understand the world and remember past lives, and even more time to be respected enough that the message might be heard.

No, it won't do at all to be reborn as a Roptralian. I'll have to be born as whatever Ennesta is. But that means . . .

Ennesta knows exactly what it means. "If you end up in the machine . . ."

This is the true worst-case scenario, being caught in the life-death cycle of Ennesta's enslaved people. And yet, it's also the best-case scenario. It's the only thing that will work.

I run a tentacle lovingly down the side of her worried face, and she covers it with a paw. "Well, then it's up to you, my love."

Ennesta nods sadly. Perhaps she would never have become a

crusader on her own, but there are a dozen-some of her people, freed and angry, onboard the ship now. And they haven't just been searching for the homeland so they can go back there and keep hiding. They won't rest until they free every one of their kind. And if this works, that will include me. I think they can do it, too. It's only a matter of time before they bring the whole InstaComm system crashing down.

"Who knows how long it will take us, though," she says. "Who knows how many lives you'll go through, and where you'll end up? What if I can't ever find you again?"

A tear falls from her eye, landing on one of my tentacles. I look at it, test it between two suckers, feel the silky saltiness of it, just like the real thing. Just like a drop in the oceans. *How does a shapeshifter do that?*

Well, maybe I'll find out.

"You found me once," I say. "Something tells me you can do it again."

"I will," she says.

It's part biofeedback, I learn a little at a time from Ennesta over the next few days. You tune into your... she lacks the word... *home* center, you know, in the... the *bluest* part of your soul. Maybe it's in your brain?

I almost give up a thousand times, every time the logical, mechanistic part of my brain stops me from achieving clarity in what Ennesta assures me is a simple meditation. There is no manual for this process.

On the third day, a breakthrough — she teaches me how to purr. Not faking it with janky breathing through my lungs or gills, but an honest-to-gravity vibration that originates from... I have no idea where. But I'm controlling it with my thoughts.

Within hours I've got it down to an almost unconscious control, almost as natural as breathing.

"Okay," I say, resisting the urge to write up the process in a bulleted list. "You get your purr on, and then what?"

Ennesta laughs, two fluffy paws held demurely in front of her mouth. "Oh no, purring is not part of the reincarnation control."

And I almost strangle her. But she talks me down by continuing on, showing me that it's a similar type of control. In another day I think I've located my "home center" and know how to program in the coordinates for Trango.

Ennesta and the other grown spheres have synthesized a chemical compound to help adapt my Roptralian physiology to the process, and now she hands me the syringe, big eyes wet with something like tears. "You are as ready as you can be," she says.

I guess that will have to be good enough. I take the syringe. It's so light! Another small thing that will change everything. "You don't have to watch," I tell her.

"Please don't leave me," she whispers in reply.

Then she shakes her head, nuzzles me, reassures me. "I don't mean that. I know you have to go and I won't ask you not to just for little me. But . . . I don't want you to leave."

Someone's always leaving, I think, chiding myself for staying bitter to the bitter end. At least this time it's me doing the leaving.

I kiss Ennesta, then inject myself.

The wave of vertigo is somehow still a shock. I swoon into Ennesta's many arms, and she catches me like she was made to do it. I want to tell her that, that and other things. There are words I'm finally ready to say. I open my mouth, but speech is already beyond me, and only a croak leaves my beak.

My brain tastes like paprika spilled on a long-forgotten tide-pool. I focus on that, on water, on tides, on Trango.

I remember to breathe, and, even though it's not part of the process, I start to purr. I focus on the mantra of numbers running through my mind as they merge, programming my soul, Gravity willing.

Vision fades, sounds grow echoey and strange, and my purr degenerates into spasms, but I can still feel the soft fur of my lover's arms and the silky tears as they splash onto my face like ocean water. *Home*, I think. *This is home.*

I want to tell her, but it's too late.

Maybe in my next life.

STORY NOTES:

This is the second story I've written in this universe. I liked Astrill too much to let zir go!

The promise of afterlives like Heaven is that we are reunited with our loved ones. Usually the idea of reincarnation does not include that promise, because though people may go on, they do so with a blank slate in a new life.

It seems to me that the losses sustained in one life are enough, and it would be a mercy to either reclaim those lost or to forget them. One of the downsides of remembering dozens of past lives in this gigantic universe would be remembering all the loved ones you would have statistically no chance of ever seeing again.

I hold out hope that Astrill and Ennesta will meet again.

The Thing with the Helmets

YOU COULDN'T TALK about the Helmets, which looked pretty ordinary displayed in a glass case in the lobby of the Smash Pad, the converted mattress warehouse where we practiced. They sparkled in all the colors of the rainbow, embossed with punny names and covered in glitter like any well-loved derby helmet, and the only hint of the eldritch Thing that happened (which no one would speak of) was a serious dent in the spider-web-patterned one on the bottom row. Well, that and the heavy-duty iron cage welded around the glass of the display case.

When the Thing happened, I was already skating at the Smash Pad basically all the time on the juniors team, and even a self-obsessed high schooler is going to notice when fifteen members of the league all "move away" or get injured or quit derby in the same month (spoiler alert: they died). The Smash Brats lost a lot of good coaches to the Thing with the Helmets.

Still, it was nothing like the rollerbugs.

Let me back up:

———

When I was eight years old my dad looked me up and down and declared that I was getting pudgy and needed a sport to keep me trim. Thanks, Dad, for the eating disorder.

But he's dead now, so whatever. I guess I have the rollerbugs to thank for that.

First we tried basketball, but I couldn't catch a ball to save my pathetic life. The same was true for soccer — who'd-a thought catching a ball with your feet wouldn't be easier than with your hands? I did like kicking the fuck out of the ball, but there was no place for such a one-hit wonder on a team.

I always liked rollerskating, so Mom thought I'd make a great figure-skater. The failure of that one was entirely my own stubbornness — I hated the cold and threw epic tantrums to get out of those classes. As part of my bargain with her I agreed to try ballet. I sort of liked it, but Dad said ballet was for sissies, and as much as I hate to admit it now, at that point I still cared about his opinion. I did my very best impersonation of a bull in a china shop, tripping the other girls whenever I could, stepping on their toes, and even kicking them with my purposely out of control pirouettes. Besides, ballet class was doing nothing good for my budding body dysmorphia. You think nine years old is too young for bulimia? Then you've never been to a ballet class.

The ballet studio asked me to leave. Mom wasn't *mad*. She was just *disappointed*. Although (sigh), she wasn't really that surprised that I'd managed to screw up again.

Finally, like a dream come true, came roller derby. Despite the tights, it was definitely not for sissies. And it was rollerskating, which I was pretty good at. *And*, though kicking and tripping were against the rules, sending another girl flying across the track with my "pudgy" hips was encouraged. I was in heaven.

———

Eleven years, two broken ankles, and about a million failed diets later, I was a proud blocker for the Smash Sisters. Mom no longer made comments about my weight because my blue hair, tattoo (happy 18th birthday to myself!), and facial piercings bothered her a lot more than the extra seventy pounds of fat and muscle I carried around under them. Dad concern-trolled me all the time, "warning" me about becoming diabetic like Aunt Peg and scowling when I ate cookies or ice cream. When he was home, that is. Which wasn't much.

It's funny how you can lose sight of the wider world sometimes. Inside Roll-a-Way rink we were in our own microcosm; music blaring and fans cheering and the yells of players and coaches echoing and whistles screeching and the bark and chatter of wheels on the wood floor were all deafening. A nuclear bomb could have gone off down in the city, and we would have missed it.

As it turns out that's kind of what happened.

The rollerbugs didn't set off a nuclear bomb. After all, they intended to live on this shiny blue planet they'd found. But they did not intend to share it with us.

Their ships tore into the sky, claws hanging from giant metal wings as they ripped their way through the city like a toddler on Christmas morning. They tore the tops off buildings and shook them until all the people toppled out. They rooted through neighborhoods like a bear tearing into a honeycomb, watching us scatter like totally pissed-off bees. Except that they were the ones flying. And stinging. They shot laser weapons that burned flesh instantly to dust.

In short, they were sci-fi fucking monsters. They had decidedly not come in peace.

Between the second half of the Beating Brontës v. Wicked Stepsisters bout and the first few jams of my team's bout against the DashWheels, my hometown was more or less obliterated.

Our first clue that something was wrong was when Roll-a-Way's roof was ripped clean off. Sunlight spilled in along with great chunks of ceiling tile and lighting fixtures. I was in the sin bin when it happened, and a head-sized bomb of debris crashed right into the NSO timing my penalty, killing him. Missed me by two feet. Dust drifted down through the slanting sunlight like snow, and through it a rollerbug craft descended.

People ran every which way, of course, like ants around a hill. Wails and cries could be heard over the music that now poured thinly out of only a few still-functioning speakers. The exits were jammed. On the track, enough debris had fallen to make skating impossible, and those skaters had all gone down.

They came up now, as I had from the box, as the women on the bench had, as the refs had, standing and staring at the new arrival with confusion and wonder.

Other alien craft were busy blasting all the scrambling people with their death rays, colored beams visible in the air like effects at a rock concert. But the first ship just stared back. After a moment it wobbled to the rink floor like a falling leaf, a ramp dropped out of it like a tongue, and we got our first glimpse of the rollerbugs.

The more astute of you might already have guessed what the aliens looked like from the moniker we gave them. We thought they were in costumes at first, because they made no damn sense — wheels for feet, knobby joints, crazy pincher hands on their withery arms, big, bulbous heads and goggle eyes. There was something vaguely insectoid about them, but at the same time it was like looking in a mirror.

They rolled out of their ship onto the track, five of them. They were smaller than us, on average, but intimidating. We assumed the toy-looking weapons in their claws would atomize us.

We stood there, mesmerized. We'd clumped together, we humans, but our curiosity — and theirs — was a bit stronger than our fear. Our team captain, Scara Thrace, picked her way forward until she was mere feet from the nearest rollerbug, who was also sidling toward us. Was Scara about to become the first ambassador from Earth to another species?

Maybe that was why she did it—maybe it was like taking your hat off for the National Anthem. Scara pulled out her mouthguard and stashed it under her left bra strap, then she unclasped her helmet and pulled it off.

The rollerbugs' reaction was instant. They jumped back as though startled, started squawking to each other in a cacophony of sharp sounds, and the weapon in that forwardmost alien hand fired.

Scara rained down to the track with all the other particles of dust.

We ran for it like scaredy chickens. What else could we do? Skates made it harder to navigate the rubble and ruin of the city, but we didn't dare stop to change as we scattered toward our various homes. My home was kind of still there, the basement part anyway, and I found Mom hiding in it with neighbor Bruce and his two little kids, watching the end of the world on their phones.

Thank all the Gods I don't believe in that it was Mom's day off. The hospital she worked at had been completely destroyed, and the only thing keeping her from running out to the nearest standing hospital to pitch in—and probably get her own self killed in the process—was keeping Bruce from going out after Kel and abandoning their kids. Thanks, Bruce, sincerely, for your lack of chill. Mom can get under my skin, but I'd go crazy if she got herself vaporized.

Who knows where Dad had been when the attack started. He never came home and neither me nor Mom really minded.

Things looked bad for humanity. We four spent the night down there in the basement, in a fort made of scavenged couch cushions and bedding, listening to water gushing from the house's severed pipes and waiting for the rollerbugs to find us.

The next day some actual news started to come in through our remaining smartphones, and I'll be damned if I wasn't part of it. It seems someone had remained in the rink with us when we *almost* made first contact, someone with the presence of mind to record the proceedings. It had gone epically viral—like I bet every human being left on the planet with access to a still-working phone and some couple bars of signal had seen it. And it was pretty clear to them, as it had been to us, that the safest way to approach the rollerbugs was to do so wearing derby gear.

So we all watched, all of us humans, as an international diplomatic team skated hesitantly out onto the tarmac of some airport like a bunch of Bambis on ice, dressed in their brand-new knee and elbow pads, wristguards, and a rainbow of round helmets. Often, they'd fall. With rare exceptions they looked foolish. It was a sad day for human dignity.

But it worked, at least somewhat.

A ship of rollerbugs spotted them and landed, and the aliens emerged like before, and this time no one took off their helmet and they hesitantly—oh so hesitantly—began the work of first contact.

———

It took months for the aliens and the humans to learn how to talk to each other. I can't remotely understand how they figured it out, but humans have been learning unfamiliar languages from each other for millennia, so I guess it's only a little more of a stretch to pick up a few phrases of rollerbug.

The upside was that in the meantime they stopped murder-izing us. We understood that the peace might not last, but for the meantime we were free to attempt surviving in our demol-ished cities without getting disintegrated. Which was nice. They were hard months, but humans pulled together to restore things like supermarkets—which were more like farmers' markets now —and we huddled together in whatever shelters still had a few sides left to keep the weather out. Folks rigged electricity and sewers as best they could.

Mom and I scavenged what we could from the house, which had been thrown into the backyard by one of those pterodactyl-clawed ships, and left the whole shebang alone. Mom wanted us to move into the shelter that had been set up at a local church, but I said *Hell* no. I pulled Mom along with me to the Smash Pad. It was entirely intact, one of the few buildings in town that was, and my teammates were already hard at work carrying sofas and mattresses and whatever else could be slept on over the torn-up streets to make a shelter of our track and lobby.

Mom's face practically turned inside out when she saw the place, but I lied and said it had been cleaner before the attack.

The lobby is where I found Skaty McSkateface, one of the meanest girls in our league, just kind of . . . staring. It burned me up to see her standing there, not working, when she was always the one squawking loudly about other girls not "pulling their weight" while giving me side-eye, as if this fathlete wasn't always the first blocker her skinny ass looked to for offense on the track.

"Hey," I said. "Barb needs help with the generator, and there's two different scavenging crews headed out now."

Her body turned toward me, but not her eyes. Those were glued to the Helmet that had belonged to Stabrina the Teenage Bitch, the star jammer from the team that had succumbed to the

Thing with the Helmets two years ago. "It was my fault," Skaty said, a bare whisper.

She turned to me. "But I can fix it," she whispered. Her eyes were like ice cubes, if ice cubes could stare right through you.

"Cool," I said, and went out to schlep mattresses.

———

None of us had been big news-watchers before the rollerbugs attacked, but once Science Barbie got the generator working reliably, we allocated one hour's worth of power each night to projecting television news on the screen we used to use for a scoreboard. It used less power than trying to charge everyone's cell phones, which most of the time had no bars anyway.

As the weeks passed, it seemed that our nation's best minds were making progress on negotiating with the rollerbugs. Usually about half the hour's news would be footage from the actual conversations, linguists in helmets trilling the phrases they'd learned with subtitles that only occasionally seemed likely to match. Things like: "potatoes are high in fiber and grow in poor soil," and "humans cannot live without oxygen." They never did seem to get around to "I'm going to remove this helmet; please do not vaporize me."

Life went on. Roller derby did not. We were still a family of sorts — more so even, since now we lived together — but now we were all committee work, no skating. How could we play, with cots on our practice track and Roll-a-Way flattened? Teamwork, drilled into us on the track, turned out to be less effective at solving problems like ants in the kitchen or taking turns at toilet maintenance.

It turns out that, like a family I guess, a lot of us didn't really like each other, or have much in common once our sport was removed.

One night, the news didn't come on.

On the scoreboard screen we saw a test pattern. No one even knew what it was except for Try Sarah Topps's grandma, who immediately started singing that it was "Howdy Doody Time." Whatever that is.

We semi-stampeded out the warehouse doors. We were a few miles from the city's mostly already destroyed downtown, but we could see the rollerbugs' ships out there again, tearing it up.

"Fuck," was all I could say. Mom was at the city's nearest semi-functional hospital, so no one remarked on my language.

"I don't think it's Howdy Doody Time," Sarah said, while Keiko mused, "I guess negotiations hit a rough patch."

But Skaty's ice-cold voice cut through all the various ironic or panicky responses.

"Get me the cutting torch," she said.

———

Skaty was the one who — two years ago now — pulled the spell-book out of a box destined for the Smash Sisters' rummage sale. But it was Stabrina who understood what it was. The glittery spiral-bound notebook looked like something in which one of the Smash Sisters' little sisters would have written bad poetry about boys or taken half-assed chemistry notes while doodling cartoon faces. But when Skaty started reading from it, sounding out what she thought were nonsense syllables, Stabrina actually covered her mouth. Like someone in a movie. Even for people who'd rubbed their sweaty skin on each other's in practice, push-ing and pulling each other and accidentally copping all kinds of feels, that felt like a violation to Skaty. She licked Stabrina's palm.

Stabrina pulled her hand away, and the notebook too.

"Next time use your words," Skaty said.

"Words, right," Stabrina muttered, flipping through the sparkly notebook. "We're not selling this."

"A used notebook? You're right, we're not."

The rummage sale pulled in almost a grand for the league, but Skaty never knew where the money went. Maybe that's where the travel team's new helmets came from. None of the home teams had separate helmets just for bouting. And no one else had been invited to the decorating party in which they'd lovingly glittered up their new headgear. Skaty told herself they deserved it, pushing herself harder than ever in hopes of making the travel team.

At first, everything was great. The travel team could not lose. Their walls were unbreakable, their jammers unstoppable, and it was almost like they could read each other's minds. They did it all without saying a word. And without laughing. Or smiling. Or sweating.

Or — maybe Stabrina was sweating a little. Anyway, her face looked odd . . .

The bout was over. The team pulled their Helmets off and, after a brief moment of blank confusion, finally shouted and hugged and laughed and cried out all the emotions they'd been holding in.

That was the first time.

By the penultimate game of the season, their faces started to look really weird. Had they painted them before the bout? Maybe their makeup was running, smearing, and that was why—

They had no faces. Photographs from the bout confirm it, showing nothing but uncanny holes in reality where their eyes and mouths should have been. The Smash Sisters' photographer chose to believe it was a film error (despite shooting with digital).

It took a lot longer that time for them to remove their Helmets. Skaty went in to hug one of the blockers — she couldn't remember who it had been — but the blocker dug low and drove her shoulder right into Skaty's sternum. Skaty tumbled onto her ass, breathless and gasping.

When she managed to look up again, Carey Barely was offering her a hand, while other members of the travel team were chasing one of their jammers, Quick Asa Bunny. Asa was quivering, juking her teammates like a thing possessed. She seemed to have more than four limbs, they moved so fast.

And then she was gone.

One last shout echoed through the Smash Pad, but the loudest sound in the world was Asa's now-empty Helmet clattering to the concrete floor.

———

Asa's Helmet was the leftmost one on the top shelf of the steel-caged display cabinet that Skaty was now cutting into. Its glitter was two-toned pink, a suggestion of bunny ears on either side.

We remaining Smash Sisters gathered around Skaty, watching while not watching (hello, cutting torch) so we all looked either bored and restless with shifty gazes, or despondent, with hands covering our eyes, or reverent, eyes downcast.

The only one not covering her eyes was T. Ann Keiko Death, who stood behind Skaty facing the rest of us. "But they still had to make it through Champs," she said. "Of course they all said they weren't going to wear the Helmets, that the risk was too high... But during the first half of their wild card bout, against some team who shouldn't have even *been* at Champs, Santa Fe or—"

"Albuquerque," someone interjected.

There was a loud clunk as part of the cage gave way. Skaty moved the torch to a different bar.

"Whatever, anyway, they were getting creamed, so at halftime they put them on. And duh, they won.

"Fast-forward to the final game of Champs, for the trophy. Those poor refs. There aren't enough penalties in the rulebook for the shit they were doing. Forget WFTDA, they were in violation of *physics*. I remember Stabrina just sort of phased through the other team's blockers and appeared on the other side. They called an Official Review and decided she must have cut the track. Fluke Cage touched the other team's jammer—just touched her with one finger—and the jammer fell asleep right there on the track. They sent Fluke to the box for a forearm."

With a huge *clunk*, the front of the cage slipped off the display case. Skaty choked the torch off and flipped her welding mask up, stepping back to let the metal grid fall forward dramatically into the lobby.

"Your summary was too long, Keiko. Here are the bullet points: we have fifteen Helmets coated in evil magic glitter. Wearing them makes you strong, more or less invulnerable, and gives you superpowers. But only for a little while before it takes over and you die in spectacular and unexpected ways. Does that pretty much cover it?"

"Ballistic Missy exploded," Keiko added.

"Right," Skaty said. "So what are you waiting for? The first fifteen get to fight the rollerbugs."

———

Is it weird that my first thought was to be proud that I was in the top fifteen for once? I stepped right up, grabbing a green mottled helmet that had belonged to Liz Ard and absently trying it on for size.

I vaguely noticed Skaty trying to stop me, but by then the Helmet's power had kicked in and it was hard to focus on what

Skaty was saying because she looked like a skeleton. I squinted at the bony arm with its five segmented digits held up in my face and the flesh of muscles and tendons and finally skin built themselves around her bones, and I heard her saying, "Wait. Not until —" but I also heard a mouse nosing along inside the wall of the lobby and wind in the trees outside and the emergency alert system bleating from a radio in a house two blocks away and, far above us, the click and trill of the rollerbugs talking in one of their ships.

I had the urge to *jump* all the way up into the sky, right through the ceiling, and get fighting. I had the urge to grab Skaty's barely protected bones and grind them to dust.

With great effort, I pulled off the Helmet.

My teammates were looking at me with fear and worry, and just a hint of the scorn/pity mix I got from the skinny bitches anytime I looked tired. So I steadied myself, hiding a headrush bordering on migraine territory, and just said, "Fits great. This one's mine."

And then the lobby's windows exploded and a pair of rollerbugs skittered into the Smash Pad.

———

We fought. I had my Helmet on in an instant and that creepy x-ray vision returned, but this time with, like, subtitles. It was like how I imagine being a killer robot would be. It was this infostream that told me the first rollerbug was about to fire her disintegration weapon at Skaty, but I guess she saw it too because she ducked her head like a charging bull and the beam glanced harmlessly off her Helmet. She tackled the first rollerbug so hard they both flew out through the shattered windows.

On the far side of her, Keiko phased out to avoid the second rollerbug's disintegration blast, phasing back in to clobber it and take its weapon. It twitched on the floor, but I could see its internal injuries and a projection popped up that told me it would be terminated in 10, 9, 8 . . . Meanwhile, Keiko darted out the shattered window in a blur.

I bounded out the gap after them, spinning in the air like a cartoon superhero, bouncing once before giving in to that urge I'd had earlier to fly. Okay, so it wasn't really flying, but I did manage to jump all the way up to grab onto one of the rollerbug ship's swinging claw thingies.

Out of the corners of my eyes — and from some directions in which I don't have eyes; thanks, magic evil Helmet! — I saw all the other Smash Sisters springing into action alongside me, flipping cars onto rollerbugs, ripping their heads off, taking their fancy atom guns and turning them back on the space invaders.

I could practically hear what they were thinking.

Or wait, I *could* hear what they were thinking.

A second rollerbug ship swooped down alongside the one I was swinging from, and my datastream vision told me it was aiming its giant atomizer cannon at me. So I did the only thing you *can* do in a situation like that, and jumped up onto the main body of the rollerbug ship. The cannon followed me and fired, but I'd already launched myself onto that second ship by the time the first one started crackling out of existence like burning cotton candy.

Sarah was already there, gripping the ship and banging into its hull with her Helmet. One, two, three hits and she was in. I followed.

It went on like that, but not for long. With the astonishing power of helmet glitter on our side, the rollerbugs had no chance.

We rid our city of them before the evening news.

But we didn't make it back to the Smash Pad in time for the evening news.

The war may have been quick, as interplanetary struggles for independence go, but it was still longer than your standard roller derby bout, and therefore longer than anyone had ever worn the possessed Helmets before. It's a beautiful feeling, wearing the Helmet, one I cannot really explain. But I'll try.

Here's the thing. When I put on the Helmet I was twenty years old. Fat. Weird looking. Rocking the community college approach to not knowing what I wanted to be when I grew up while still living at home with judgy parents who were unimpressed with my life choices. The only thing I'd ever been pretty good at was roller derby, and as you may have surmised, I wasn't even that great at derby. I'd aged out of the Smash Brats two years ago and even with the fifteen best players in the league dead (as I now knew), it still took me over a year to get drafted to the travel team. I wasn't convinced my teammates actually liked me.

But with the Helmets on, it was different. With the Helmet on, I felt like the best in the world, and furthermore, with all of us wearing them I felt I really, truly belonged. Sure, each of us went off on her own to take out rollerbugs in individual feats of glory, but even more often we worked together, coming at them from all angles with vicious, beautiful combo moves.

When it was over, we landed in unison on a rooftop with only a few holes in it. We faced each other, and if there was a moment we could have taken off the Helmets it was right then, our mission complete, having won our bout.

A piece of information pinged in my head, lighting it up like a flare in a cave: stragglers. Rollerbugs, a handful of them, alive in the city.

We didn't even need to look at each other before off we went.

Our Helmets told us where to go. They told us everything we needed to know: how many there were (five), where they were (outside Hillside Hospital), and whether they were armed (they weren't). We swarmed that parking lot like hungry lions, cutting through a crowd of injured people to reach our prey.

Everything else was muted. I could see everything, inside and out, in extreme close-up or backed out to an impossibly wide view. But none of it was important save the glowing bones of the rollerbugs. We would smash them into dust.

But other bones came into my x-ray view, human bones, suggestions of beings that were, inexplicably, *protecting* the rollerbugs. They said words to us in their human language, words like *not a threat*, *injured*, *help*, but we were so far beyond human that we could hardly understand them. We had squad goals. Destroy. Win.

We broke into an offensive formation, screening and hitting our way through the blockers between us and those alien jammers. Nothing could stop us. Except—

"Helga Prudence Syvertson!"

The syllables were familiar. They got inside my head like an itch. I blinked, looking at the bipedal form whose mouth had shaped them. It too was familiar. I blinked again.

Bigger than the itch was the hum of my teammates, urging me on. We had each other, and needed nothing more. I kept going, through the squawking being. "What is wrong with you?" it said.

And that, even more than the other syllables, was familiar. I recognized that as a question this being had asked me many times, over many years. A question I had asked myself. Those . . . words . . . brought a kind of . . . feelings-pain . . .

Nothing is wrong with you, my teammates seemed to say. The Helmet seemed to say.

And oh, oh how I wanted to believe it. But as strong as the pull of camaraderie was on me, *what is wrong with me* pulled harder. The datafeed slowed, my x-ray vision got blurry, flickered colors, the real-world vision flickered colors. I heard a wail of mourning coming out of a mouth that was in my face. I reached my hands up to blot out that sound and found the buckle of a chinstrap. Those hands — my hands — pressed into my face and up and up and the pain was so intense I thought my head — my head! — would explode. *Ballistic Missy exploded,* Keiko's voice in my head helpfully told me, and then it was all their voices, the whole team, and oh, they were so *disappointed* in me, and the pain! My head was ripping in two!

I blacked out. Luckily.

But I vaguely remember hearing one last voice as I did. "I'm proud of you," it told me.

She told me. The nurse. Mom.

———

I don't actually know what happened to Skaty and Sarah and Keiko and Barbie and all the rest of them after I lost consciousness, because Mom won't tell me. She says I don't need to trouble myself with such ugliness, which of course just makes me want to know more. Did they kill those injured rollerbugs? Did they explode?

I never saw them again.

All Mom will say, over and over again, is that she always knew those roller girls were a bad influence.

"We did save the world, you know," I tell her, and she just tsks. Honestly, I think to her the world-saving just barely makes up for our foul language. She hasn't told me again that she's proud.

Just the opposite: she nags me about going back to school (it's not even rebuilt yet) and taking up a new hobby to keep active. Something safe, wholesome.

Maybe cheerleading, she says.

STORY NOTES:

This was the last of my stories that my mom got to read, and before I let her, I needed to make it super clear to her that the Mom in this story wasn't her. Just because she was a nurse. And wielded her disappointment more effectively than anger. And hated swearing. Unlike the Mom in this story, Real Mom was always supportive of me as I was.

I'd been playing roller derby for eight years when I wrote this story. The jargon is real. The derby names are my own invention, but that doesn't mean they're not in use. Back in the old days of derby, when we had two-whistle starts and major and minor penalties, there was a name registry to prevent skaters from having names that were too similar. By the time of this story, the popularity of the sport was such that all attempts to manage or even track names seem to have been abandoned. I did check the registries and do some quick googling before using these. If Scara Thrace, Skaty McSkateface, Stabrina the Teenage Bitch, Try Sarah Topps, T. Ann Keiko Death, Ballistic Missy, or Fluke Cage are reading this, I like the way you think. Let's be friends.

Scara Thrace was one of the names I considered for myself. My actual derby name is V. Lucy Raptor.

The Taking Tree

THE BOY, who was an old man, did not stay long. As he hobbled out of the forest, the tree, who was only a stump, watched his cane of burnished wood. Her wood.

It all came back to her: the roaring of the chainsaw, sap bleeding from her wounds, the torment when the boy dismembered her, taking her limbs for a house and her trunk for a boat. She remembered watching her felled body dragged away across the forest floor.

After the old man limped away the tree never saw him again, and she was very sad indeed. Life as a stump was boring. She missed the chittering of squirrels in her branches, the feeling of wind rustling her leaves. The tree wished for death. After all, what was an apple tree without apples and leaves and branches or even a trunk?

But a strange thing happened. The tree's roots lived on, a twisting, spreading mass of subterranean life, and as the years passed they shot up saplings that ringed the stump. These saplings grew and grew until they united into a massive, gnarled apple tree, their flesh becoming one. The tree was the mightiest in the forest, and though she was alone she was pleased and proud.

Birds and chipmunks and other forest friends returned to her, and the tree, at long last, felt happy. They nested and nuzzled into her, and the tree vowed never to take these true friends for granted. She taught them which apples they could eat, and they never took too many or strayed too close to the tree's hollow heart.

Her long years of misery had changed the tree in many ways.

———

One day a child came to the forest: a little girl, whose blonde hair reminded the tree of the boy she'd once loved. For one weak moment the tree hoped she had found another human friend, someone who would climb her trunk and swing from her branches and eat her apples and love her.

The girl paused, looking up into the tree's leafy canopy as if into her soul. She eyed the beautiful red apples with hunger.

And something bitter twisted the tree's heart. *This is how it begins*, she thought. She bent one branch toward the girl, loading all her anger and venom into the darkest of her apples, then watched with glee as the girl plucked it and sunk her teeth in. Pale juice dripped down her chin, and a look of joy spread across her face.

And then, stricken, the look on the girl's face turned to one of pain and horror and fear. She doubled over, vomiting until her heaves produced nothing but a thin bile like tree sap. When she was done, the girl got unsteadily to her feet and staggered away, out of the forest.

The tree's leaves quivered with laughter.

———

Summer's leaves browned and dropped and birds flew south. Snow blanketed the forest, and then melted away. Another child came into the forest. "What a marvelous tree," the boy said, and he immediately started climbing its knobby trunk and swinging from its branches, just like that long-ago boy had done.

The tree looked to her animal friends for support, but they

had fled when the boy arrived. And that was all the advice she needed. She could still feel saw-blades ripping through her bark and flesh, tearing her limbs away. She remembered the years of loneliness.

The tree shook with that remembered agony. She shook and shook until the boy in her branches could no longer hold on, toppling from her heights through her lower limbs to land with a thump and crack on the hard-packed dirt surrounding her.

She hardened herself to his cries and before long he crawled away from her, unable to use one of his lower limbs. *Better him than me*, the tree thought.

Again the tree was left alone with her animal friends. Seasons passed and she nurtured clutches of small beings and felt at peace. But they flew away every year; they had such short, flighty lives.

Summer came and another boy approached. He scrabbled all over her branches, scaring the critters away. He picked up a bird's nest and peered at it before tossing it out into the woods. And then, near the core of the tree, the boy crouched on a wide branch and pulled a folding knife from his pocket. He pressed its tip into a smooth patch in the tree's trunk and carved.

The tree felt those scratches like the deepest of violations. Chainsaws revved in her mind, and she heard the echo of her trunk crashing to the forest floor. *No, not again*, she thought.

The tree shook more furiously than ever before. The boy lost his balance and dropped his knife to the ground below. He clawed at the tree with his fingers, trying not to fall. But fall he did, right into the tree's hollow core. The space in the center of the tree was only a little wider than the boy. The bottom of it was the flat, sawn top of the old tree's stump, ringed with the saplings that had grown together around it.

The walls of the space were sheer. Though the boy tried and tried to climb out, each time he fell back to the bottom, bruised and scraped. His shouts for help reverberated through the tree, making her feel pleasantly full.

The tree thought that at last she had found a friend who would never leave her, never hurt her. The power was hers now, and she would never be lonely again.

STORY NOTES:

The two pieces of children's literature that most traumatized me are both by Shel Silverstein: the poem "Melinda Mae" and the book *The Giving Tree*. I have yet to process the former trauma into fiction, and perhaps I never will, but the latter seemed easy enough to fix.

I know I'm not the only one who was deeply disturbed by *The Giving Tree*. It's hard to believe that this is still presented to impressionable children as a straightforward tale of generosity rather than a harrowing cautionary tale about setting boundaries.

I wish the tree in the original story had slapped the boy with her branches instead of offering them to him for his stupid house. I wish the tree lived in an orchard of other trees and never needed or wanted the companionship of an ungrateful human. I wish instead of being "happy" to let the boy sit on the stump he'd made of her, she could have unleashed her roots like the tentacles of a land-kraken and pulled him under to a dirty grave.

I couldn't give her those things, so instead I gave her rage.

Oneirotoxicity

ANOTHER DREAM HAD GONE BAD.

I knew it by the color of the liquid in the tiny vial. When Dreams 4 Life delivered the doses each afternoon they looked for all the world like water, but this one was swirled with rusty brown and darkening even as I looked.

"Shit." It didn't convey the weariness I felt. It was the fifth one this week, and too late in the evening to do anything about it now. Thankfully the other four in the day's batch looked good. I sniffed them to make sure—orange blossoms and sea salt—then loaded the clear vials into the slots on the front of Kyle's Dream-Catcher. A row of empties waited in the rear slots to seal away his natural dreams before they could hurt anyone.

When the machine had been programmed and the little needle-arm poised over the first vial like a cat's paw over a koi pond, I stuck the rotten dream in the pocket of my velour sweatpants and shuffled back out to the living room.

"Only four today, but they're all set whenever you want to go to sleep." I'd finished talking before I realized that Kyle was already asleep, curled up on our oversized couch with computer print-outs cascading off his lap and onto the floor. Bad dreams in half-cc vials were lined up in color-sorted regiments on the coffee table, flanked by pill bottles, a glass of water, remote controls, a plastic tray of office supplies, and a neat pile of used Kleenex. Kyle's hand looked pale even against the sheets of paper it rested on.

What I wanted to do was climb onto the couch next to him and wrap my arms around his bony frame. We could sleep intertwined, like we did before the fevers and chills, before the bruises. Before the worry. The thought held me rooted to the spot, toes digging for support in the flokati rug. After a moment I knelt in front of the sofa and started collecting the papers—research for his dissertation. When I reached for the one under his hand, he startled awake with a "No! It's not ready!"

"It's okay. It's just me."

He blinked at me, true consciousness flickering on, and pushed himself higher on the sofa. "Of course. In my dream someone was trying to take my research. He was really mad. And possibly a lizard." He laughed, then coughed. I swiveled to grab his water glass for him.

"Thanks. I didn't want the lizards to have my research, but you should see it. There's a compound that keeps popping up in the bad donor dreams. I don't know what it is, but the markers aren't consistent with any of the dream types we've catalogued before. It's not in all of them, but..." He started coughing again, and this time the fit seemed to go on and on. My own chest hurt from it, though I think it was my heart that ached rather than my lungs.

"You should go to bed," I said when it was over. "Your Dream-Catcher is all set."

Kyle looked alarmed. "I don't want donor dreams tonight."

I sighed. This old fight again.

"It's not helping, Mara."

Wearily, I replied the way I always did: "It would help if you stuck with it." *And if the dreams stayed viable*, I thought, but did not say. "Why are you so stubborn?"

"As a result of my obviously deficient brain chemistry." The answer was sarcastic, but he smiled wearily. "Okay, I'll be a good boy and take my medicine."

I helped him off the sofa and he was able to wobble his way into the bathroom and into bed without much help.

He slept so much lately. I only wished it was doing him some good.

When I was a child, even before the discovery of oneironutrients, conventional wisdom held that sleep was restorative. My mother told me over and over that I needed beauty sleep, but I never seemed to get any more beautiful, no matter how much of the day I slumbered away. My skin stayed blotchy and my eye sockets deep and dark like a zombie's.

It was also widely accepted that everybody dreamed, whether or not they could remember their dreams. But it wasn't until Dr. Musoka at UCLA's Center for Sleep Research first captured a dream that it became clear just how varied the quantity and quality of human dreams were. And just how important they were.

By the time I met Kyle, as undergrads, scientists had identified over two dozen ONs, and linked deficiencies in several of them to disease susceptibility. Clinical trials on dream-replacement therapy started almost immediately, with astonishing results in fighting certain cancers and auto-immune disorders. Kyle could explain it better than I — it was his undergraduate advisor at Stanford's Center for Human Sleep Research who developed the first dream-diffuser. I was just another uninspired artist with one flopped gallery event and a room full of untouched canvases to show for my BFA in art.

Oneirotoxins were discovered a few years later. High levels

of these seemed to be correlated to disease, especially auto-immune and mental health disorders. Dream-replacement therapy showed early successes in those applications too.

By the time we were married, the field had been so thoroughly explored that Kyle was forced to research the finer points of dream "types" for his doctorate in Oneirology. The FDA had approved the use of donated human dreams for a host of ailments, and the national dreambank system had been established. Which I guess was lucky for us, since Kyle's ON-deficient leukemia was diagnosed just three years later.

With Kyle sleeping—perchance to dream—I collapsed onto the couch where he'd been. I stared at the detritus on the coffee table, willing the Kleenex to get up and march into the wastebasket. It didn't move. For a long time, neither did I, but eventually I sat up and started tidying the papers that had fallen to the floor. They were print-outs of analyses of dreams—long columns of numbers and abbreviations and symbols that represented the components of the dreams he ran through the machine in his office. He had told me what it all meant, many times, but I still had trouble understanding it. Lately he'd been spending a lot of time working with the sour dreams from Dreams 4 Life, an obsession that I wasn't sure was related to his dissertation.

Every page was marked up in Kyle's looping handwriting, numbers circled and underlined and double-underlined in four different colors of ink. Kyle wanted me to follow his work; he feared he wouldn't live to finish it. But when I looked at those messy pages of symbols and codes and truncated notes, I knew I'd never get it.

With the living room neat and the Kleenex disposed of, I followed Kyle to bed. He flinched when I switched on my bedside lamp, and the feathery tendrils hanging over his head trembled, but he didn't wake. His eyes were moving—he was dreaming—so I didn't dare touch him.

I reprogrammed my own DreamCatcher, making sure I had enough empty vials in the collection slots, and quickly shut the light off. That night I wasn't going to save any dreams for myself. It was a long shot, but I thought whatever paltry ONs I could produce might help Kyle, even if only a little. Arranging the soft wires around my head, I looked up into the machine's grid-like collection plate until I fell into a sleep of my own.

At first I thought I was screaming. My heart was pounding. Snatches of hypnagogic speech trailed off before I could grasp them, until I realized I was awake, it was morning, I was in my bed, and so was Kyle. And *he* was screaming.

I swept away the intruding wires of my DreamCatcher, then did the same with Kyle's, placing my hand softly but firmly to his face to wake him. Through a layer of stubble his skin felt clammy, like damp Velcro. The screaming stopped as he shook awake, swiping at my hand.

"It's just me." I waited for the wild look to drain from his eyes.

He inhaled sharply and seemed to realize where he was. "I'm sorry," he said in a dry voice. "Nightmare."

"I figured."

He pushed himself up in the bed, then lurched over the side and vomited. I couldn't tell from my side of the bed whether he'd hit the wastebasket this time.

I swung my legs out of bed and into my sweats before I knew why I was doing it. He already had everything I could get for him huddled together on his nightstand: Kleenex, water, pills. I came around the bed anyway, just as he was straightening back up and groping for a Kleenex to wipe his mouth with. He had hit the target. We were getting good at this.

"What was it?"

He shook his head, falling back into his pillow, and I knew it would be just like the other times, and he wouldn't remember. I looked at his DreamCatcher, making sure all four bottles were spent. Kyle reached for his water glass and he looked so weak that I picked it up and held onto it until it was steady in his hand. When he was done I set it as close as I could on the bedstand, sliding the dream machine over. My own hands shook.

I'd picked the plastic liner out of the wastebasket and was on my way out of the room before he spoke. "It was . . . shadows." I set the bag down by the door and went back to the bed, crawling up beside him from the foot until I lay on my stomach and elbows looking up at him like a little girl waiting for story time. Scary story time.

His smile became a frown as he tried to recall the dream. "Shadowy things . . . moving around me. All dark and gray. No eyes." He shrugged. "I can't remember now why it was so scary."

I shrugged back, though because of the way I was propped this consisted of lowering my body rather than raising my shoulders.

"Dreams are that way, I guess. No real logic." I remembered my own DreamCatcher. I didn't remember having any dreams, but then you never did if they'd been collected. I looked hopefully at the row of tiny jars, but only two had any liquid in them, and one was a shady shade of sepia. Rats. I slouched lower into the bed.

"Just a feeling of dread," he said. "I'm sorry I scared you."

I put on the best smile I could, climbing all the way up so that our faces were close. "You can't scare me," I lied.

Kyle still had the straining-to-remember look on his face. "Why am I still so tired?"

My smile wavered. "It's okay. Just go back to sleep." I put my hand on his scratchy face — drier now — and moved in to kiss him.

"I taste like vomit."

I didn't care.

Before I left, I pulled the blinds closed and loaded my one viable dream into Kyle's machine. I stuck the other vial in the pocket of my sweatpants, where it clinked against yesterday's bad dream.

I took both of them to Kyle's office. One thing he *had* taught me was the importance of record-keeping. Using his notation system, I affixed both tiny jars with tiny labels and entered them into his log. Kyle's corny saying was that in our house, bad dreams made good data.

————

I spent all day chewing my nails to shreds and waiting for the delivery driver from Dreams 4 Life. Kyle slept almost all day, and I alternated between frenzies of pointless activity — organizing my fabric swatches by color and texture, throwing out oil paints dried up from disuse, picking the layer of paint off of all the house's light switches — and fatigue so deep that even changing the channel on the television seemed an impossible task. A few clients called, but I let the phone go to voicemail. The idea of drawing any more stuffy modern living rooms or kitchens made me feel physically sick.

The only useful thing I managed to do was to pour a few drops of food-color-tinged water into empty dream vials to give to Dreams 4 Life. They insisted on collecting the bad ones for "proper disposal," but Kyle wouldn't part with any of them.

The doorbell rang sometime after six. I'd been practicing my complaint all day, but when I opened the door and saw the harried look on the driver's face, I hesitated. But then, so did he. I imagined two slack and haggard faces staring each other down, caught in an infinite loop like reflecting mirrors.

"Wow," I said. "You look like your day's been as bad as mine."

The driver — Matt, his nametag said — blinked at me. He chuckled, then looked like he felt guilty for chuckling. "Well, I have been feeling sorry for myself. I probably shouldn't." He handed me a small tray with five clear vials, still cold from the onboard cooler. I peered into each one, looking for the faintest hint of color. They looked clear, but I would have bet our house that some would turn before bedtime.

"How many bad ones?" Matt held his clipboard in his left hand and clicked his pen repeatedly with his right.

"One," I said, setting the new dreams on a table inside the house and handing him yesterday's tray, with its four empty vials and one of brownish water. "But it's five this week, and" — I looked back into the house and lowered my voice — "he's so sick. I'm so worried. What am I going to do?" I felt a note of instability entering my voice and stopped, though there was more, much more, that I wanted to say.

Matt looked somewhere below my eyes. My neck, maybe. "I really can't say. I'm sorry." I knew it was true, too; he was just the messenger.

He held out the clipboard and pen so I could sign for the delivery, then retreated down the brick steps of our porch to the driveway where the company's hatchback idled, generic sunshiney logo mocking me with its horrific mustard and cyan color scheme and Comic Sans font.

Dreams 4 Life really was the worst of the dream providers. But also the cheapest, and therefore the only one our lousy insurance would cover. In the Wild West of dream-replacement therapy there were a lot of operators, with widely varying quality. It was such a new field that regulation and oversight really hadn't caught up with practice.

The first tears were leaking from the corners of my eyes before I shut the door. A part of me wanted to run after Matt and invite him in for a drink, just to have someone to talk to.

It wasn't that I had no friends, but lately it felt like it. All of my *best* friends were scattered across the country, dealing with their own troubles—children and unemployment and ailing parents—and the people we knew locally were mostly Kyle's friends and colleagues. He hadn't wanted them around since he'd gotten so sick. He hadn't even told his parents how serious it was. So aside from my clients, whichever driver Dreams 4 Life sent, and Chloe, the nurse who came in twice a week to check on us, I was on my own.

"Do animals dream?" I asked Kyle on one of our early dates.

He launched into a rambling answer about what it meant to dream, which I half-listened to. All animals that had yet been tested produced ONs and OTs, to a much more predictable degree than humans. "For example," he said, "every mouse whose dreams have been collected produce roughly 80% ON-L and 15% ON-A." He went on to talk about the fluctuating of the other 5%, and the reliability of sampling methods, before getting back to my question: "But they aren't *dreams* the way you probably think of them."

When humans had tried mouse dreams, nothing happened. They didn't dream of cheese. They didn't have nightmares about cats and mousetraps. They just got a reliable dose of ON-L. Human use of animal dreams was banned almost immediately, though, so no one got to find out whether dogs really do dream of chasing cars. As far as I knew, the FDA still hadn't decided whether it was safe.

"Their fear is just a knee-jerk reaction," Kyle always said. I knew he tried whatever dreams came his way, animal or human. He'd try serial killers' dreams if they were available.

Kyle had long been distracted from his proposed dissertation research into the "types" or substrata of dreams, focusing instead on the nearer-to-home problem of dreams souring. Some dreams were born bad, heavy with oneirotoxins and deeply discolored. But the only ones that seemed to change over time were the ones from Dreams 4 Life, a fact that puzzled Kyle.

He had analyzed hundreds of dreams, both from the dreambank and from individual donors, and though he hadn't found the answer yet, he had made some discoveries. One was that the chemical makeup of the dreams didn't change as they went bad. If it was made of ON-D and K when it was fresh, it still was when it stank like a month-old fish. Another was that the oneironutrients he received in his daily doses were startlingly regular. Which, of course, puzzled me. If they still had ONs, why wasn't he getting any better?

But Kyle just waved that question away in favor of a more basic mystery. He posed the problem to me as a logic puzzle: "Everyone you know is on ON-replacement therapy, right?"

Well, not *everyone*. But they were prescribing it an awful lot, for everything from depression to lupus to leukemia.

"And everyone needs at least a dream or two per night, including donors?"

Right.

"And they can't be split, or stretched, or synthesized."

Okay, if you say so.

"So where are all these dreams coming from?"

It seemed to me that the math still worked. There had to be enough strong dreamers, putting out eight or even ten dreams a night, to cover the demand. But what did I know?

I asked an executive with Dreams 4 Life about it once, but the company was about as transparent as a brick wall. Their sources were confidential, she said.

———

Two of the dreams were already bad by ten o'clock. Kyle had come out to the living room and thought he could handle some dinner, and when I had my head in the fridge I saw the dreams' discoloration.

"Fuck, fuck, fuck!"

"What is it?" Kyle called from the couch.

I stepped into the opening between rooms. "We're out of to-matoes."

Kyle squinted at me as if to say, *I know you better than that; what is it really?*

"It's the damned dreams again. Two of them." I looked up at the ceiling, staring down the uneven line between ceiling and crown molding. My lower eyelids felt heavy. "At this rate there won't be any dreams tonight. Or worse, more nightmares."

Kyle sighed. It was a loud sigh, carrying all the way across the room, over the drone of a Discovery Channel narrator.

I looked at him.

"You know it doesn't matter," he said. "They're not helping, and I suspect they're making it worse."

"How can you say that?" I asked. "You know the research bet-ter than anyone. You've seen your tests. Your illness is caused by deficiencies of ON-D and K. If you're not getting better . . ." I couldn't finish. I'd never allowed myself to vocalize my theory, that he'd done this to himself testing distilled and mixed dreams before the practice was regulated, or depriving himself of his own "native" dreams so he could study them.

I'd never allowed myself to *blame* him for dying on me.

Not out loud, anyway.

Kyle's words were quiet, but they carried right into my soul. "It doesn't matter," he repeated. "Nothing's going to help now."

My eyelids overflowed, first one then the other. I blinked, and when I looked at the room again everything was blurry and Kyle was lost in the haze. I wiped my eyes with my palms.

"It *does* matter," I whispered.

I went back in the kitchen and made my best tomato pasta for dinner.

———

Once Kyle was back in bed with the two remaining dreams loaded in the DreamCatcher, I started making phone calls.

I was a long time out of the loop for dealers, but through friends of friends by one in the morning I was on the phone with a guy calling himself Nocturn. He quoted me a ridiculous price per unit, and we agreed to meet in an hour. He promised me nothing but high-quality individual dreams, none of the "gruel" we were getting from the donorbank. "You don't want that shit," he said. "All the individuality mixed right out of it; all processed and packaged like fast food. My shit is five-star farm-to-table cuisine, organic and gluten free." He didn't fill me with confidence, but I was out of ideas. I made sure Kyle had everything he needed on the bedside table, and left before I could lose my nerve.

Kyle didn't share my reservations about illegal dreams, but I still didn't tell him where I was going. He'd been one of the early dream traders, collecting and diffusing dreams with a machine he built from Internet plans. He mostly did it for research, but even before medical testing started, people were getting high on each others' dreams. I don't think it was even a year after Dr. Musoka captured the first dream.

The craze hit my college hard, but it scared me. Even though I'd always been a weak dreamer—or maybe because of it—I didn't like the idea of having another person's images in my head.

Then came the horror stories: people becoming dream junkies, sleeping their lives away; people developing schizophrenia from their first try; people dying from overdoses or rotten dreams. People were mainlining them, and the problems spread. You couldn't know which ONs—or OTs—were in a given dream, so you couldn't trust them. It became illegal to deal dreams.

I did try it once, despite everything. My roommate went on about her fantastic dreams so much that I finally relented and let her share one with me. All I remember about the dream is that everything shone, and I could fly.

For the next three days I felt like I could fly, to the point that I almost tried it. My skin felt flushed and everyone I saw around campus looked like a stranger. Colors seemed brighter. I painted like a madwoman, and made some of my favorite pieces (the same ones that would bomb in my gallery show). I skipped classes. I stared at ceilings. I couldn't sleep. I couldn't think about anything else. It was the most intense three days of my life, but I recognized a dangerous path when I saw one. I requested a room switch.

So it was with shaking hands that I traded cash for a brown bag of clinking vials under the chrome-edged table of an all-night diner. I left my milkshake three-quarters full on the table and hurried home.

———

I really didn't know what the sound was that greeted me when I opened the front door, not at first. But the stink of shit and vomit and sickness was unmistakable. I dropped everything but the dreams on the parquet floor, kicked the door shut, and ran to the bedroom. That was when I recognized the sound as crying.

Kyle sat on the floor next to the bed, a puddle of watery shit staining his pajamas and spreading onto the floor. He held his head in his hands, leaning against the nightstand. The wastebasket was on its side halfway across the room, and everything from the nightstand—from the DreamCatcher to the Kleenex to the pill bottles to the now-shattered glass of water—was on the floor all around him.

"Are you one of them, or are you Mara?" he asked, looking at me through his hands.

I set the bag down by the door and knelt in the wreckage by his side. "I'm Mara, honey." I put my hand on his arm and he flinched.

Finally his face softened as he recognized me.

"Oh, you are. Good."

He reached for me with his thin arms and I held him as tight as I dared. My eyes felt as wide as two flatscreen televisions, broadcasting static into the dark room. I was too shocked seeing him cry to cry with him. "What happened?"

"I fell. It was the shadow people again. They didn't leave, even after I was awake."

"It's okay." I thought about the size of the bruise he'd have tomorrow. I wondered if we should go to the hospital.

Kyle pulled back from me. His eyes were so red. "Why do you keep saying that, when you know it's not?"

I thought for a long time about an answer, but I couldn't find one. "I don't know."

"I'm scared," he said.

My heart broke. I felt it seize and snap, felt it replaced with an icy weight. "I am too."

We sat for a while that way, arms around each other in a dark room, in a puddle of excrement, vomit, and broken glass, rotten dreams. The sky was lightening by the time I'd gotten him and myself and the room cleaned up, Kyle's dream machine loaded with five guaranteed excellent unique dreams, and into bed.

In the morning he was dead.

The only thing I remember clearly about that day is waking up in the dim daylight thinking of shadowy forms. I sensed immediately that the room was one soul short, and I rolled over and put my hand on his stubbly face—gently, as if to wake him. He didn't startle.

After that I must have called people because his body was gone and my mother was in the house, along with a number of other people I don't exactly remember, and they were cooking and cleaning and telling me to sleep and to eat, and offering me pills and hugs and telling me to sleep some more. Days must have passed this way.

I don't remember crying, but my face hurt all the time. It felt new, ill fitting. At one point I went around the house turning all of the pictures on their faces. Hanging ones I covered with scraps of fabric. For good measure I covered the mirrors too. We weren't Jewish, but it seemed like the thing to do. I didn't want to look at my tear-mottled face.

One thought bubbled up through the haze over and over: I killed him. With the illegal dreams, or with my own worthless dreams, or maybe just by not being there when he fell. I killed him. The refrain played on endless repeat, only beat down temporarily by my mother's distractions or food shoved in my face or utter fatigue.

There was a funeral. It was unremarkable. My mother slathered my makeup on thick but still I could see the lie in every face that told me how good I looked. I cried every time someone told me how strong I was, so I guess they were wrong about that too. My chest hurt and my bowels felt like water.

After the funeral, it seemed like everyone in the world was in my house.

Kyle's friends from school were there, skulking about looking geeky in ill-fitting suits. One by one each of his professors shook my hand and told me, in slightly different words, how smart Kyle had been, and each time it felt like a slap in the face.

His parents were there too, of course, and after too many drinks his mother started yelling at me for not taking better care of him. His father tried to calm her down and get her away from me, at first, but when she yelled, "You should have told us he was dying!" he apparently decided she was right. In the end, my mother rescued me by pretending not to be able to find the extra toilet paper, and I almost loved her for it until she whispered, "You really should have told them."

Some of my friends from college made it, although not the ones I really missed, and they clumped together drinking and reminiscing. One kept peeking under the fabric-covered pictures and paintings. Another brought her camera and actually took pictures. None of them had known Kyle well.

But Kyle's brother was the strangest of all. He had always been a dedicated and talented musician, playing whatever instrument he picked up with ease. I had expected him to play at the funeral, but he declined. He told me later that he hadn't been interested in music for a while. It didn't sound right, he said. He'd been on dream-therapy, Dreams 4 Life, and it was changing his life. He felt better than ever before, and he realized how selfish he'd been and how trivial his life was. In fact, he told me, Kyle's death had made him realize how fleeting life was, and that was why he was going to do something meaningful with his, and join the Army.

Almost my only crystal clear memory from that day is telling him, "Your life *is* meaningful. Don't sacrifice it in one of these stupid wars." He shook his head at me, as though I just didn't get it. Though he smiled, his eyes looked haunted.

I collapsed into my bed with the house still full of irritatingly normal conversation, but thankfully when I woke up the next day, everyone was gone. Only their casseroles remained.

My mother had left notes by the phone with all of my messages sorted into two categories: clients and condolences, and I wanted to sweep them all into the recycling bin. I went into the room that had been Kyle's office. *You killed me*, it seemed to say.

I shut the door and went into my office. It was a mess of unfinished sketches and paintings, mostly of rooms in my rich clients' houses. The blank canvases stared at me like a room of mirrors, and I hadn't enough fabric to cover them all. I shut that door too.

The fridge was jammed with neatly wrapped food I was unlikely to eat. Behind it, though, I saw three trays of Dreams 4 Life dreams. They'd apparently kept delivering for a couple of days, and had neglected to collect the unused and rotten dreams. The ones in the fridge looked to be about half viable, not that it mattered now.

In the living room, the remote controls were missing. I looked in the couch cushions, under the couch, and behind the television before I remembered there was a drawer in the coffee table. I opened it to the most terrific clatter of glass on glass, like a brief hurricane through an ill-tuned windchime. My mother had transferred everything from the coffee table into the drawer, preserving the arrangement of the bad dreams in neat lines. They fell against themselves like drunken soldiers when I pulled the drawer out. Some of Kyle's notes were there too, his multi-colored scrawl all over them. I grabbed the remotes and shut the tinkling drawer as quickly as I could.

The first few nights I slept raggedly and woke tired. During the days I pattered around in my sweatpants, avoiding my clients and ignoring calls from friends who were still in town and wanted to do lunch. Eventually those stopped. A few times I picked up paintbrushes, but when I looked at the white canvases all I saw were the walls of my clients' homes. I thought in wall colors: Navajo white, Wimbledon white, eggshell, ecru, espresso, pale taupe.

It could have gone on like that forever, but finally I got hungry again. I pulled a saran-wrapped baking dish of macaroni and cheese out of the fridge and behind it were the Dreams 4 Life trays, and it occurred to me that an ON boost certainly couldn't hurt me, and just might help. My natural ON levels were never dangerously low, but they weren't particularly high either.

Of the original fifteen dreams, six looked clear. I loaded two of them into my dream machine.

———

I woke in the morning feeling like I'd forgotten something. The world looked like I was viewing it through a blue filter. I walked out to the living room, feeling how cold and hard the wood floors were against the soles of my feet.

That morning I couldn't remember why I'd been avoiding my clients. I went right through the messages my mother had taken and called them all back, setting up consultations and design meetings for the next week. Then I got to work, sketching rooms, pulling fabric swatches for upholstery and window treatments, and researching a new kind of cork flooring I'd heard about.

My heart still felt like a frozen boulder I dragged behind me, tethered to my chest. But I was less aware of it. If I didn't look over my shoulder, I forgot my burden for a while. Sometimes, though, I thought I saw shadows moving in my peripheral vision, and I started to be afraid. When I looked, they were always gone. Just my brain misinterpreting the fabric draped on the walls or the darkness that clung to wooden furniture.

On each of the next two nights I loaded two more Dreams 4 Life dreams, pleased that no more had gone bad. Maybe there was a time curve to dreams rotting? I wished I could tell Kyle about it, give him more data for his dissertation. It hit me like a physical pain that his dissertation would never be finished. Like falling through a trap door, I was thinking of Kyle again, and my guilt and sorrow were back, more vicious than ever. My hand could almost feel the curve of his jaw under the skin. I fell asleep crying that night.

And woke screaming. In the dreams, gray figures lurked behind me in doorways, followed me through the house, found me even when I hid under the bed. They were chanting something, or maybe just moaning. As I woke up the details drained away, until I found myself alone in bed, clutching the blanket to my chin, scanning the corners of the room for uncast shadows.

I got up and went to work, but I felt strange. Haunted. My mother called to check up on me and I have no idea what I said to her, but I must have lied well because before she hung up she told me I was "healing just fine." I'd jumped so much when the phone rang that I left a line of fine-point Sharpie all the way across my sketch of a client's new bathroom.

I was standing in the kitchen holding a Tupperware of dubious-looking chicken when I swear I saw something cross the living room. Nothing was there when I looked, of course, but that same terrible thought that had shadowed me since the morning of Kyle's death had re-emerged: I killed him.

Suddenly I wasn't hungry at all.

I put the chicken back in the fridge and slid the deli tray all the way out. I was strangely relieved to see my crumpled bag of illegal dreams still there. There were several left over, and on impulse I unrolled the bag and dumped its contents out on the tile counter. I held the vials one by one up to the light, studying each one's clear crystal shine, beautiful as diamonds refracting. Were they deadly?

I thought of pouring them down the drain. Instead I loaded one into my DreamCatcher. If it had killed Kyle, it could have me too.

In the dream I was a spaceship captain, travelling through time, bringing democracy and feminism to medieval societies. I woke laughing, and looked around the bedroom as though I'd never seen it before. I felt like a set of eyelids I hadn't known I had were finally open. I remembered the sensation from college. I felt awake, really awake.

I went right to my office and started to paint. I painted galaxies and comets and planets; I painted royal processions and all-woman pirate ships. I painted until I got hungry and stopped for lunch—the chicken was still good after all—then I finger-painted a spaceship on my dirty plate using mustard and relish and raspberry jam. It would have been a good painting, too, if I'd had any blue condiments.

I felt fantastic until about seven in the evening. The dream had faded away, and the house started to look familiar again. I went to the kitchen to scavenge for dinner, and noticed the light on my answering machine blinking.

Eight new messages! I hadn't even heard the phone ring. One was from my dentist, and another was from a friend. Three were from clients, asking about this and that. Can we make the bathroom a darker red? Are the throw rugs washable? And so on. But the other three messages were all from the same client, ranging from impatient to angry to concerned that I was late, later, and apparently never showing up for our meeting. I had completely forgotten.

Suddenly I felt deeply fatigued. Everywhere I looked I saw work that needed to be done, and there was nothing in me that could do it. But that wasn't all. I wanted to sleep. I *craved* a dream. The horror stories of my youth replayed in my head, but despite it all I considered reloading the DreamCatcher — maybe two dreams instead of one would get me all the way through the day tomorrow.

I stalked around the house for a while, trying to make up my mind. Finally I wandered into my office and was shocked to see the paintings I'd worked on all day. They were terrible. All garish colors and bold lines, with nothing to make them meaningful. They looked like children's drawings. It made me wonder about the show I'd had in college, the dream paintings I'd done then. Out of disgust I'd thrown the unsold ones away, but I'd still thought they were good. Now I wasn't sure. Had I *ever* been an artist?

I took the remaining illegal dreams from the fridge and poured their droplets down the kitchen sink, washing the vials with soap. After that I got a bunch of rags and solvent and wiped as much of the still-wet oil paint as I could off of the day's canvases. If only all mistakes were as easy to erase.

For a week I went without dreams, save my own. I didn't remember these, but that wasn't unusual. Without the ecstasy of the illegal dreams or the boost of the donor dreams, life was hard.

I stepped right back into my grief like it was a movie I'd put on pause. I moped and I paced the house and I tried to work, with little success.

A few weeks after Kyle's death, two of his colleagues came to the door, shuffling about sheepishly. "How are you doing?" one asked. I was about to send them away when the other one spoke. "We're here for the school's equipment."

When they were gone, I stood in Kyle's now half-empty office. I hadn't been in there since I'd shut the door after the funeral. It had always been minimalist, but now the place felt desolate. All that remained were piles of Kyle's notes, rudely scattered across his desk; a couple of filing cabinets; his bookshelf of scientific texts; and his computer. Even his particular smell was gone.

The pages of notes with their multi-colored scrawl mocked me. *I'll never be done*, they seemed to say, *and it's your fault.* I should have paid more attention to Kyle's explanations of the science. Hadn't he been trying to show me something right before he died?

I went to the coffee table where his last notes had been hastily stored. A column of letters was circled, with a note at the bottom that read, *where are you coming from?* I couldn't answer that question. I didn't even understand it.

Kyle's army of dead dreams still resided in the drawer, organized by color. I selected one of the lighter-colored ones and unscrewed the cap. The stench hit me with surprising force — it still had the sweetness of orange blossoms, but with a sickly undercurrent of something acrid, like burning hair or rotting flesh.

Even so, I loaded it into my DreamCatcher.

———

I didn't wake until after noon the next day, and when I sat up my head pounded like an unbalanced washing machine.

I almost lay right back down, but I made myself get out of bed and work on a design for an ultramodern living room that was due in a few days. I saw blurred shapes on the edges of my vision, but I tried to ignore them. The pain was glorious. It shrieked in my head like an ill-behaved pet parrot, demanding attention. My grief could barely be heard over the din. But it *could* still be heard.

So every night I uncapped a rotten dream and loaded it into my machine. Every morning I woke up feeling a little more tired, seeing a few more shadows, with a headache that throbbed a little more vigorously.

On the fourth day of bad dreams I was staring at a sketch of a living room and kitchen when I saw the shadowy shapes coming out of the drawing. They peered around the sketched-in fridge and crouched under end tables, their fingers like tendrils reaching, for what I didn't know. I got out a charcoal pencil and traced them before they moved, outlining their dark forms on the drawing. When I was finished, I held the piece at arm's length. I kind of liked it, in a creepy way. Then I realized I'd ruined the sketch I'd meant to show the client, and I kicked myself. I set it aside and started working on a replacement.

The next day, I came back to the ruined sketch. I'd woken up feeling like something dark was sitting on my chest, sucking my breath out. The bed had been damp with my sweat. Looking at the creepy sketch, though, I felt something like pride. I rooted through the assorted sketches in my office until I'd collected a pile of the ones I couldn't use for work. Staring at each one, it was as if the shadow people were actually in the rooms; all I had to do was trace them.

By the time I had to leave to meet my client I had dozens of sketches, including quite a few I wanted to turn into paintings.

I ran a comb across my aching head, gathered sketches into my portfolio, and shoved what I'd need for the meeting into my satchel.

When my client came to the door, she looked surprised. I heard her suck in her breath as she hesitatingly opened the door to let me in. I guess I must have looked amiss—I still hadn't uncovered my mirrors, so I didn't know—but I didn't care. I wanted to show her the designs and get back home to my paintings.

We sat in front of a picture window and I showed her sketch after sketch of new living room ideas. She liked all of them, and I was getting frustrated by her indecision, when I pulled a wrong sketch out of my portfolio. By chance it was her house, with monsters.

She gasped as I placed it on the table in front of her, and I guess it shows how messed up I was, but it took me a while to realize what was wrong. To me, *all* the sketches looked like they hid ghostly forms.

"I'm sorry," I said finally. "I don't know how that got in here."

"What are those things?" she asked, shivering. She was looking rapt at the sketch; it was more attention than she'd paid to anything I'd shown her.

I didn't know how to answer. "I've been calling them shadow people."

She stared at the sketch for a while more. "It's amazing."

I *really* didn't know what to say.

"I didn't know anyone else . . ." She turned her face to me, eyes following after as though stuck on the sketch. "I want one of these for my house. However we end up doing the room, I want a painting like this to go in it. Can you do that?"

I found my inner professional at last. "Of course," I said, trying to make it sound like I had paintings commissioned every day. A voice inside me was shouting joyfully, for the first time in I didn't know how long.

Of course, it only took one thought to turn joy to sorrow: *I can't wait to tell Kyle.*

That night I loaded two bad dreams into the machine.

————

Days and weeks became blurry again. I went back to one bad dream per night, but they were getting worse: darker in color, stronger in odor. I kept thinking of them as full of OTs, until I remembered what Kyle had learned—the actual makeup of dreams didn't change.

The headaches got more intense, and sometimes I woke screaming and vomited over the side. The wastebasket was on my side of the bed now. The shadows transfixed me and frightened me but I pinned them to canvas with my paint, and people liked them. I was baffled by the way people looked at them; it was more like recognition than anything else.

My client had spread the word about my painting. Soon other clients wanted them, and before I knew it I was having another gallery show.

My mother was so proud she flew in for the opening, but when she came to the house the look on her face wasn't pride. She'd hardly set her suitcase down before she headed to the kitchen again, and she would have started cooking right away if I'd had any ingredients in the house. As it was, we were late for the opening, and she made do with doing my makeup. I'd almost forgotten about makeup; I still hadn't uncovered my mirrors.

"You're not getting your beauty sleep, are you?" she asked me, holding my chin as she painted the space under my eyes. I looked up into her face, wondering where I'd have to look to see her facelift scars. She moved my face to one side, and the monster in my head shifted and growled. Reflexively I closed my eyes. Dark shapes menaced.

I couldn't answer her question. I was getting some kind of sleep, but it wasn't beautiful.

Mother didn't mention the fact that all my pictures were still turned to the wall. She didn't mention the mirrors, or the closed door to Kyle's office. She didn't mention Kyle at all. But when she left after two days, my fridge was full of food again.

And then, inevitably, I was down to my last bad dream. It was almost black, almost opaque, the way my turpentine looked when I'd been rinsing brushes in it all day. When I opened it the reek hit me like a physical thing. The orange blossom smell was still detectable, barely, under heavy waves of sulfur, rotting garbage, and gear oil. It made my eyes water, yet my only thought was worry about what I would do the following night.

I painted my heart out on that last day. And ended up with a portrait of Kyle that mixed memory of his ghastly near-death appearance with the shadow people in an impressionistic wash. I cried almost the whole time, tears blurring my vision so I couldn't even tell if the damn thing was any good.

I stashed it in a corner, face to the wall.

Cold turkey was harder than I thought. On my first dreamless morning I woke up disoriented, hearing voices whisper in a language I couldn't understand. I didn't remember having a nightmare, but a feeling of horror clung to me all day.

After that, things felt stalled. I still painted at first, but it was only momentum that carried me. The headaches started to fade away, and I recognized that as a blessing. But I passed my days like a ghost. I stopped answering the phone again. Every day I tried to paint, but some days I just sat with a brush in my hand for hours before giving up and turning on the television.

I hadn't realized how much the bad dreams had affected me until their effects started to wear off. After the first few days I found myself thinking more clearly. I was able to focus more on my design work, though I still found it hard to paint. The shadow people were slinking away from me, keeping to the shadows where they belonged. Perhaps they'd never been there after all.

As my mind cleared, it hit me, like a slap, that there were still a few dreams left in the house. When a person used a Dream-Catcher to take what Kyle called "non-native" dreams, that person's own dreams were bottled. When the donor system had first started, Dreams 4 Life collected those dreams, but at some point the courts ruled that they couldn't force people to surrender their dreams, even if they were diagnosed as unhealthy. Kyle used his dreams for experiments, but there were still a few left. I found four of them in Kyle's horribly empty office, and lined them up next to my DreamCatcher.

I was hesitant about taking Kyle's dreams; it seemed like an invasion of privacy. Also, selfishly, I feared what taking one of his dreams would do for my art. I needed *bad* dreams to paint, and while his were supposedly unhealthy, they were all clear and smelled like a summer's day, even after months unrefrigerated. Finally, I was a little afraid of what I'd see. Was it a good idea to jump inside your dead husband's unconscious mind? What if I learned something I could never unlearn?

I was a coward. Those dreams sat on my bedside table for at least two weeks.

I was sitting in my office with a paintbrush in my hand, staring at three paintings of rooms I'd designed. The clients had all commissioned shadow paintings, but I couldn't see the shadows anymore. The phone rang, and it startled me but I ignored it and kept glaring at the uncooperative paintings. Our phone didn't play the outgoing message out loud, so the only place I heard Kyle's voice was in my mind: *You've reached Kyle and Mara's phone; leave us a message.* I wondered if I would ever be able to change that message.

I jumped when the phone beeped and a singsongy male voice filled the room. "Mara, it's Kent from the gallery. I'm just calling about the new series. We can't wait; people are talking; very big buzz on the next show. Hope it's going well. You know where to reach me." I wanted to scream. It wasn't going well at all. I was a fraud who'd done one thing that people liked, and I couldn't even do that any more.

I put down the paintbrush and tore through the room, looking for any sign that I was an artist after all. What I found was Kyle: the painting I'd done of him under the influence of bad dreams. I'd almost forgotten about it. Looking at it now I felt like someone else had painted it. Edvard Munch, maybe.

It felt wrong to be proud of making such a ghoulish image. But I was. Out of a swirl of angst and ennui, Kyle's eyes stared with something like humor.

It made me smile. I missed him so fucking much.

That night I loaded one of Kyle's dreams into my Dream-Catcher. I dreamed that I was at a cocktail party in a huge blank space. People wandered around like ants, shaking hands with each other, and sometimes when they did, both people jumped like they'd stuck their fingers in an outlet, and a wispy form emerged from their clasped hands. I recognized the forms. I had painted them many a time.

In the dream I — as Kyle, I guess — walked around the party, shaking hands and occasionally getting shocked. It was probably Kyle's mind that was trying to find a pattern to the shocks and shadow births. Eventually he figured it had something to do with the clothes people were wearing. He/I only got shocked by people wearing hats.

I woke laughing, but my face was wet with tears. The dream was like a hug from a loved ghost—it seemed like pure Kyle, fear of parties and all. It also seemed like a clue to the mystery of the shadow people, and perhaps by extension to the bad dreams. I wished he was there to interpret it.

I wished he was there, period.

That day I dared, with trembling hands, to turn one picture around. It had always been a favorite of mine, a perfect embodiment of my geeky love, taken at the Very Large Array in New Mexico. We'd spent minutes setting the shot up so that it looked like one of the giant radio telescopes was coming out of his right ear. His hand was held flat next to his head, gently cupping the bottom of the massive dish. There were a few photos with this pose, all with different facial expressions, but the one I'd framed showed him with a knowing look, as if he was receiving a great cosmic secret.

Looking at the picture didn't hurt as much as I'd feared. I just hugged it to my chest and cried.

The next night I took another of Kyle's dreams, but I didn't remember it in the morning.

The third dream took place in a huge house with big blank rooms. There were lines to get into all the rooms, populated with a shocking cast of individuals, from midgets to giants, in colors from human skin tones to green and purple. Many of them seemed more like animals than humans. When the people went into the rooms, though, they all became the same. One feature at a time, the individuality was stripped away until the people themselves were nothing more than shadows.

But there was one room where the people stayed individual. There wasn't the same variety in that room—they all looked like people, for one. But what uniqueness they had, they retained. I went into that room and asked them why they weren't changing. "Why, don't you know?" they all replied at once in eerie harmony. "We're already the same."

When I woke that time, it was like a lightbulb had gone on in my mind. I ran to Kyle's office to see if I was right. I pulled a beginning textbook on dream science from his shelf and skimmed through it until I found what I needed. *Each person has a dream type, like a blood type, that is distinct from the oneironutrients or oneirotoxins contained within. However, unlike blood types, these seem to be compatible with one another.* The book went on to explain, as if to a college freshman, that this meant that a person could safely take a dream from someone with a different dream type.

Well, I thought, *what if they're wrong?* The lightning bulb flashed even brighter, like a nuclear bomb going off.

I called the Dreams 4 Life executive I'd spoken to before. "I only have one question," I said, heart racing. "Do you mix the dreams?"

"Of course we do," she answered. She sounded put out, like she'd been asked if bears shat in the woods, and wondered why she was putting up with someone so stupid. "If we didn't, people would get actual dream images, and the ON formulations would never match prescriptions. How many donor dreams do you suppose meet a patient's needs exactly?"

"Of course. But they're strictly from human donors, right?"

The woman paused. Finally she said, "You know very well that human use of animal dreams is prohibited by the FDA." It wasn't an answer.

"Of course." I hung up.

My next call was to Kyle's advisor, Dr. Glenn. He came right over to look at Kyle's notes, and I watched him read through it all with great interest. He was like a little boy reading a new comic book, gasping and laughing his way through it. "I think you're right," he said in the end. He hugged me, and I started to cry. He said what I was thinking: "If only Kyle were here for this."

Dr. Glenn worked quickly to fill the gaps in research that would prove Dreams 4 Life was mixing animal dreams into their products, causing dream type reactions including shadowy images and behavioral changes. We worked on the paper together, but Kyle was given first author credit. In the school's opinion, this represented a genuine addition to the body of scientific knowledge, and Kyle was posthumously awarded his doctorate.

The story hit the papers before graduation, and mail came pouring in. Even while Dreams 4 Life was refusing to release any of their files, while they were vigorously denying any use of animal dreams, I started to get fan mail. And hate mail. Dreams 4 Life dreams weren't working the same way they had been, and people were angry.

One day I came home to find my front window broken, and half a dozen live chickens flapping and squawking and shitting in my house. One of them had a note tied to its leg, carrier-pigeon-style, telling me both that I *was* a chicken and that I should dream chicken dreams (which were highly toxic). As intimidation went it was pretty hilarious, but messy.

The saddest, yet most redemptive letter I received was from Kyle's brother. He was in the Army, on rotation spitting distance from Iran. Things were scary, he said. Since entering the Armed Forces the feeling that had pressed him to enlist had faded, and now he could barely remember the clarity. He missed it, and he was angry. But our research (it touched me that he thought *I* had anything to do with it) had showed him why he'd felt that way. He'd written me a song, and as soon as he could get back home he'd come play it for me.

He didn't mention anything about his and Kyle's parents. I hadn't spoken to them since they'd yelled at me at Kyle's funeral, and whenever I thought of that it hurt like a missing body part; we'd been close once.

The school let me accept Kyle's doctorate diploma for him. I ordered his robe and regalia, his silly graduation hat, but I didn't invite anyone to the ceremony. It wasn't mine. Kyle's name was called and I walked across the stage with a big smile, somehow not tripping and falling on my face. I shook Dr. Glenn's hand and hugged him tight, and he whispered, "Listen": the audience was quiet, but a few voices shouted with wild acclaim.

I shaded my eyes against the lights but couldn't see who was making the ruckus. Not until afterward, when I was trying to sneak out of the reception, and found myself face to face with Kyle's parents. Before I could even squeak out a greeting, his mom had wrapped me in a fierce hug.

"I'm so sorry," she said.

"No, I am," I croaked, starting to cry.

We could have gone on like that, fighting over who should feel worse, but thankfully Kyle's dad stepped in. "None of that matters. We missed you, Mara. You look well."

His mom nodded. "You did great. Kyle would be proud of you, and I'm so proud of you both."

———

But before all of that — before the story of animal dreams hit the news and the resulting stir put Dreams 4 Life out of business, before chickens forced this decorator to redecorate, before graduation—I had one more dream. I put off using it for weeks, partially because I felt I'd solved the mystery Kyle's unconscious mind had been working on, but mostly because it was the last part of him that still lived in my house.

I was feeling better all the time. I'd started eating, and really focusing on my clients and their stupid houses. The work was interesting enough, most days, and it left me with time to paint on the rare occasions when I felt inspired. I even started calling some of my friends back and venturing out into the world.

I uncovered the mirrors, and was only somewhat startled by the way my appearance had changed. My hair had grown long and unkempt, with a startling white streak near the front. My face was pale and thin. But I knew I'd looked worse, and I knew I'd look better again.

I uncovered the pictures one at a time, giving myself time to adjust to each one. Eventually the only picture I couldn't bear to look at was our wedding photo.

It was the anniversary of our first date, and loneliness weighed heavy on me, so I decided to load that last dream into my Dream-Catcher. I was terrified that I wouldn't remember it, that I would have saved it all that time for nothing. But it was amazing.

In the dream I, as Kyle, stood on top of a hill overlooking a city. I remember feeling the joy of having walked all the way to the top, the thrill of a healthy body, and I knew the dream must have been from near the end of Kyle's life. It was twilight, and the lights of the city were twinkling on like Christmas lights, as the stars echoed them above. But something was missing. And then I saw myself—Mara—walking up the hill toward me. I ran to her and we held each other there, between the earth and the sky. I looked into her face and I loved it.

When I woke up, I went to my favorite mirror, an antique that hung in the hallway between my office and the now empty room, and tried to look at myself through Kyle's eyes. I felt like I knew who I was, white-streaked hair and all. I approached the last covered photo and pulled the shawl away slowly, letting it fall to the floor like a theatre curtain in reverse. There we were: young lovers stepping hand in hand off of a stage and into a new life together. That life was over now, but I didn't cry.

With one finger I touched the glass over the side of Kyle's jaw. "I love you too."

STORY NOTES:
I first started working on this story at the Clarion West Writers Workshop in 2009, and I can't remember much of what sparked it, other than possibly sleep deprivation?

Dad's Christmas Presence

IT'S A STORY as old as time: a father's desire to create a special Christmas memory leads to a tragic chimney accident. Yes, we thought it was strange that Dad missed the frenzy of gift-unwrapping. Yes, we noticed the smoke from our cozy fire backing up into the room as though the flue were closed (but it wasn't). Yes, we thought we heard a sort of muffled screaming. But then we'd always suspected the old house was haunted.

It wasn't. Not then.

I guess it took Dad long enough to die that he got sort of bitter about it. Jimmy and I were just kids, engrossed in the gimme-gimmes, which I think should have given us a pass. Mom... honestly she's just not that bright. I mean, neither was Dad. Obviously.

Ghost-Dad started haunting us as soon as the decorations came down, which was right before his funeral. Mom swore we would never celebrate Christmas again. We shoved the lights and ornaments into boxes in the attic, dragged the tree into the back-yard, dressed in our family portrait clothes, and then there he was, all hovery and see-through and still dressed as Santa. Jimmy ran right for him, tackling for a hug, but sailed through the apparition and bonked his head on a doorknob instead. He wailed and wailed and we were late for the funeral, and Mom made me hold the ice pack over Jimmy's giant goose egg.

Ghost-Dad was a real jerk. He would pull the rug under our feet at the top of the stairs. He'd make the light switches shock us. He was the reason our garbage disposal never worked: one time it "jammed," and when Mom reached in to clear it, it started up again. She only lost the tip of her ring finger, but we never trusted the sink monster again.

Jimmy had it worst. Ghost-Dad could make him fall for the trap almost every time. He'd go in for a hug and come out bruised or bleeding.

Mom and I started fighting about Christmas in November. I understood that she had painful memories — we all did — but didn't she understand that it was *Christmas?* We were still kids, and we needed presents, decorations, cookies, all of it... with the possible exception of a visit from Santa.

I took it upon myself to sneak the holiday into the house. I went up to the attic, a task made much more daunting by Ghost-Dad, who wouldn't allow the light to stay on, or a flashlight to work, or even a candle to stay lit. I felt his malign presence as I struggled to stay on the little causeway of plywood and not fall through the ceiling. I reached a box I suspected contained Christmas stuff, opening one dusty flap and pulling out the first thing my fingers found, a cool sphere.

Immediately the lights came on, and with a moan the likes of which I hadn't heard since last Christmas, Ghost-Dad was gone. I held a shiny red ornament, paperclip hanger still attached. With the box open, I located the other boxes, dragging them toward the pull-down stairs. With the box closed, the lights went out again, and my feet were pulled out from under me, and down into the house I fell.

Nothing was broken. None of my bones, anyway. One box of Christmas had tumbled down with me, and I found myself surrounded by shattered glass and tangled string lights. But Ghost-Dad was gone again.

After I cleaned up the mess, Ghost-Dad returned. But I'd been thinking in the meantime, formulating a theory. Jimmy took one wobbly step toward Ghost-Dad before he remembered what I'd told him to do. He pulled out the Santa hat I'd given him and put it on his head.

Before Ghost-Dad dissolved, he screamed and covered his eyes in terror. Yep, Ghost-Dad was afraid of Christmas.

A demonstration convinced Mom to let us celebrate, and we did so in relative peace. Ghost-Dad didn't bother us, but our memories of Real-Dad did. We missed him, maybe for the first time. Our presents to him had been packed up with the rest of Christmas, and there they still were, wrapped and ready. We put them under the tree, where they remained through the whole sad holiday.

New Year's came and went and our decorations stayed up. Then Valentine's Day. I think we were all afraid to take them down. Jimmy wore his Santa hat almost all the time, and Mom had to steal it from him in the night to wash it every now and again.

When the tree was fully dead we threw it out. We un-decked the halls as much as we dared, leaving a garland here and a stocking there to ward off Ghost-Dad. It worked.

But those three presents weighed on me until one summer day I covered up all the decorations. I held my gift to Dad in my hands, obscuring its reindeer paper, until Ghost-Dad appeared, still wearing his Santa costume.

"I want to show you something," I told him. He rattled the windowpanes. "Still mad, I guess. I get that. I'm sorry we didn't save you. But look, I made you a present." I unwrapped the paper and crumpled it up, then opened the little box.

It was a *lame* present, one of those things we did in school every year, but I hadn't had any better ideas. An ornament made of our family portrait, decorated with glitter and ribbon and love.

The curtains blew in an unearthly breeze, then settled down. Ghost-Dad took the ornament out of my hand and hovered it to the mantel. He smiled and climbed right up the chimney.

We still keep a few candy-cane candles and sprigs of holly on side tables, but I don't think we'd see Ghost-Dad even without them.

STORY NOTES:

I've always had a vague dislike of Christmas, so when I was asked to submit something for *Every Day Fiction*'s holiday lineup in 2015, it wasn't going to be a heart-warming tale. Unless you count hearts on fire. The opportunity to give it a punny title was just the icing on the burnt Santa-shaped cookie.

No Alphabet Can Spell It

FOR LACK OF A BETTER NAME, I call myself Laika. We've both been shot into space and abandoned, though not necessarily in that same order. But unlike the original Laika, I intend not to die.

To that aim I rouse Belka. She swings at me, but her arms are tangled in her cocoon's elastic straps, so I don't have to dose her with the tranquilizer I hold behind my back. After a minute the wildness dissipates out of her eyes. But it stays close, held in by the gravitic mass of her insanity. She looks through me. "We must be there, huh?" she asks, as though I'd come to offer her another gray and mushy frozen dinner instead of a wide-open planet under a real sky.

I nod, and she extricates herself from the sleeping pod and moves toward the *Wildest Dreams'* flight control area. She seems compliant, so I retrieve the syringe cap from a zippered pocket and stow the now-capped tranquilizer in another pocket before she can see it. But I keep my distance. The image of Albert trailing behind us into the frozen void, the sound of Belka's hysterical laughter, will be with me for however many centuries I live.

A lot of things didn't survive the forty-five-trillion-kilometer voyage to CelBod, the planet now hanging hugely before we three remaining Fixies like a gray-blue waxing marble, furry-edged against the black of space: the flavor of real food, comms with Earth, optimism, Belka's sanity, and Albert, to name a few.

Gordo is waiting for us by the wide forward window, and I let the zero-g tides pull me to him as they always do. We hold hands nervously, as if we were still pre-teen orphans in NASA's strictly controlled dormitories and not fifty-something Fixies mere hours from colonizing an exo-planet. Assuming Belka doesn't decide to crash and kill us all.

Something has apparently gone wrong with the dual-particle transmitter between Earth and CelBod, because according to mission specs we're supposed to be bouncing messages to the planet for instant relay to Earth. But it's not working. It's hard to say exactly when the problem started, because we were somewhere in the middle and there was still an awfully long lag between us and either side of the DPT, but the last transmission we did receive didn't exactly fill us with joy. The woman on the other end was distracted, and asked us to wait a minute (which was funny, because I think we were waiting almost two years at that point anyhow), and then she looked offscreen and said, "What the hell is that?" And then all we saw was static.

I have been clinging to the idea that the transmitter on CelBod just needs some tweaking that the CREATORs and AIs can't handle. Gordo doesn't disabuse me of that thought, even though he is the mission engineer and knows everything about the DPT, and even though we all know that the robots built the damn thing in the first place and probably know how to fix it better than any human.

But I try to put those thoughts aside. Through the front window, Celestial Body #8972642158 is so gorgeous that I could almost call it Eden or Goloka or Valhalla or Shangri-la or any of the other names romantic Earthlings tried to stick on it. CelBod shimmers as we dive toward her, two moons hiding behind her like shy children.

I hope the planet is more eager to meet us.

The landing doesn't kill us, even with no support from Earth or the AIs seeded on this world, and despite Belka's wild cackling as she pilots us through the planet's bumpy atmosphere. In fact, we land within a few kilometers of the targeted landing zone, on a huge volcanic flow that looks eerily like the barren stretch of New Mexico we trained in. The land we can see out our windows is smooth reddish-gray, with rocks that rise high above the *Wildest Dreams* like ocean waves. All of it is bathed in light from the yellow sun.

I want to jump out of my chair and pop the hatch and run to the settlement that the AIs and CREATORs have been building these past decades, but gravity immediately makes its presence known, and everything becomes hard. It takes me a few tries just to get my hands up to the buckles on my harness. I barely manage to lift them out of my lap, and then I overshoot and hit myself in the face. Then I laugh, watching Belka and Gordo struggle with their own gravity.

"Gravity is such a downer!" Gordo yells, laughing like a maniac as he tumbles from his jumpseat.

I finally stand up on my wobbly fawn legs. They don't immediately snap, so I take a few steps. The world is heavy and I am weak, but there's a familiarity to it that's also solidly reassuring. After a few minutes we all manage to stand and stretch, and before we can stop her, Belka opens the hatch latch. Fresh air streams in, ruffling our hair, and we breathe deeply.

"It's a good thing the O2 reports the AIs sent back were right," Gordo says, still laughing a little. "How funny would it have been to get all this way and die when we opened the hatch to poison air?"

"Hilarious," Belka says, but despite the flatness of her voice, I think she means it. I can easily picture her laughing breathlessly even as she asphyxiated.

I just shake my head, turning my back on the two comedians and heading for the ramp. I am the first one down, but I have no momentous words. Actually, right then gravity catches up with my bladder, and I urgently need to pee. It's such a perfect mockery of our whole epic undertaking that I start to laugh too, joining the chorus of hyenas that we astronauts have become. We giggle like schoolchildren, getting our land legs as we run and cautiously jump and spin around on the blood-red rocks. Which is, of course, exactly what we must look like; none of us were older than twelve when we were Fixed, decades ago.

As we finally sit, giddiness ebbing, soaking in the warm rays of sun through atmosphere, reality starts to sink in. We are here. We're on an alien planet, breathing alien air, and sitting under an alien sun. These things are subtly different from those we left behind: the air a little thinner, the sun brighter, the sky a darker, almost indigo blue. But after a decade in the tiny vessel behind us, it's like home. Which is good, because it *is* home now.

"Can you believe we live here?" I ask, another wave of hysteria threatening to overcome me.

The others shake their heads. Of course, we actually live eight kilometers to the southwest, near the shore of a brackish ocean. Gordo and I debate the merits of walking that distance to the settlement, the conditions of which are unknown. Our alternative is to spend yet another night in the goddamn *Dreams*, and even if any of us could stomach that thought, the ship is only outfitted for zero-g sleeping. With the ship on the ground, I'm not sure any of our bunks will be usable.

Gordo pushes hard for the hike, almost yelling in his squeaky voice, but Belka silences us with one quiet word. "Listen," she says. She is sitting far from us, near the top of a wavy ridge, but we hear her and are immediately silent. At first I don't hear anything, and then I do: a little crack, with a little echo. "What is that?"

The sound comes again, and Gordo looks at Belka with what I call his "imminent tantrum" look. "It sounds like a twig snapping. So what?" he asks.

Before words can come, I'm on my feet, walking past Belka up the rise. "This planet doesn't have trees, remember? So how can there be twigs?"

"And if they're not twigs, what are they?" Belka adds ominously. "Not to mention the question of who or what is stepping on them." She opens her eyes wide, and I know that now she's just trying to scare us. We may have watched too many horror films in our years aboard the *Dreams*. In a spaceship, *everyone* can hear you scream.

From the top of the volcanic wave, we have a panoramic view all the way down to the coast. It's breathtaking, but not in a way any of us expected. The distant sea shines greenly, topped with whitecaps. Next to it, we can just make out the cylindrical units of the settlement, built by the CREATORS from native minerals and parts shipped ahead. And in between here and there, where there should only be swirls of striated rock and wispy alien shrubs, is a vast field of trees.

That would be strange enough. Due to spotty info from our early robotic scouts, questions of what flora and fauna should be unleashed on CelBod were to be left to me, the mission biologist, upon our arrival. But the strangeness doesn't end there.

Imagine an orange grove, with trees in orderly rows. Imagine the already round trees shaved into perfect spheres atop oddly straight and uniform trunks. And then imagine that they aren't orange trees. Oh, some are — I can see a row of them stretching diagonally down until I lose sight of the orange fruits peeking from the leaves—but there are also apple trees, and other fruit, and pines shaped like designer Christmas trees. The lines of trees display a level of perfection that's flat-out unreal. And between them, ribbons of water glimmer in rounded right-angle formations, like the printed paths of circuit boards.

"Um...," Gordo says.

The cracking sound comes again, off to the left, and we all snap our heads around to look.

The robot's body is short and spindly; it stands on four long legs with a cylindrical midsection resembling a fuel tank and a smaller head stacked on top of that. This seems to be tipped at a quizzical angle, with two lens-like eyes pointed in our direction. In its two long arms the robot holds a stick, and as we watch it, it snaps the stick in two and inserts both halves into a hole in its thorax.

I find myself unreasonably frightened. The thing doesn't look unfriendly. In fact, it looks like a misshapen mechanical dog trying to understand its master, and I don't immediately see anything weapon-like on or around it. But goose bumps raise the hairs on my neck and arms.

This robot is not from Earth.

As I'm staring, slack-jawed, Gordo's hand slips into mine. I pull my gaze from the surreal sight and see my shock reflected in his face. I squeeze his hand, and he smiles vaguely. And then from the creepy orchard more of the robots emerge, one by one, until a line of them gazes up at us from the tree line.

I'm racking my brain thinking of things we can use as weapons, but we came in peace. I still have the syringe in my pocket, a less-than-useless weapon against a metal foe. We have tools, perhaps, that could be used as clubs. These are stowed both inside and outside the ship, but the ship is behind us and I don't know how fast robots can run. But then Gordo starts to laugh. He's trying to contain it, but I can feel his mirth through his slightly sweaty grip as he draws himself up and addresses the legion of robots. "Take me to your leader?" he says.

As it turns out, robots are good carriers. They easily tote everything we need from the *Wildest Dreams*, and I get the sense that they could have carried the whole damn ship on their shoulders, like robotic ants, if there'd been a wide-enough passage between the manicured trees. Their limbs telescope in addition to bending at joints, and they navigate the terraced landscape as gracefully as ballerinas, their heads always level. We walk alongside them as they mutely lead us down the steps and over the thin streams of water to the settlement. We stay quiet too, in some mixture of awe and fear. The robots stop sometimes to break errant twigs away from the trees or to pluck them from the ground, which is clean and smooth and flat, with no rocks or leaves to be seen.

With perhaps a mile to go to the settlement, we are ambushed again.

Figures swing down from alcoves in the increasingly odd-shaped trees. The noises are terrific: shrieks and beeps and something that might be a purr or a growl. Instinctively I reach for Gordo, and he for me. Behind me I hear Belka emit a squeak.

I don't know what I expected. Some kind of alien monkeys, maybe, or agile and noisy robots. But then I see the ambushers, ringing us in a slightly menacing way, although their hands are empty. They have hands. They are human beings.

Teenagers, to be exact. They are taller than us, taller even than Earth teenagers. They are naked, their secondary sex characteristics dangling here and there for all to see. Breasts. Armpit hair. The works.

For a long moment nobody speaks. Our robot porters continue on without a pause, even though we've stopped dead. Some of the teens are still making an assortment of noises that sound more mechanical than animal. One girl, looking me right in the eyes, beeps angrily. And then almost at once, as if on an unseen cue, they erupt in laughter. "It's just a couple of kids!" one particularly tall boy calls out. His accent is strange, kind of staccato. "Where did you come from, little kids?" asks another. "What's wrong with your skin?"

They don't wait for answers. They're all around us, and all we can do is move with the herd. I tilt my head back to see how Belka is, but she's gone without a trace, just like Albert. I do not mourn her loss, though I miss *him* intensely right now. He was our psychiatrist.

The teens lead us into the settlement, which looks better than I'd dared hope. Some of the pods Earth sent ahead seem to be missing, but there are other buildings made from metal and glass and what looks like silk, in bright if childish patterns. Some of the buildings are tall, some scarcely above ground, but all are what I would describe as whimsical, covered in spired turrets and domes and ladders and catwalks and some features I don't have names for. Among them I recognize some of the pods and the looming Eiffel Tower–shaped antennae of the dual-particle transmitter. All in all, I feel like Dorothy seeing Oz for the first time, surrounded by tall munchkins in a gaudy new place.

But I also feel relieved, and I'm not the only one. "The transmitter!" Gordo practically yells in my ear. He starts to run toward it, but he's stopped by the naked children.

"No TV," says a girl's high voice, followed by a lot of giggling.

Another girl comes toward me, reaching with slender but calloused fingers toward the arm of my jumpsuit. I stand still, thinking not to startle her, as if she were a wild animal. And so it is a moment before I notice her enormous nude belly.

She is pregnant.

Pregnancy has always fascinated me, because it's something I can never do. As a Fixie, I'll be physically twelve years old for as long as I live—which might be two hundred years. When the *Wildest Dreams* left Earth, the oldest living Fixie was 142 years old and still running marathons. His skin was wrinkled and a bit spotted, and he'd had cataract surgery many years before, and he'd had some trouble with his liver (which was attributed to an excess of liquor), but he was healthy as a clam otherwise. The trade-off, of course, is puberty. We don't have it, and thus we can't reproduce. In my case, this choice was a no-brainer. If I'd have finished puberty, the docs told me, I had a 90 percent chance of dying from a hereditary thyroid disease called Storgen-Childs. Whee.

I twist my hand toward her belly. Her eyes—an otherworldly green—lock onto mine, gaze broken only by chunks of evenly clipped hair falling across her face. As my fingers creep toward her belly, and hers pet the thin fabric that covers me, I think I see her smile slightly.

But then an ominous hush overtakes the crowd of children, and she draws back as if shocked.

What now? I think. I'm getting pretty sick of first contacts already, but when a huge, spider-looking robot roves into view, I almost faint with relief. It's a CREATOR, one of the robots Earth sent ahead. "Let. Them. Through," it says, bleating the words out with its antiquated speakers.

As it scuttles away, Gordo and I follow through the parting crowd of youngsters. They wait until we are past them before chirping and whirring and laughing, a cacophony like feeding time at an outer space zoo.

CREATOR leads us to one of the old pods, which is buried at the end of a curving metal staircase that goes down I'm not sure how far. CREATOR is too big to get down the steps, so it squats on top of the cellar door like a giant spider guarding its web. The walls are sheer, almost glass-like cuts of stone, and at the bottom is a cold chamber with a lot of flat-panel screens, all of which show nothing but static.

Gordo makes a beeline for a computer terminal and starts typing away. I am momentarily overwhelmed with gratitude for him. If he'd been the one Belka sent on extended spacewalk, or if he'd been the one to succumb to space ennui and withdraw, I doubt I would have made it to CelBod with my own sanity intact. And now, watching him commune with computer systems, I'm grateful in another way. *Thank the universe for my engineer*, I think. My own redundancy training in computers is like a faint memory, and whatever is wrong with the dual-particle transmitter, I'm sure I could never fix it on my own.

I'm startled when the computer starts talking. "OMG, John?" it asks in an almost human-sounding female voice. The screen Gordo's using fills with a sideways emoticon—in other words, a smiley face. "I've been waiting for you for ... calculating ..."

Gordo cuts it off. "Yes, it's been a while." He turns to me, a look of vague worry on his face. For my part, I am shocked by the computer's use of Gordo's legal name. I'd almost forgotten it.

"And Jane!" the computer fairly shrieks. "Can we play games now?"

My brow wrinkles so tight it hurts, and I force my face to relax. I'm reaching way back into my memory, back to the training days at NASA, when we and the other prospectives met the AIs. Of course, we never met the first one to leave for CelBod; that was before our time. But I do remember playing chess and other games with a version of the AI that left later. All of the software was designed to mingle and learn from disparate experiences, so a later arrival must have remembered us.

AI theory said that if we fed them enough data (which we did — practically all of the knowledge humans had ever gleaned), gave them a purpose (which we also did, by entrusting them with the preparation of CelBod's settlement), and left them alone (which since the transmitter died had obviously been the case), they would mature.

As I watch the smiley face bob up and down on the screen, shifting mouths and eyes, I'm starting to think this hasn't happened.

Eventually I realize that I should respond. Thankfully, Gordo already has. "Computer?" I hear him asking. "Can we play games later? I'd like to get a little work done first."

The emoticon on the screen changes rapidly, so fast I'm not sure what characters it's using. But the effect is a distinct eye roll. "Okay," it says. "What can I do?"

"I'm trying to re-establish communication with Earth through the dual-particle transmitter," Gordo says. "Can you tell me what's wrong with it?"

"Oh," the computer says, her emoticon mouth turning into an O, then returning to a smile. "It's not broken. Can we play now? None of my children have the patience for Go." On a nearby screen, the static turns to an even grid, a Go board.

"What do you mean?" I blurt out, ignoring the computer's request. I put my hand on Gordo's shoulder for comfort.

Gordo, with remarkable restraint, says, "Not just yet, okay? If the DPT is working, then I'd like to talk to mission control. Can you connect me?"

"No," it says. The smiley face shoots up off the screen, replaced by a flatlined face. "Earth is gone."

———

Gordo and I spend the rest of the day underground, glued to the multiple monitors of the comm center. All of the streams coming from Earth have been recorded, up to the point at which there are no more. So we scan newscasts, because the NASA comms, which stopped almost six years ago, say nothing, nothing, nothing. "What the hell is that?" And the question is never answered.

Between requests for games, the computer tells us that it's just as well Earth is gone. It tells us about lying to NASA, what spoilsports they were. Its emoticon winks at me, and even Gordo's arms around me can't stop my shaking.

The newscasts stopped coming in only a few months back. Leading up to the final broadcasts, there is talk of political tensions between countries. It doesn't seem any more fervent than what I saw in my sheltered life as a NASA orphan and biotechnologist. There's no real warning before the news blinks off, and it looks like all countries went off the air within two weeks. At first we try to establish a chronology, but soon we give up. What difference does it make?

Earth isn't talking. And it's far enough away that we can't know what's happening, now or ever. We don't have equipment sophisticated enough to even see the planet from here. I think the computer was exaggerating, and Earth is still there. I even think there are probably people on it. There have to be *some* people, right? But they've lost the will or the ability to communicate with us, so the spirit of its statement remains true.

We are alone.

Or at least we would be if it weren't for the horde of children. They are standing at the top of the stairs when Gordo and I emerge, chittering like a flock of grounded birds. The sky is a twilight purple, though the sun has already set. Above the eerily level tree line I see a huge half moon like a yin and yang, black side clearly visible against the not-black of the night. Below it the second moon rises redly, like a harvest moon. It could almost pass for Luna, if it weren't for the behemoth above it. A chill runs up my neck, though the air is mild: this is an alien world.

The children have us backed up against the doorway, and it occurs to me, not for the first time, that they intend to murder us. *Well, it was fun*, I think bitterly. Four boys stand at the forefront of the crowd, puffing their naked chests. "You don't belong here," one declares. Another asks, "Are you going to *tell* on us?" and a squeak on *tell* betrays his nervousness.

"We came from Earth," Gordo says, trying to muster a deep and authoritative tone. It's clear these teens don't respect us; there's no way for them to know we're in our fifties. "And we come in peace."

To his credit, he says it with a straight face. The crowd of teens is divided between laughter and eye rolling and awe. "Yes," the apparent leader says, moving menacingly close to us. "We saw that movie too. Annie loves movies."

"Well, it's true," I add meekly, arms spread placatingly.

"Give me your lunch money," the tallest one yells, to more laughter. He is standing right on top of us, puffing his chest out and bumping into Gordo, knocking his footing off balance.

I look around at the crowd, noticing more and more. For one thing, all of the kids seem to be within a few years in age. They're clearly older than ten years old, which means that the AIs started growing them before the *Wildest Dreams* even left Earth. I suppose that's not surprising, given the established trees. The other thing I notice, scanning the crowd, is that the four males in front are the only ones. There are at least a couple dozen girls, maybe thirty or forty. Which also makes sense, if the goal of the AIs was to start a breeding population as quickly as possible. My eyes search for the pregnant girl I saw earlier, and I eventually recognize her by the ridiculous clarity of her green eyes.

But not before I see several other bulging bellies.

The other obvious thing is the two separate groups: girls in a ring behind, boys alone in front. Yet I don't think the boys are dominant; in fact, they seem a little afraid of the girls.

"What do you mean?" Gordo asks, looking a bit worried. We're surrounded, and the boys are pressing closer all the time. My hand drifts to my pocket, where the syringe still waits. I don't want to start out on the wrong foot here, but I also don't want to be crushed in what appears to be a power struggle with savage hormonal humans who shouldn't even be here. When the boy leans in again, looming over me like a gorilla, I hit him in the abdomen with my needle and push the plunger home.

He drops like a bag of rocks, almost crushing me in the process. Silence ensues. Then whistling like steam from a kettle, and high-pitched sounds that I take as approving from the ring of girls.

And then they whisk us away once again, to the living quarters where our belongings have been thoroughly rooted through and then stored neatly in cubes. There's a bed for us in one of the cylindrical pods, which seems smaller than the ones we trained in and around on Earth. We're apparently expected to share the bed. I think I should protest, but I don't want to. The sight of the soft mattress makes me realize what a long, long day it's been. The same must be true for Gordo, because as soon as the children and the spindly robots leave us alone, we lie down together and fall into a dead sleep.

But not before I realize how wonderful it feels: Gordo's warmth and weight next to me, the evenness of his breath. *We're home*, I think. I wrap my arms around him and close my eyes.

—————

The same waxy light is filtering in through the pod's windows when I am shaken awake, and I open my eyes to see two sets of eyes glowing whitely back at me. Two of the naked girls crouch by my bed with urgent expressions on their faces. It's all I can do not to scream.

"M-1 says you're just a child, but it isn't true, is it?"

I look over my shoulder to Gordo, who is still sleeping with his mouth wide and his arms flung above his head. I shake my head, then notice the girls' puzzled looks and whisper, "No, we're not children. But how did you know?"

The one on the left points skyward. "We saw your... arrival. It was a thing beyond our grasp. Like the machines, you must be more than you seem."

The logic has me stunned. I wish I hadn't wasted so much time obsessing over Earth and had spent more learning about the facts on the ground here. I still don't know why the AIs decided to grow people without authorization, or how they raised them, but for the moment I'm impressed.

The girl on the right beeps a few times, very fast. "Yes, and stories. Talk later. F-3 needs us."

They both squeak, and I am practically pulled out of bed to a harmony of eerie whistling. I think to wake Gordo, but he looks so peaceful, and he deserves the rest. The girls and I walk under the light of two moons until we reach a ladder that spirals up into a tree so tall that it's hard to believe it's not native—except for its rigidly straight trunk and round branches. We climb up, way up, onto a platform that looks rough and unstable. Broken limbs of trees and scraps of metal are laid jaggedly like driftwood, wedged into nooks and tied with crude-looking rope. In other places, hammocks sag from holes in the floor, and on one end of the platform, the torso of one of the spindly robots is wired between two horizontal branches to make a chimney.

I can see at once that this is their place, fashioned with human hands.

Girls sleep on every available flat space, and some that aren't so flat. Near the robot-stove, though, a group of them huddle around one figure writhing on a bed of leaves. It is the pregnant girl, the one who touched my clothes.

One of the ones who brought me here—F-8, she tells me—leans down to whisper, "F-3 is...we do not know. Annie only says that she makes a new life. But she looks like the other thing."

"Annie?"

"Annie," the other one says. She is tall, almost too tall for the tree house we're in. "The director, the mother, the intelligence."

"The teacher," another says, a girl I'd thought asleep near my feet.

"The maker."

"The one from before."

And then they are saying words too quickly for me to make them out, interspersed with the name and a lot of beeps and trills. The only dissenting sound is a wail of pain from F-3. A contraction. I go to her, stepping carefully around holes in the floor and the naked limbs of beeping girls. She looks at me with her piercing eyes wide and white all around. Her skin is clammy and cold, and she shakes all over.

The next few hours are a blur. I am a biologist, not a doctor, and my training in creating human life was focused on the laboratory end, the vat growing that I would do to seed this planet. Our doctor went for a spacewalk somewhere between suns and never came back. Not for the first time it occurs to me how unprepared we are, despite it all. I try my best, with no equipment and no way to communicate with the AIs — Annie — and their nearly infinite store of information, telling myself that women have been doing this for millions of years.

Of course, they've been dying in the process for just as long.

F-3 gives birth in the relative dark of night, with only one half moon for ambience. It's a girl. She wails as the other girls rush to clean her off, and I show them how to support the baby's head. They beep and click and whir, cooing to her in the strangest baby talk I've ever heard. They seem interested and frightened in equal measure, and it's the first time I really register their similarity in ages. They have no little sisters and brothers, and have probably never seen a baby. It's another mystery: why Annie would make only one round of children and then stop, given the enormous store of genetic material Earth sent to CelBod. But I am exhausted, up to my elbows in blood and the other offal of birth, and I'm in no mood for mysteries.

I turn back toward F-3 and am shocked by her pallor and the cloudy cast of her eyes. *Maybe it's the moonlight*, I think. But it's not. I try my best to save her, calling up old redundancy training in medicine. I look for tears and try to stop her bleeding. But the problem is inside, beyond me.

By the time I stop trying the sun is rising, filling the thin air with light that filters through green leaves. F-3's body is as cold as space. "What happened to her?" one of the girls asks me.

I shake my head. "I'm sorry," I say. "She's dead."

The hush that follows is thick, broken only by the baby's mewling. All eyes in the tree house slowly turn my way.

"Dead?" one says, as if testing out the word. I feel my eyes getting wet, and I can only nod.

"Is she broken?"

"Scrap metal?"

"Obsolete?"

I want to say no, she is more than that. But I just nod again, a gesture that they don't seem to recognize. A few of the girls have come over to look at the body and prod it with their fingers, and then they seem to get it. I let out a breath, grateful that I don't have to try to explain death. Or to understand it.

Some of the girls start to carry F-3 away, loading her into a pulley system that goes over the side of the tree house. Others cluster around the baby, who continues to whine. I look over to see the infant's fingers locked around one of a pregnant teen, who beams down at her. "What should we call her?" I ask, aiming for a cheery tone.

Some of them look curiously at me, heads at an angle like the robot in the woods. Many of them seem to have Fs on their lips, looking around the group as if counting. "No, no, no," I say, shaking my head uselessly. "A name. Let's give her something a little more . . . meaningful?"

The girls are stumped. They look wildly around them, obviously trying to pick names from the tree's branches, like fruit. F-6, the tall one who came for me, asks, "What are you called?"

And now I'm stumped. I almost tell them to call me Laika, the name I took on the *Wildest Dreams*. But those dark thoughts of abandonment seem wrong for this place, so I hesitate. My official name seems wrong too. Jane Doe. It's as bad as no name at all.

Eventually I shrug. "I don't really have a name either," I say. "I guess I need one too."

But that thought just hangs there among the branches, because the baby starts wailing again, loud and demanding.

"She needs food," I say. "Milk." I wonder briefly if they have milk before reasoning that these people were once babies, and obviously ate something. A few of them are themselves pregnant, so I guess there'll be milk soon, assuming I can keep some of the moms alive.

The girls nearest to the baby start to move, picking her up and heading toward the long ladder. A chorus of noise spreads from them, with the letters O and K at its core. The creepy sensation that these alien teenagers give me is coming back. They remind me of a flock of birds, or a hive of bees, a colony of ants. Something not quite human.

At that moment I think of Gordo, who is surely awake by now and wondering where I've gone. I feel it like a shot of pain, and I start to follow the girls to the ladder. But F-8 stops me with a tug at my sleeve. "How did this happen?" she asks. "How did that... baby... get inside F-3?"

So I find myself giving the birds and bees talk to a group of birds and bees. They know shockingly little, despite being raised by information itself with a steady diet of movies, and despite living as naked as monkeys. And yet, they've obviously been experimenting. When I tell them the connection between intercourse and pregnancy, a knowing look enters F-8's eyes. She pats her abdomen absentmindedly, and I notice the beginning of swelling there. Others look worried, frightened beyond belief.

I try to reassure them that the process isn't usually fatal, but I don't think they believe me.

"How do you know these things?" one asks, a tiny girl who's sitting with her arms around her knees. "You look younger than me."

I start at the beginning, then realize I have to go even further back. "I'm much older than you," I say. "I'm fifty-three years old. And on Earth, our years are a little longer than here."

"You're a Fixie," one offers.

"Exactly," I sigh, grateful to be momentarily off the hook. A ripple of mechanical-sounding wonder moves through the crowd, and now many of them look at me the same way they did at the baby. It's been an illuminating day for them, and the sun's only just risen. I'm tired and extremely hungry, so I shrug off all the questions and head toward the ladder and, hopefully, some kind of breakfast. If nothing else, our extra provisions from the *Wildest Dreams* are around here somewhere.

I'm climbing onto the top rungs, twisting around to descend, when F-8 says, "So, when are you going to get un-Fixed?"

And my foot slips.

I find Gordo in the kitchen/living room pod, which has been modified and added on to, making a huge cafeteria with tables and benches that pop up out of the floor on telescoping legs. He's in the middle, surrounded by a lot of the naked girls. They leave a berth around him, but it's obvious that they're split pretty evenly between interest and fear. There are no boys in the cafeteria.

Gordo is stuffing his face as fast as he can. He has three square plates in front of him, piled high with fruits and vegetables and bread and even what looks like fresh meat. He's so focused on the food that he doesn't notice me approaching, and jumps when I touch his shoulder, food juice dribbling down his chin.

"I guess I shouldn't have worried about you worrying about me," I say.

He looks up at me guiltily, and I grin. Then I slide onto the bench next to him and start eating food from his plates. It's delicious, and not just compared to ten years of freeze-dried whatever. Whatever else "Annie" has been up to, she's done a great job getting food production up and running. It seems like everything we need to make a go of it is already done.

"Info spreads fast in this place," he says. "Without words, often. Have you noticed how they use other sounds in their language?"

I nod, enjoying the hell out of something resembling bacon. For the moment I'm not concerned that I haven't seen any pigs for it to be from. "Have you been hanging out with the 'Ms'?" I ask, employing air quotes for punctuation.

Gordo shakes his head. "They don't want anything to do with me. Unless it's to loom over me brandishing their wispy mustaches. The 'Fs' seem a bit skittish too, although they all really wanted to watch me take a leak."

I can't help but laugh. "Well," I say. "They learned a lot about men and women today. They probably just wanted to see which one you were." I ruffle his hair, which looks oddly flat with a planet's mass tugging it down.

"Yes, well. I guess they've decided it's neither. For now, anyway. Did you hear that we can un-Fix ourselves?"

I'm not laughing now; my heart starts beating fast. "Yes," I say carefully.

"It was one of the last things Earth sent before it blew itself up or whatever."

I just nod. It's refreshing to be around someone who under-stands body language. Hell, Gordo and I know each other so well after forty-some years together, we could probably communicate with *only* body language. So I can tell that neither of us wants to be the one to ask. It's so awkward that I give in. "I don't want to," I say. Even if my thyroid wouldn't probably kill me, I still wouldn't want to. Once, long ago, I longed to grow up. To have boobs and hips and make steamy love with beautiful people. To have a family. But not in a long time. Our bodies may not mature, but our minds and our hearts do; they learn to long for other things.

Now Gordo nods, relief and a touch of frown on his face. "Yeah, me neither. Let's see how old we can get instead."

"That's right," I say. "I want to be around to see F-3's baby's grandchildren. As long as I don't have to deliver them."

Gordo laughs, and it seems genuine now, the same little-boy smile that kept me sane across the void. "Okay," he says. "We'll have 'Annie' train some doctors."

It's gotten quiet in the cafeteria, even the little beeps and whatnot noises hushed. I'm in mind of a forest when a preda-tor nears, but I'm sure there aren't any predators here. The little naked children wouldn't have stood a chance.

But the girls surrounding us all have firm grips on their cut-lery, from knives to spoons, and their mouths are set in determi-nation. Thankfully, those looks aren't aimed at us. In terms of table manners, a decade in zero-g has left us less civilized than these kids, and therefore unarmed.

I look where they're looking, toward the door, and see the tall-est boy entering. M-1, I presume. He almost has to duck to get in the doorway, followed by the other boys close behind.

Things happen fast. I feel motion and Gordo's arms around me, and I see the girls turn into a blur of anger and flesh. They spin together like a tornado, silverware flashing. I hear yelling and gnashing noises and cries of pain, and somehow under that I even hear the sickening impacts of metal into flesh. I smell blood.

One more sound emerges from the melee: a maniacal laugh that haunts my dreams. I look around wildly, taking in the flailing arms and kicking legs, and in all the motion a still face at a window catches my eye. An impish little girl's face, beaming with madness. She's gone in an instant, but I know with a clarity I can't explain that this chaos is Belka's doing.

And then I realize that I'm on top of the table with Gordo, and that it's become a tall platform, lifting us above the melee. Near the door bodies slump on the floor, and I can't tell if they're breathing or not, only that they're bleeding. *Not again*, I think. But it's not the same: this time the bodies, at least the ones I can see, are male. The crowd starts to disperse, and I see an army of the spindly robots coming in with scrubbing attachments on their hands and feet.

"How many boys are there in this place?" I whisper to Gordo. He is silent. "How many?" I ask again, with greater urgency.

"I've only seen four," he finally says. At which point he gets my point, and uses the control panel at the side of the table to lower it back down.

But it's too late. The wild girls know how to wield their cutlery, and all four boys are dead or dying from stab wounds. Gordo and I press towels into their wounds, but they still die. The robots carry them away, presumably to join F-3, maybe to become bacon. Who can say?

In the whir of machinery only a few girls remain, tending to their sisters with bruises and cuts. I see F-8, pushing against a robot that's trying to clean blood spatter off of her like one would with an overly friendly dog. "Why?" I ask her.

She looks at me with red blood against red cheeks, but no

emotion in her eyes. "One of them broke F-3. And maybe many more of us too. They needed to be taken out of service."

It's so ridiculous that I can't even think. Until now, I haven't let myself consider the big thoughts. I haven't thought of Earth and the billions of people presumably dead. I haven't thought that we on CelBod might be all that's left of humankind, charged with the task of continuing that legacy. Thinking it now makes my soul hurt.

I cling to Gordo in the blood-spattered room, feeling young and old.

———

Colonizing a new planet could never be simple.

NASA spent years, with international partners, assembling a massive ark with embryos from hundreds of thousands of animal species and thousands of human individuals and seeds from millions of plants. They sent them in "bullets" to CelBod, capsules that could rocket through the black faster than anything big enough to support human life. And most of them arrived. The pods came the same way, compressed like IKEA furniture. So did the CREATORs and Annie, though she wasn't called that.

All of these things had to arrive and work together to prepare the planet for the slower-moving, fragile humans (us) to arrive. Even so, we were limited by cost and space to four humans, and tiny ones at that. We've known since the first Mars base that Fixies make great astronauts. We're small and we don't eat much and we suffer less from hormonal needs and sexual tension. Oh, and we live for-goddamn-ever.

All we can't do is populate the bases once we get there.

Hence the multi-stage plan that was the colonization of distant Celestial Body #8972642158. It hasn't gone according to plan, but it can still be saved.

After our bloody breakfast, I head to my laboratory to see

about making some more humans: male ones. Populating the place was always supposed to be my job, and now that Annie's experiment in free-range children has gone so very wrong, it's my turn again.

The plan is fucked.

I expected to find a lot of the seeds and embryos gone. Obviously a number of them have become people and trees and presumably animals.

I did *not* expect to find all of the human embryos missing, their little tubes empty and clean and neatly slotted into racks in an unpowered freezer. I can make elephants and raccoons, dandelions and redwoods, alligators and catfish. We have plenty of those. But I cannot make humans. I am doomed to watch our race wither to extinction.

Gordo finds me weeping, curled under a lab table wishing I were back in space. Gravity numbs my shoulder and heavies my heart. To his credit, to his never-ending credit, Gordo doesn't ask me what's wrong. He looks into the freezer and gently shuts that door, then crawls onto the floor behind me, holding me until I cry myself dry.

After a long while he sighs hugely. I know what he's about to say, and unfairly I already hate him for thinking it. "You know," he says, "there is one more way to make children on this planet."

I know, I *know*, that he means it for the benefit of the human race. I know that he's not just interested in sleeping with every naked teenager on CelBod, of being the Adam in this ridiculous Eden. I know that it doesn't mean he doesn't love me or that he wants to leave me. He probably won't even have intercourse with them—we have much better technology than that.

But it breaks my heart. I turn away from him so he won't see me cry, even though I've been crying for an hour. "Of course," I say with mock lightness. "Some of the girls' babies are sure to be male." Which is true, of course. But even so it would mean waiting many years to breed the next generation, wasting the current Fs' most fertile years. It's a gamble with the entire human race for stakes, and furthermore it's definitely not what Gordo and I are thinking about.

His silence says, *I will not let you make me say it.* His words say, "Do you think Annie has introduced ice cream to CelBod?" And of course I love him again.

Of course I always will.

There are no graves on CelBod. It's not a custom most of the children, as I persist in calling them, understand, and with resources still slim, burial isn't a sensible option. And anyway, I'm not sure what name I would put on a stone. John? Gordo? Or the series of whirs and beeps that the children use? I have no alphabet for it. So I hike up to the lava flow to grieve. Looking over the tops of the odd trees to the stars, I can imagine that I'm looking back toward Earth, if Earth is still out there.

Thankfully, a few of the Fs' original children were male, so the population of CelBod wasn't *immediately* inbred. Now there's a fifth generation brewing in some of the planet's bellies, and so far they seem okay. It looks like the human race might make it, which means my mission is accomplished, and it's time for me to lay down my head and rest, next to the bald, spotted head of my old true love.

Only I can't. I'm only about 115 years old, give or take, and the end isn't even in sight.

Most of the original Fs are dead now, and Gordo and I long ago programmed nonwords out of the robots' vocabulary, but the clicks and chirps and beeps have persisted in the language of

CelBod. I hear it now, coming toward me like a wave surging up through the crystal streams to this crest of red rock. I still don't know what most of the sounds mean; it seems like birdsong to me, even after all these years. But as the voices climb toward me I hear familiar patterns that might be words, might be curses, might be prayers to the gods we thought we left back on Earth.

One of the children, actually a child just a few years younger than I look, runs up to me ahead of the pack, whistling a tone that I often hear. Though I can barely voice it, I've come to think of it as my name. She hands me a leaf that she probably picked up from the forest floor. "Thank you," I say, accepting it. It *is* beautiful, red and pointed like a star. She squeaks out a trill of delight, and then repeats the first sound louder, facing back toward her mother. "Momma, she's here!" she calls.

The crowd repeats the tune, a couple of short beeps and a long one that growls into a purr. They don't understand the way I react to death, but they know I'm sad and I think they've come to comfort me. *What am I to them?* I wonder, not for the first time. I'm not sure. But I know who they are to me. They're my family.

I may never know what they see up there, but together we look up into the bright night sky.

A Matter of Scale

An Account by Dr. Riley Lovegood

YOU KNOW THAT THING where you become aware of something, then suddenly you see it everywhere? Like, maybe a year ago I saw *cavatappi* on a menu, and I had to ask the waitress what it was. The day after that, I was at the grocer and the only pasta on the shelves was cavatappi. Or anyway they had more than one brand of the curly noodles in stock, when I only just learned that they existed. It must have been there all along, right? Because the other alternative is that cavatappi was in the store *because* I was now aware of it, and that model of the universe is one I simply cannot live in. If that's the kind of universe we live in . . . well, I'm getting ahead of myself.

Let's assume these things have been around since the beginning.

I want to go back to the beginning. And that is my family crest.

Many of the older families of the Miskatonic Valley have shields with lions or gryphons or other beasts. Ours — it's sort of a symbol. It has a few sharp lines that seem familiar, like a rune or Cyrillic or Chinese character (but it's not — trust me, I've looked). It's bulbous and symmetrical and yet deeply *wrong*. It resembles an animal if you squint a certain way. If you ignore biology and allow for tentacles to replace most other body parts. If you accept that eyes are windows to the bottomless, meaningless, dark, soul-devouring depths of space.

But that's only if you accept that those things on the crest are eyes.

The symbol is like a Rorschach test, telling more about the beholder than itself. Furthermore, it's like cavatappi. Once you see it, you can't stop seeing it everywhere. Come to think of it, it even *looks* a bit like cavatappi.

Father saw it in the ocean. He thought a beast slumbered below, trapped on an undersea island. Actually, he thought it was a god, and that it was his destiny to find and awaken the god, who would then go on a rampage and destroy the fragile sanity (and home planet) of insignificant humans. I don't know why Father thought this was a good idea.

He sold the scheme to Miskatonic University as a scientific survey to discover what creatures live in the ocean's depths. Giant squid, perhaps. Not the Kraken, or Leviathan. Certainly not Cthulhu.

He didn't find it there, and returned a broken man.

It was Mother who identified the god Father sought as Cthulhu. She introduced him to a cult worshipping this and other demon gods, where his family crest was sensibly taken as proof that he was a chosen one.

I dismissed their obsessions. If I'd believed in their apocalyptic gods, I suppose I'd have feared them — I certainly fear the other cult members, with their worship of gibbering madness.

But I had more important things to worry about than sunken continents and mythical monsters. Rural New England escapes the scrutiny of, say, Appalachia, but a real problem of poverty surrounded us. Nutrition was an issue, as was hygiene, safe drinking water, and disease. So rather than devote my life to the search for ineffable evil, I became a doctor.

I kept a small office at the MU teaching hospital—mostly so I'd have an excuse to "run into" Gina, in Research—but most of my work involved visiting patients in their far-flung homes, bringing basic medicine to folks who really needed it.

———

There is a lake just outside our town where children swim and old men fish. Nestled between craggy hills choked with mouldering pines, Needle Lake was shady all hot summer long, and frozen solid all winter. I always hated it. It was one of those lakes where one step off the bank puts you knee-deep in frigid water, a second step gets you waist deep, and by the third step you're swimming. The water was murky and, to my mind, menacing.

Who knew what was down there?

Legend said Needle Lake had no bottom, but I always knew it did. A lake that had no bottom would pass right through the Earth, and you couldn't just have a hole in the planet like that. Magma and other stuff would bubble up and fill it, and certainly water wouldn't stay in it. The truth was that no one knew how deep the lake was, until a few months ago. A team of cartographers from old MU finally surveyed it and came to the shocking conclusion that it was 1,666 meters deep, or 5,466 less evil-sounding feet deep. It was the deepest lake in the world.

Considering the lake's small size, this was even more shocking. Its sides must truly drop straight down, as though a giant bored a hole in the Earth. MU was determined to (literally and figuratively) get to the bottom of this mystery.

Of course, Father and his cult of lunatics were even more excited. This explained why he hadn't found slumbering Cthulhu in the ocean! All this time the god had been in our own backyard! His eyes lit up with manic fire when he heard the news.

Miskatonic still had Father's equipment from his failed ocean-ographic voyage, so they enlisted him to guide the deep-diving submersible, nicknamed DeeDi, into the bottomless pit, cata-loguing what they found there. We were alone on the boat when he winched her aboard — none of the undergrads MU had as-signed could stand to work with Father, so he'd roped me in as an assistant.

DeeDi swung to the deck with a gentle scrape, dripping mud and an ichorous green slime like putrid seaweed. Nevertheless, Father ran to it like a long-lost lover, hugging and nuzzling it like a kitten. "What eldritch secrets have you brought with you?" he whispered.

I turned my head away in revulsion, as he smeared lake-gunk all over himself. The trees on the nearest shoreline shook in a breeze. To me they looked like multi-limbed figures crossing themselves against a great evil. For the barest of moments, I glimpsed the symbol from my family crest among them, before flexible branches bent another way and the mirage passed.

I'd been watching the video feed as DeeDi explored the lake, so I knew no colossal monster slumbered there. There were barely any fish either, though they may simply have been nimble enough to stay out of DeeDi's headlights. The deeper she went, the less we were able to see through the stagnant murky water.

But that very murkiness told us that *something* was down there. When we putted into the dock, the first thing the undergrads did was hose DeeDi off with a high-pressure hose and decontami-nants and retrieve the sealed samples she'd collected. They hosed Father off too, eyes darting askance at each other as they did.

I never knew for sure what DeeDi dredged up, as the Univer-sity never released that information. I cannot actually prove that what came next came from Needle Lake.

But it did.

It took a while to notice the change in Father. He'd been nuts for years, maybe always, and he surrounded himself with people who supported and reinforced his insanity. When he started speaking in tongues, *Ph'nglui mglw'nafh Cthulhu R'lyeh wgah'nagl fhtagn*, and so on, he was at a cult meeting. The others simply joined in.

Soon, though, he became ill. He couldn't eat, and when he did he could keep nothing down. He spiked a high fever and shook with the chills it wrought. I carted him in to the MU teaching hospital after a day of this, but we couldn't save him.

Mother buried him in an ornate coffin, carved with the family crest. The day was drizzly and flat gray. And when I looked at the crest in the cemetery, clods of dirt raining upon it and turning to thick, dark mud, it looked like a virus.

Oh no, I thought. *What have we unleashed?*

Father wasn't the only one it was too late for. By the time he died, the hospital was full of people like him, ranting in a consonant-heavy babble and vomiting up their lives.

———

After Father's funeral, I went straight to the lab at the hospital. I didn't even change out of my black dress, just threw a lab coat over it, swapped heels for sneakers, and knocked on Gina's window. She looked up from a microscope, frowned, and then waved to me with gloved hands. She stood and stripped them off, opening the door with a geeky smile on her face. People were dying, but she had a mystery to solve, and her enthusiasm for her work couldn't be hidden.

I smiled back at her, despite a growing cold fear in my stomach.

"Riley," she said. "You've got to look at this." She stood behind

the wheeled stool she'd just vacated, gesturing to the microscope's eyepiece.

I was terribly afraid I'd see a familiar shape. "Dammit Gina," I
tried to joke, "I'm a doctor, not a microbiologist."

She didn't laugh. She just grabbed me by the shoulders and
gently pressed me onto the stool. I bent my head to the microscope and saw — I really couldn't say. It didn't look like anything
I'd seen before and, to my immense relief, it didn't resemble my
family crest.

My relief was so immense I almost laughed. To think I'd almost believed in Father's end-of-the-world nonsense!

As I watched, one of the little blobs shivered and stretched
and split into two. It seemed to happen very fast, but what did I
know?

Gina explained to me, very impatiently, that this microbe be-
haved unusually. It seemed able to manipulate the host's DNA,
yet it replicated using mitosis and a lot of other highly technical
stuff that I mostly failed to follow. The kind of doctoring I did
largely comprised prescribing antibiotics and ointments and referring patients to specialists. Joking aside, I was rusty on the
biological basics.

I tuned back in when she said she could develop a vaccine.
And then it was all I could do not to kiss her like that soldier in
Times Square. Maybe for lots of reasons.

———

Gina delivered the vaccine in less than a week. Many people died
in that week, and MU was losing control of their carefully tended
secrecy. Rumor had it the CDC was on its way to take over if we
didn't clamp down on our disease STAT.

Gina tested it on herself, because she is a real-life hero. It
worked, so we gave it to everyone. It even worked, in slightly

modified form, as a treatment for people who'd already been in-fected. Overnight the death rate from the new disease dropped to zero, and everyone in the Miskatonic Valley sighed with relief.

I did a round to all of my rural patients, vaccinating all of them. The county made the vaccine mandatory in schools and offered it for free at the library and post office and all the chemists.

With the danger behind us, I took a break to mourn my father. We hadn't exactly seen eye to crazy eye in life, but I found I missed him. Insane or not, it was nice to be around someone with that kind of certainty. Without him life seemed ordinary. I often found myself drifting off, eyes locked on the crest above our fireplace.

A phone call snapped me out of distressing thoughts. "Help, Dr. Riley," the voice said. My phone's caller ID said Mike Maguer-rin, but it didn't sound like his voice—it was discordant, almost inhuman in its depth, like there was a growl underlying it.

I asked a few follow-up questions, but he was unresponsive. I suspected tonsillitis or strep throat, made sure I had tongue de-pressors and flashlight, and set out to help poor Mr. Maguerrin.

It was dark when I got to the Maguerrins' house, and quiet as a grave.

I rapped on the screen door, and for a long moment heard nothing. When sound came, it was in the form of an otherworldly wail that loosened my bowels. I admit that I almost dropped my medicine bag and ran like a ninny back to my car. But I'd taken an oath, and furthermore curiosity compelled me to see what was inside the house, even if it was some form of monster. I felt my father with me, his apocalyptic curiosity tugging me forward.

The screen door creaked open, and behind it I found the door unlocked. I pushed inward very slowly, calling out for Mike, or

Clara, little Belle, and even baby Billy. All I heard was a sort of whimpering from down the hall. I fumbled on the wall for a lightswitch, finally flicking on the porch light. It did little to illuminate the house, and much to lengthen all the shadows into eerie monstrous forms. But it was light enough for me to pick my way across the living room floor toward the hall.

The living room looked like it had seen a fight. A shoddy armchair had been overturned, and books and other detritus littered the floor. A lamp lay broken on the floor, still plugged in. "Mike!" I called again. "It's Dr. Riley. I'm coming toward your bedroom."

A grunting murmur was my only answer, and a scuffling that got louder as I approached the door. And then a little girl's voice from behind me nearly scared me out of my skin. "Dr. Riley," it said, and of course it was only Belle. I turned and saw her in the low light, a silhouette of a little girl clutching a baby doll in one hand. And yet something about it seemed off. I groped again at the wall for a lightswitch, and this time when I found it the light was almost blinding.

And what I saw... Words fail me. Belle was a little girl still, but she was also... not. Her skin was a bilious shade of green somewhere between mucus and seaweed, and her once-long hair was gone. In its place—and, indeed, in many places on her naked body—tendrils sprouted that waved and groped in the air with unspeakable intelligence. I could swear that some of them were eyelessly watching me. Her eyes were not a child's any longer. They were black pits deeper than the murk of bottomless Needle Lake. They were abominable eyes.

I recoiled, and stumbled backward right into Mike and Clara's room. In here, too, the light was off, but what spilled in from the hall was more than enough to reveal the unutterable horror that lay within. It was a monster. The very monster I'd feared through childhood, the very monster from Father's fevered dreams. It writhed like a mass of snakes, shifting like a mirage of hot pavement. Its skin looked similar to Belle's, but with more maggoty limbs and more of the...tentacles...that sprouted from its head and torso and other parts I could not name.

Worse still, this creature that writhed and moaned and seemed unable to right itself—it had two heads.

"Doctor," Belle said, now quite near to my side, and her voice sounded rough and low, as though she were coming down with strep throat. "What's wrong with Mom and Dad?"

"Where are they?" I started to ask, but then I looked to Belle, festering and slimy-looking. I looked back at the two-headed thing in the room. As I watched, the heads grew closer together, like mitosis running in reverse. Ripples spread through the palsied, tentacular body, as mass shifted. And just then, one appendage flailed toward me, and as it did, a glint of gold caught the light.

Against all sense, I stepped toward the hideous limb and grabbed it, feeling my way toward what passed for fingers, where I'd spotted the gold. I had an icy weight in my stomach, already sure I knew what it was.

It was a wedding ring.

I threw the limb away from me, shrieking incoherently. If poor Belle was looking to me for help, she would be severely disappointed, for I could think of nothing but escape. The heads of the figure in the room shifted even closer to each other, blobbing into one. And for a moment, before the terrible heads resolved into one, I saw in the figure a shape so burned into my brain that I could never stop seeing it. But it was really there this time, big as life: two-headed Cthulhu, the Lovegood family crest.

But the horror didn't stop there. When I finally found my

quivering legs under me and turned to run, for the first time I clearly saw the doll that Belle was holding. It wasn't a doll at all; it was baby Billy, his skin as leprous as the rest of theirs, but his head bashed in on one side. And she wasn't holding him by the hand either; their hands had grown together into one deformed appendage, linking them like paper dolls.

———

I drove without knowing where. But I wasn't surprised to end up at the hospital, rapping on the window of Gina's lab. I *was* surprised to find her there, it being late evening, and the crisis, as far as anyone knew, solved.

"I need to see it," I said by way of greeting. When her only response was a puzzled look, I gestured to her microscope. "The vaccine. Show it to me."

She nodded. "We've had some very... weird... reports of side effects. Rashes and such. Psychological effects. It's like nothing I've seen before."

I couldn't respond. On the one hand, to call what I'd witnessed *side effects* was the most enormous understatement ever. But on the other hand, I'd expected her to disbelieve me. I'd *wanted* her to disbelieve me, because I wanted to be wrong. Here in the hospital, under the harsh fluorescent lights, none of it seemed possible.

It took Gina a few minutes to prepare a slide, and in that time I doubted myself. Surely I'd imagined the whole thing. After all, madness ran in my family. I had seen a thing because I was looking for it, was always looking for it, thankyousomuch Father. I scratched absently at an itch on the inside of my leg.

When the slide was ready I leaned toward the microscope, prepared to laugh at my foolishness. I closed my left eye and squinted into the eyepiece with the right.

And there it was.

It wasn't exactly the same as the family crest, or the monster I'd seen at the Maguerrins' house. Not at first. But watch these wee beasties long enough and they'll show their fanciest trick. One of the cells in the slide stretched, parted, and slowly cleaved in two, replicating. And as it did, for a two-headed moment, it was the symbol from my crest, the missing puzzle piece in my descent into madness.

I stared long enough to watch it happen again and again. And more. The monstrous cells divided, but then they converged, and just as Mike and Clara had, they merged into one. The resulting cell was the same as the others, only larger and growing larger still the more of its neighbors it consumed.

An itch on the back of my hand brought me back to the present. I scratched it with my other hand and felt skin peeling off in thin strips under my nails. My eyes snapped down and, to my horror, I saw three perfect strips of scaly reptilian skin beneath what remained of my own flesh.

———

I knew immediately how the story would play out. Mike and Clara Maguerrin had already become one, and Belle and Billy were well on their way. I had no doubt that it was happening in all the houses of town, in each one where people had been inoculated against Father's disease.

The cure was much, much worse than the disease.

They'd rise from their various homes and wander out, and when they met one another, they'd merge like mercury beads coming together. They'd merge and merge until — *Ph'nglui mglw'nafh Cthulhu R'lyeh wgah'nagl fhtagn* — until Father's vision, his — *my* — destiny was fulfilled, and Cthulhu rose.

Logic told me that Father would want to be a part of it, so there was only one sensible thing to do. It wasn't easy with my skin flaking away, but I enlisted Mother and the surviving members of the cult, and they helped me dig. I injected his body with the vaccine, hoping it would take hold despite the formaldehyde in his dead veins. The cult members took it from there. They chanted and held each other as their flesh putrified and they became one.

But I had other plans. Oh sure, I knew we'd all be together in the end, serving the Great One. But before that happened, I figured I had one last human choice to make, the most human of all choices, really: I could pick who to be nearest to.

I chose Gina. I ran to the hospital, and this time I was not surprised to find her in her lab, her skin like a puddle of quavering jelly. It was hard to tell, with her face transformed into a blasphemous, throbbing mass framing eyes like infinite malevolence, but I swear she opened her tentacles to me.

BIO:

Dr. Riley Lovegood, daughter of esteemed astrophysicist Corina Elderbaum and marine researcher Thomas Lovegood, earned her M.D. from Miskatonic University and went into private practice. She's run several marathons and charity races, including a few zombie runs. These days, Riley spends most of her time with partner Gina as part of the ineffable evil overtaking New England.

STORY NOTES:

I've never been big into the Lovecraftian mythos, but when I was asked to submit to a *Mad Scientist Journal* anthology I couldn't resist. That was years ago, but even then I felt that the only thing scarier than a big monster was an incredibly tiny monster, so tiny you couldn't see it until it was far, far too late.

I am writing these notes on Day I Have No Idea of the Covid-19 pandemic, which I hope by the time you're reading this is just a terrible memory of that time we were all a bit lonely. But suffice it to say that this story seems even scarier to me right now than it did when I wrote it. And that bit about developing a vaccine in a week? I guess this story goes to show that some things shouldn't be rushed.

It also goes to show what can happen when you *really* ignore physical distancing during an outbreak.

Snow Angels

THE SNOW STARTS late in the morning, flakes like white rose petals rushing past my window onto the grime of Pioneer Square: pterosaur weather.

Whoever had theorized that dinosaurs were cold-blooded had been about as dead wrong as anyone could be—with the possible exception of the scientists who thought cloning them was a good idea. They were dead, as well as dead wrong. As it turned out, dinosaurs loved cold weather, especially the flying ones. Massive Quetzalcoatlus seemed to love striking like lightning out of dark clouds, plucking pedestrians to their deaths.

"It won't stick," says Fay, drifting past me with her mug of horrible coffee from the break room. She pauses, leaning against my desk to peer out the window. "It never does. Snow here is just a big tease." Fay looks like something of a tease herself. Even on the coldest day of the year, she wears a short skirt and a low-cut top. Her one concession to the weather is a pair of furry boots over black tights. She slurps her coffee, embracing it with her whole mouth, licking a drip from the side of her yellow mug. But I am not thinking about her mouth, not anymore.

"Of course, everyone in the city will lose their minds," she adds casually.

I look past her, out the window. White flakes against a sky the color of aluminum. With a hint of leathery wing? I shiver.

———

Cities are pretty safe from the dinosaurs: like all wild things, they prefer the wild. Only occasionally do you hear about a flock of

Procompsognathuses taking the subway into Manhattan or Chicago to terrorize the native rats. The cores of cities — like the business district of Seattle where I work—are even relatively safe from pterosaurs, who don't like to chance the alleys between tall buildings.

Still, I hope to see one. Their smaller cousins used to visit us at our Southern California house, landing on the roof and frightening Lani awake. "Make a wish," I'd tell her. To me, spotting a dinosaur was like glimpsing a shooting star.

I call home after lunch. Lani answers with a cheerful "hello," but I hear sleep in her voice and I have to bite my irritation back. I imagine her as a mountain of blankets, distant and immovable. Yet also strangely compelling.

"How 'bout this weather, huh?"

A pause. Bedsprings squeak as she scoots to the window. "Oh my goodness," she says, and I imagine her looking out onto the backyard of our rented house, seeing it transformed into a rumpled bed of shapeless bushes and rusting lawn furniture. I see her donning a bathrobe, running one hand through bed-flattened hair.

She'll stay inside all day, wisely avoiding the chance to become prey. We live on top of Queen Anne Hill, after all, and the elevation and low buildings make it a prime hunting ground for Quetzalcoatlus. And Lani has nowhere in particular she needs to go.

Sitting at my steel desk, lunch-cart sandwich and burnt coffee eating holes in my stomach, I try not to hate her for it. But I do. I hate her for this cold weather, hate her for my cubicle, hate her for this whole city, *her* city. I want to go home.

"You better come home right away." Now she sounds agitated, finally wide awake. "You'll never make it if you wait."

"Okay," I say. But I'm not really listening. Some of us have to work, cannot simply leave any time we like. Can't lounge all day in a warm bed, soft skin against flannel sheets. I can picture her there, and the image is so beautiful that it makes my hatred waver.

Outside, the air swirls.

By five p.m., drifts pile high against buildings, covering the city's debris like draped sheets in an unused room. In the streets, cars slush through brown snow, honking and belching steamy exhaust clouds. Intrepid or foolish cyclists weave between them, exhaling clouds of vapor and ire. The panhandlers in the square wrap dirty blankets around their shoulders as they shake torn coffee cups of change at passers-by. They huddle in the shelter of doorways and under the wrought-iron and glass portico in the square. My own jacket feels inadequate, wind biting through in gusts.

A few hipster types in ironic wool caps with ear flaps are building a fort in the alley, packing snow into venti-size paper cups then mortaring the resulting blocks into their wall with more snow.

The snow stuns me. Sure, I've seen it before: I've been skiing, and once it even snowed in the desert town of my birth. It didn't stick, though. It was just a tease.

This is different. I start to think Lani was right about getting home. I briefly consider abandoning my car to the lot it's parked in, taking a bus home. But then I think of the walk from the bus stop, imagine being plucked by my head into the air, bony beak squeezing as I flap my arms uselessly, and the car seems a better option.

Before I get ten feet from the office, Fay calls after me. I turn to see her skipping my way, scarf trailing behind her. Her short leather jacket is unzipped, and I wonder how she can stand the cold. But when she nears I feel heat radiating from her. The snow seems to evaporate around her in a foggy haze. Talk about not cold-blooded.

"Are you really driving home?" she asks. She looks at me like I'm a lunatic. But when I nod she laughs, puffs of dragon's breath wafting up to me. "Thank god. Can I have a ride?"

"Sure," I say immediately. Not thinking of her apartment, her bed.

"You can just drop me at the bottom of the hill," she says. "If we make it that far." She winks, and my face feels warm.

We drive through a city made strange. Traffic is backed up everywhere, but though the roads are slick I manage not to slide into cars or trees or suicidal cyclists. Fay babbles about the snow, about growing up in Montana and living in Los Angeles, about so many other things that I can't keep up. She tilts her head against the window to look up into clouds the color of bruises. But she reports no sightings of pterosaurs, only three-headed snowmen and cross-country skiers.

I have to crack a window. The defroster is no match for Fay's monologue.

Finally we reach the area locals call Lower Queen Anne. Home is a straight shot from here, up one very steep hill. But it may as well be Mt. Everest. At the bottom of the hill, cars are pushed off the street at odd angles, piled in drifts like giant metallic snow. Like the middens of shells dropped by gulls, writ large. I imagine they were left there by an even larger pterosaur — one larger than any yet discovered, let alone cloned — something immense enough to grab cars right off the road and drop them onto the asphalt, breaking them open to reach the soft meat inside.

As Fay and I watch from a side street, a huge accordion bus slides backward, jackknifing. It sails past us, just missing my front bumper on its way to the junk heap farther down. People run toward the spectacle, crowding the sidewalks on both sides of us like spectators at a ski jump. There are so many of them that I again consider my chances of walking home, using the crowd for cover. The very thought chills me to the bone as I remember the icy wind and my thin jacket. I sigh.

Fay laughs, the cackle of a joyous witch. "You're not getting home tonight," she says. She reaches across the parking brake and squeezes my thigh, and her heat goes right through my wool slacks. She smells like palm trees and sand and—is it my imagination?—suntan lotion. Skin and Christmases at the beach. Home. The steamy look in her eyes fills me with a mix of fear and excitement, but in that moment I know I will follow her heat anywhere.

"Let's make snow angels," she says.

There's not much room on the streets, but I manage to back the car out of traffic and park near where I imagine the curb to be. We get out and the cold air assaults me. Reflexively I look to the sky, but all I see is the city's light reflected on clouds. The buildings around us, I judge, are high enough for safety.

The snow melts into icy water when it hits me, cold rain dripping down my neck. Fay leans her head back to catch flakes on her tongue, but I doubt any of them get that close to her without evaporating.

She falls backward onto the snow-covered hood of a parked car, flapping her arms, leaving an imprint of angel wings. "Come on," she beckons. I look around, but her wingspan covers the hood. And the thought of plunging into snow makes me shiver.

So instead of leaning back, I lean forward. Fay rises to meet me, pulling the lapels of my coat. Her mouth meets mine, and I stop shivering. We fall together onto the car's hood, grasping at each other as pedestrians pass by and the occasional crunch and shout from Queen Anne Avenue tells of another car accident.

No one is getting home tonight.

My frozen fingers find the space between Fay's skirt and her top and she gasps. But it only makes her pull me closer, and I fall into her as if through broken ice.

When my phone vibrates, it shocks me like a cold splash. Jangling tones play: Lani's ring. I picture her waiting for me in our warm house, our castle atop the hill. I am hours late already. I imagine her peering out a foggy window, pulling the curtains aside to look for me coming up the driveway, delicate eyebrows knit into a squiggle of worry.

I draw back. Fay lies between her angel wings, hair fanned out like a halo in a Byzantine painting. "Stay with me," she whispers.

But it isn't only guilt pulling me away from Fay. Her halo, her wings mock me as I turn. Angels aren't the only things with wings.

"You'll never make it," she calls after me.

"I know."

My Honda starts to slide even before I nose out onto the steep, icy street. But I rev the engine anyway, pushing hard to get up the hill. The watching crowd shouts to me as I go, mostly with derision. They're right, of course. All of them. I *am* an idiot.

My wheels spin and I start to lose momentum. Slowly, the car comes to a stop. Then gravity takes control and I slide backward, sideways, down the hill toward the jumble of cars at the bottom. Steering is useless. Braking is useless.

And then I see it in the sky, the huge dark outline against glowing clouds. *Make a wish*, I think, and step on the gas one more futile time.

I won't make it. But I don't regret it. I had to try.

STORY NOTES:

I wrote this story as a bit of literary fiction, perhaps a last gasp of the overwrought feelings-based stuff I thought was good in my twenties. But it never really worked that way; it needed dinosaurs. I was given the prompt "quetzalcoatlus" by a sponsor in the Clarion West Write-a-thon in 2012, and it was a marriage made in . . . well, surely not heaven.

And for those of you who've never experienced Seattle in a snowstorm, all of this is accurate.

Down in the Woods Today

TODAY IS THE DAY.

At dawn we wake from our paralysis, Mr. Wuzzy and I. He pushes himself up off of his face and stretches, wiggling his embroidered nose, then jumps down from the shelf above your desk, Cherie. He lands gracefully, lightly, as though his age is no factor. I shimmy my own self out from under your arm and your pink comforter and slide to the carpet, and together Mr. Wuzzy and I creep out of the house. I stand on his head to reach the doorknobs.

"Goodbye, Cherie," Mr. Wuzzy whispers, when we are far enough away that you won't hear him speaking. "Do not search for us." Do not search for *me* is what he means. And to some degree, I share his view. Despite the honor and privilege it would bring me, I do not really wish it to be you, Cherie. You keep me safe on your soft bed, and you are rarely rough with me, holding me by the ears or snout or tail.

At the clearing we meet other bears, hugging old friends so hard our stuffing shifts in our bellies. There are bears no bigger than your palm, and some who must be bigger than your whole self. They tower over Mr. Wuzzy and me, but they are still soft and sweet. We beat them every time at hide-and-seek.

Some bears look worse for the year past, but I feel svelte and smooth. My fur is soft and clean; none of my seams need to be restitched.

The day is spent in a spirit of joy, for we know that at dawn the paralysis begins again. We run and tumble and exalt in movement. Some bears do nothing but eat and drink. Some are drunk as plush skunks by sundown. Others climb the oak and maple trees, rustling about in the branches like I imagine real bears must do.

An ancient Teddy Talks-a-Lot hobbles through the long grass, his beak-like mouth opening and closing soundlessly. I think he is singing, but he must have been out of batteries for years. He will never be chosen. At the edge of the clearing, as usual, a clique of Caring Bears share a joint. When I pass by them a Hope Bear yells, "Cheer up!" and the others laugh.

Mr. Wuzzy and I are playing ball tag when the creeping sensation crawls up everyone's backs, making the fur of our scruffs stand on end. Humans are watching.

We are pros; every bear drops instantly, simultaneously. The forest is now a silent place, littered with lifeless toys. Light slices through the trees at a long angle. The ball bouncing through the long grass and off into the trees is the only movement.

I sense a juvenile human weaving through the trees toward us, and I know that it is you. Mr. Wuzzy knows it too; I can see the panic in his plastic eyes from ten feet away.

You could still remain safe. But then you step into the clearing.

It is all any of us can do not to gasp. The excitement that runs through us is electric, almost palpable. You step right over Mr. Wuzzy and his matted old fur. You step over a dozen bears on your way to me, so gentle, so careful not even to kick any of them. In this moment we all love you, but I love you most of all because I know you are mine.

"Mr. Fuzzy," you say, bending over to pick me up, "what are you doing out here?" You scoop me sweetly up into your arms, not even tugging me by a paw, and pluck a leaf from the fur of my face.

For an instant I'm not sure I can do it.

I look into your innocent face, questioning me as though you already believe I could answer. Then I rear my head back and bare my teeth, pointy and sharp and crowded as a shark's. I wait for your shock; need to feel it. Perhaps I am trying in my own way to give you an escape. But you do not drop me.

And then I bite.

My poison acts fast. You drop like we do, like a rag doll onto the forest clearing, still cradling me in your arms like a precious baby.

In the next moment the bears come to life, cheering and pumping their paws in the air. A few bears look disappointed, kicking stones and muttering things like, *I thought it was my year*. But they do not complain.

Only one bear is truly upset. As I step down from your paralyzed body, Mr. Wuzzy approaches me shaking his head. "We should let her go," he says. "She's been kind to us and doesn't deserve this."

"You're just jealous," I say. I run my paw through the fur on my head, smoothing it down. "You're not her Mr. Fuzzy anymore and now you never will be."

He looks like he wants to say more, but we are interrupted by last year's Chosen Bear. Cuddles is an old bear, taller and thinner than Mr. Wuzzy and me, with the lumpy misshapen look of a comfort object. His fur is even more matted and stained than Mr. Wuzzy's, and one of his plastic eyes fell off long ago and was replaced with a gray button. He grabs my paw with his and lifts it into the air like I'm a boxing champion. All the other bears cheer again. In the corner of my eye I see a Joy Bear clapping her paws across her rainbow-embroidered tummy. She catches my eye and winks.

Cuddles turns back to me when the crowd starts to disperse. "Congratulations, Mr. Fuzzy. What a year you'll have. I must have seen the whole world! It will be hard for me to go back to the stillness again." His plastic eye takes on a faraway look as he rambles, but his button eye holds fast to me. He claps me on the back. "Enjoy the rest of the picnic, son. I'll get everything ready."

And so I step away from your body. I have a Joy Bear to find, a Mr. Wuzzy to ignore, and a picnic to enjoy.

It is difficult to lose Mr. Wuzzy, who follows me around jumping up and down like a young human who has to pee. "You don't understand," he says, but I do not listen.

It's easier to find Joy Bear, and when I do at last old Mr. Wuzzy gets the hint and goes, head down, out into the crowd. Joy bear is forward, nuzzling her pink heart nose into my neck even before we sneak away from the clearing. Already I enjoy being the Chosen Bear.

When the black sky starts to lighten, we gather for the ceremony. You are bound hands and feet in the center of the clearing, and when you see us gather around you your eyes grow wide with fear. It seems now you understand: it's lovely down in the woods today, but safer to stay at home.

Cuddles stands beside you, as does Mr. Wuzzy. He strokes your face, staining his fur with your tears. When the crowd's murmuring dies down Cuddles speaks: "Another year of paralysis has passed. Another year begins at dawn. But before it does, we make this offering so that next year we may again gather here."

He turns to you, gesturing with one paw. He has a flair for the dramatic that I'm trying to memorize. Next year it will be I saying these words. "A human has come here, of her own free will. Who will testify to it?"

The crowd erupts as almost every bear raises a paw and shouts his testimony. Cuddles gestures to me. "Mr. Fuzzy, Chosen Bear, is this your human?"

"Yes," I say. Mr. Wuzzy scowls at me.

"And are there any challenges?"

I am surprised when Mr. Wuzzy raises his paw. "I challenge," he says. A gasp ripples outward through the crowd like a wave through water.

Cuddles looks confused. Never have I seen a challenge, even though it's usually the case that more than one bear is linked to the human in question. The honor belongs to the Chosen Bear. "She is your human too?" asks Cuddles.

"Yes," Mr. Wuzzy says.

The crowd is loud with speculation. *What happens now?* I hear some ask. A female voice says, *Maybe they can* share *the heart.* But I look into Mr. Wuzzy's eyes. He does not want to share. He wants to set you free. I wonder if you know the depth of his devotion: without a sacrifice none of us will be released from our paralysis next year.

And so I don't wait for a judgment. "I am the Chosen Bear!" I shout. "Her heart belongs to me." There is a moment of silence before the crowd reacts, but when they do it's clear they are on my side. They cheer for me, and I feel powerful. I bare my teeth at Mr. Wuzzy, running my tongue along each thorn-like point. I do it to make him angry, and it does.

Mr. Wuzzy jumps across your squirming body and tackles me, his own needle-teeth snapping in my face. I am on my back in the grass, but I manage to get all four paws under him and push him away, and he falls back. I charge him like a bull, but he is quicker than me. He grabs me and before I really know what he's doing, my face is in the dirt. I think he is stepping on my head, twisting and grinding until I feel the stuffing breaking apart inside, feel the dirt working deep into my fur. Over it all I can hear your scream.

Suddenly the pressure is gone, and I stand up. All around me is chaos, bears hitting each other, grabbing and pulling at fur and ears and tails, stabbing at eyes and biting with their sharp, sharp teeth. The crowd has pulled Mr. Wuzzy off of me, and now they surround him, so many people attacking him that they're hurting each other by accident.

I brush the dirt from my face, afraid of how badly my fur's been damaged.

Cuddles breaks free of the melee and jumps onto your tummy, waving his arms in the air. "Quiet!" he yells, with such force that it cannot be ignored. Bears freeze with paws drawn back mid-punch; they freeze with mouths snarling open.

"The sky lightens," he says, softer now. "We must proceed."

Looking chastened, bears get back into order, helping each other up and murmuring apologies. A battered-looking Mr. Wuzzy brushes himself off, even as other bears stand around him like guards.

"Chosen Bear," Cuddles says. "As custom dictates, I leave the honor to you. It is up to you to decide if you'll share with the challenger."

I nod humbly to Cuddles, then glare at Mr. Wuzzy. "I will not."

"Then on your word we begin."

I step toward you and you twist away. "No. No. No," you chant through the tears. Standing on your chest I stroke your face with my paw as Mr. Wuzzy did, and when I look at you I understand how he felt. It didn't have to be you, and perhaps I would even have been happier if it were not you. I do not like to see you so sad and afraid.

But it was you.

"Yes, Cherie," I say quietly, only for you. Then, "Yes!" I say louder. The bears strike as one mass, fast as a pack of snakes. Shark-like teeth surround you from all sides, and we devour you quickly. You do not scream for long.

We eat until there is nothing left, crunching through your bones and licking every last drop of blood from our fur and the grass in the clearing. In our frenzy we even eat your clothes and the ropes with which we bound you. Yet your heart is mine alone, and I eat it slowly, savoring the year of freedom it buys me.

The sky is very light when the last bears leave and I worry that they will not make it back to their homes or stores before paralysis sets in. I am in no hurry. I dawdle, deciding where to go, when I hear a soft moaning from just outside the clearing.

Mr. Wuzzy crawls toward me from the woods. I see a new rip along his side seam, and I think his left eye looks loose. "Mr. Wuzzy," I say, "did I do that to you?"

Mr. Wuzzy laughs. "No, Fuzzy. I don't think you could."

I reach down to help him up, checking the sky in alarm. The sun will peek over a distant ridge any moment; Mr. Wuzzy should be home by now. Even as I worry about the sun, another thought occurs to me. "Did you get any of the . . . of Cherie?"

He shakes his head. "Couldn't get through the crowd. For some reason they were mad at me." He smiles again, but weakly, and I realize how much I'll miss his sense of humor. Even during paralysis, Mr. Wuzzy was a pal.

I run to the center of the clearing where the grass is matted and trampled. "Maybe there's some blood left!" We may have missed some in the low light, I think. But I see nothing.

"It's okay," he says. "I was asking for it anyway."

"But the paralysis! Next year—"

"It's okay," he says. "Just take me ho—"

The sun has climbed into the sky, and Mr. Wuzzy is inert again, just a toy. He falls limp onto the ground and I run over to squeeze him, shake him. It's no use. I want to cry, but of course I cannot.

It's hard work, but I carry him all the way back home. There are people about, so I have to stop frequently to act like a toy. It's noon by the time we get to your house, a household in pandemonium. Your humans are frantic looking for signs of you, but they will never find any, Cherie. I looked myself, but not a drop of you remains.

I use the confusion to enter unnoticed. Your door is closed, so I stand on Mr. Wuzzy's lifeless head to reach the knob, then I carry him the rest of the way to the neatly made bed. It was never rumpled last night. I push him up onto the bed and arrange him just-so against your lacy pillow, just the way you used to place me.

I whisper, "Goodbye, Mr. Wuzzy."

I take one last look around the room before I go, memorizing everything. Like you, I will never return.

STORY NOTES:

I wrote this story at Clarion West based on a classmate's musing about sinister interpretations of the teddy bears' picnic (thanks, Persephone!). I turned it in for critique the same day our instructor for the week, editor David Hartwell, went on a long digression about how you can never kill children or dogs in your stories, and definitely never ever write in second person.

A few people thought I'd done both, though on closer inspection this story is in first person (I = Mr. Fuzzy) but addressed to a specific person (you = Cherie). Mr. Hartwell conceded that the violence against a child somehow worked in this piece. Rules are made to be broken?

When this story was published, I had to file the serial numbers off the other commercially trademarked bears at the picnic, for legal reasons. But I really didn't try that hard, and any late Gen Xer or early Millennial should be able to identify them pretty easily.

I still think that song is vaguely menacing.

A Fairy Tale

THE CHORUS OF "Happily ever after" roused me from my stupor. Even from the living room I could hear the bored edge in Elise's voice; it was as predictable as Kari's enthusiasm or Allan's sing-songy tone, and as strained.

Storytime was finished. I headed to Kari's room to say good-night, but paused outside the door when I heard her speak. "Daddy," she said, "is that how it was for you and Mommy?"

I held my breath, sincerely wondering how Allan would answer. But it was Elise who answered: "Of course not. Mom's not a princess."

Kari laughed, but Allan didn't miss a beat. "She is to me," he said.

I crept away as quietly as I could, unsure whether the sound I suppressed was a sob or something more like bitter laughter.

It was a over a week later, and storytime was definitely over. I tried not to think of Allan as I stared into an expanse of prairie grass. It spread like a yellow-green ocean from the light on the back porch to the end of the known universe, losing color the farther it went into the night. Finally I could see nothing but the phosphorescent glow of hundreds of lightning bugs: the deep water. There be monsters.

I sat on the kitchen's island cradling a glass of Pinot Grigio, and without thinking of Allan, I contemplated how I had gotten myself stuck in a place like Ohio, anyway. No, not *stuck*, my editor-mind corrected: *marooned*. Marooned and emotionally mutinied by a pair of pirate daughters who had always loved their daddy better.

The glass of wine sweated in the evening's heat, drops of cold water running down the stem and over my fingers. I wiped my hand across my forehead just as a wave of breeze skimmed across the ocean of my back lawn, in through the open window, and over my face, turning me suddenly cold all the way through. The screen door slammed on the back verandah and I jumped up to face my girls.

"Mom!" Elise shouted. She held something behind her back as she stood shifting with excitement from side to side. "You're never gonna believe what Kari and me found!"

In my editor-mind I cringed, thinking *Kari and I,* and wondering if ten was too young to start correcting the finer points of my daughter's grammar. But I figured she'd pick them up with or without me; it seemed all she did was read. I tried to smile. "Did you catch some good lightning bugs?"

Little Kari, hands over her mouth, looked as though she was about to burst. But Elise continued over her sister's muffled snickering, strangely sober. "Yeah, Mom. And something ... else." She brought the object out from behind her back without looking at it, and I was so focused on her scrunched-shut eyes that it wasn't until she re-opened them with a little gasp that I saw what she meant.

She held the mayonnaise jar high in front of her like a trophy. Ragged holes had been punched in the plastic lid and the peeled-off label left only smudgy streaks of glue to obscure its contents: three agitated fireflies, their green butts blinking on and off like living Christmas lights; a few leaves and a bumpy twig; and, sitting on the twig with her elbows on her knees, a tiny winged person.

I looked from my older daughter's stunned face to my younger daughter's suppressed mirth to the mayonnaise jar to the glass of wine in my hand, took a sip, and set it down on the counter behind me. I took the jar from Elise, still studying her expression. My mind was struggling to convince me that I couldn't have seen what I thought I had. Not a fairy; not a real one. Probably some toy I gave them and forgot about, I thought. I laughed at my gullibility, and raised the jar for a closer look.

The figure sat turned away from me, presenting me with coppery hair and greenish wings. Delicate, almost translucent wings which, I now saw, moved gently in and out as if to the rhythm of a creature's breathing. Holding my own breath, I turned the jar around.

There she was, not a toy at all, cast in intermittent lightning-bug light. About three inches tall, fair-skinned and naked, she sat on the twig with her bare feet on the glass bottom of the jar and her head in her tiny hands. One of the lightning bugs—to her the size of a barn owl—buzzed around her head, and she shooed it away with a violent wave of her arm.

She picked her head up and fixed me with fierce green eyes. "What?" she said, in a surprisingly big voice.

My grip on the jar slipped. It fell a few inches before I caught it again, and the fairy—or whatever she was—fluttered her wings in the jar's airspace before settling back down onto the twig. I set the jar on the kitchen counter.

Kari scrambled up onto one of the stools on the other side of the counter, perching on her knees with her elbows on the formica countertop. She peered into the jar like a cat looks into a fishtank, still grinning. "Can we keep her?" she asked.

The tiny woman threw her hands up in the air. I shook my head, feeling like I was moving underwater. "I think . . ."

"What's your name?" Elise had scooted onto the stool next to her sister to regard the fairy, though with a less predatory look on her face.

The little creature stood up in her 32-ounce world. "What's yours?" she asked, pointing her whole arm at my daughter.

"Oh. I beg your pardon," she said, and I smiled proudly. "My name's Elise, and this is my sister, Kari." Kari waved quick as a hummingbird, and Elise gestured across the counter to me. "And that's our mom."

The fairy turned toward me and inclined her head slightly. "Hey, Mom," she said.

I laughed, reaching for my glass of wine. "You can call me Deb."

"Iris."

"What are you?" asked Kari, and her wide eyes narrowed as Elise punched or pinched or kicked her under the counter's edge.

"No," said Iris. "I have a few questions for you. Question one: which one of you slack-jawed gawkers is going to free me from this lard-smelling prison?"

"Will we get a prize? A wish granted?" In her excitement Kari didn't seem to notice the dirty looks she was now getting from both her sister and Iris.

Iris turned toward her, her voice syrupy sweet. "What would you wish for, little girl?"

Kari squealed with joy, talking a mile a minute. "A new bike, or to be the prettiest—no! Three more wishes! Or just for Daddy—" She cut off abruptly, and the joy fell away.

"I can do that," said the fairy.

Kari and Elise gasped in unison.

"But I'm not going to. Wishes, wishes, wishes. Nope, not this time." She laughed a squeaky, cackling laugh.

"Now hold on, Iris," I said, setting the nearly empty wineglass back on the counter.

"What?" she asked. "You don't like me fucking with your kids?" One of the fireflies dived at her head and she ducked, swiping at it with both arms.

Elise and Kari giggled, and I wondered if it was about the bug or the naughty word. I don't think they knew what it meant, only that it was off-limits. "Iris," I began, aiming for an authoritative tone. "I'm going to have to ask you not to swear in front of—"

"Hey," she said, flapping her wings. "Do you know what kind of fucking powers I have? Maybe I can destroy you with a snap of my fingers." Squinting, I saw that her tiny fingers were poised to snap. Once again she was dive-bombed by a lightning bug, but she simply pointed at it and the bug blinked out of existence. She leaned one hand against the jar's wall for a moment, head down, then looked up at me with a dark expression. "You don't know, do you?"

I shook my head.

"Then I call the shots. Open lid, now."

Her arms were crossed over her naked chest, her foot tapping impatiently. With a shrug I reached over and unscrewed the mayonnaise jar's lid. Iris flew out, stretching her wings, as did one of the lightning bugs. The other bug seemed content to throw itself repeatedly against the glass wall of the jar.

"Iris," Elise said, a waver in her voice. "How did you make that bug disappear?"

The fairy paused in mid-air, looking at Elise. "I told you I had powers, didn't I?"

Elise seemed to consider this, eyes rotating in their sockets to follow Iris, flying in loop-de-loops in our kitchen. She looked more than a little frightened, Elise, and I thought I should say something to comfort her. But what was there to say? Eventually she continued: "But where did it go?"

I re-screwed the lid, locking the remaining firefly inside. In a small way I mourned its missed opportunity for freedom. *You snooze, you lose*, I thought, and with that, unbidden, came thoughts of Allan. He'd flown right out of the jar that was our marriage—vanished, or maybe just escaped—and I could still hear the buzzing sound as I banged my head against the glass.

Iris flew around, floating like a butterfly with her nude legs trailing behind. She hadn't answered Elise, and it didn't seem like she was planning on it. "Can you bring it back?" Elise asked.

Iris set down on the counter, stretching upwards with her arms. Kari reached her arm across the countertop to get my attention, whispering loudly enough for everyone to hear. "Mom? She's not wearing any clothes."

"No she's not, honey," I said, looking at Iris's tiny white butt as she bent to touch her toes.

"No she's not," Iris echoed. "An astute observation, little girl. And no, I don't want any of your doll's clothes. You people are all the same." Suddenly she twirled around and pointed at me. "Hey, how 'bout a drink?"

I shrugged, looking into my own empty wineglass. "Wine okay?" She nodded. "What can I put it in for you?"

Iris sighed loudly, and I imagined I could see her roll her bright green eyes. "A thimble is traditional," she said. She paused, while I mentally searched the house for a thimble. I wasn't exactly a seamstress. "If you can't manage that, the cap from the toothpaste tube will do." She sounded incredibly put out by the whole thing.

I nodded to Elise. "Will you get a cap for our guest?"

Elise hurried off in the direction of her bathroom.

"Wash it out real good!" Iris called after her. "That shit tastes horrible."

Really well, my editor-mind said. Wash it out really *well*.

It took forever to get the kids to sleep that night; fairy tales didn't interest them, especially not ones read by Mom. "Can we keep her?" was all they wanted to know. I told them it wasn't really our choice, but I did eventually get them to bed with the assurance that Iris would still be around in the morning. Relieved, I crept out to the back porch with an opened bottle of Pinot Grigio, and lit a cigarette.

"Blow that my way," said Iris, as I dropped into one of the padded deck chairs. She sat on the edge of the table between them, legs swinging in the night air. "That's one of the things I miss out on, being so small. Cigarettes. There's just no way to shrink those."

I exhaled a lungful of smoke at her, watching as she basked in its carcinogenic fog. "Yeah, but at least you're a cheap date." I pointed to the toothpaste cap in her hands, filled with a few drops of white wine.

She laughed, leaning back on her elbows on the table. A few caps of alcohol had made her far less cantankerous.

"And you have magical powers," I added. "I think I'd like that." Iris said nothing, her shiny green wings moving slowly in and out like a fan. "Iris?"

"Yeah."

"If you could make that lightning bug disappear, why couldn't you get out of the jar?"

"Who says I couldn't?" she said, an edge entering her voice.

I put my hands up, backpedaling. "You're right. I shouldn't

assume." I sipped my wine, then quietly: "I just thought if you could've gotten out, you would have."

She glared at me. Her eyes seemed to be made of emerald light; sometimes they shone, other times they pulled light into them like twin black holes. "You think magic's like turning on a light switch?"

"I don't know."

"Not even a light switch is like a light switch. You just think it is because you don't see what it takes to get the power into your house. Somewhere coal is burned to turn water into steam to spin a turbine to make electricity, which travels for miles to get to your house. You flip a switch and the light comes on, *like magic.*"

"Okay, so . . ."

She sighed. "So I'm having an off day."

I raised my glass in a toast. "I hear that."

Iris leaned back again. "It's pretty out here," she said. "Calm."

I looked out at the waving field of prairie grass, trying to see it as anything but a wasteland. The lightning bugs had all gone to sleep, along with the few neighbors we could see, and it was quiet, quiet, quiet. In the town behind me lay the college campus with its old stone buildings and its suddenly unfunded and unstaffed literary magazine, all folded in for a summer's hibernation. Sometimes I thought I could hear it snoring, rumbling like an approaching summer storm. Soon it would wake, breaking open like a hatching egg-sack with motion and noise and youth, and I knew we'd see Allan then, at least. He wouldn't turn his back on a tenure-track position, even if he had no problem turning it on me.

"So what would your wish be?" Iris asked, turning over on her

234 · EMILY C. SKAFTUN

side. Her wings out of sight behind her, she looked just like a woman in miniature.

"I don't know," I said. "World peace? Naw, that's boring. I really don't know. Money wouldn't fix anything. I don't even think having my job back would." I took another drag from my cigarette and blew the smoke over Iris's recumbent form.

She shivered in delight. "You want him back?"

"Can you really do that?" It didn't occur to me to ask how she knew about Allan in the first place.

She laughed. "No, not really."

This time I laughed too. "Oh. Well, he always comes back eventually. Not that it matters much. Seems like he's not here even when he is here." I paused, sipping from my glass. Iris did the same, then extended her toothpaste cap to me. I took it, dipped it into the wine in my own glass, and handed it back to her. "I guess my wish isn't so much that he'd come back as that it would matter if he did."

"That's a tough one."

"I know. So how 'bout you? What's your wish?"

She looked at me, startled. "I—I don't know." She turned toward the ocean of green grass, wings moving subtly in the breeze, but before she did I thought I saw a new look on her tiny face, a darkness that I couldn't quite identify.

The next morning I woke to the sounds and smells of breakfast, and for an instant I thought Allan had returned. *But he doesn't make breakfast*, I thought. And then I remembered the previous evening.

I stumbled downstairs to the kitchen, where Iris was flying above the stove. Under her command, breakfast literally made itself, spatulas hanging in the air waiting to turn slices of French toast and bacon. She was still naked, of course, and I wondered how she avoided splatter burns.

Kari busied herself setting the dining room table—four plates, but only three with glasses and silverware. On the fourth plate sat Iris's toothpaste cap. Kari scurried past me holding a carton of orange juice and a jug of syrup, while Elise huddled next to the stove, watching intently as Iris hovered over the frying pans.

Seeing that there was nothing I could do to help, I sat down at the table. Before I could even pour myself some orange juice, Iris and my girls came into the room, preceded by floating plates of food that somewhat unsteadily set themselves down on the table.

"Good morning, girls," I said. And to Iris, "Looks like you're having a better day."

She smiled, breaking off a crumb of French toast with her hands and carrying it to her plate. "Your girls have been helping me."

"I set the table," said Kari, her face already smeared with syrup.

"I see that, Kari," I said. "Thank you." Elise's eyes remained focused on little Iris sitting cross-legged on her floral-print plate. "Elise, how were you helping?"

She just shrugged and stabbed a piece of French toast with her fork. I looked to Iris, hoping to catch some sort of answer in her gleaming eyes. But her head was bowed away from me.

Ebullient and oblivious as always, Kari broke the silence. "What's your family like?" she asked, showing everyone her partially masticated breakfast.

Iris looked around as though she wasn't sure the question was addressed to her. As her attention settled on my younger daughter, her wings drooped. "I don't really have one . . . anymore."

"What happened to them?" asked Kari.

The little fairy shrugged, moving wings as well as shoulders. "What happens happened. The world is big; we're small. It's easy to lose things."

Her sadness was palpable, so many times bigger than her. It hovered around the table as if borne by transparent wings.

"It's okay," said Elise, finally starting to eat her breakfast. "You can stay with us."

She didn't ask me if it was okay, and the parent in me wanted to protest on principle. Nonetheless I was glad when Iris answered, "Maybe just for a little while."

When we finished eating, Iris cleaned our plates with one sweeping wave of her arm. Like that, the syrup and crumbs and the little white strings of bacon fat that Allan used to eat but none of us liked were dispatched, perhaps to some other realm. "Beats the dishwasher, don't it?" she said, winking at me. I heard myself giggling, imagining the dimension of banished items. A land piled high with table scraps and lightning bugs, but also with secret treasures stored for safekeeping, with precious children and irritating lovers.

Echoing my own thoughts, Elise asked, "But where does it go?"

"Would it bother you if I said I didn't know?"

Elise shook her head and Iris watched her, an appraising look on her face. "I think it's just gone."

"Can you bring it back?"

The fairy was grave. "Disappearing is easy, but bringing things back is hard. It may be the hardest thing in the world."

———

Iris had been with us for a week, which meant it had been eighteen days since Allan had gone, and I still wasn't thinking about him. Not enough to pick up the phone, anyway, and once again be the first to crumble. It had always been easy not to answer when his cell number appeared on the caller-ID; the calls were never for me. This time, though, he hadn't called. But it seemed like even the girls missed him less with Iris around. Who needed Allan when there was magic in the house, a little more magic each day?

With Iris's help, the housework got done in a snap: dirty socks floated merrily into the washing machine and streaks simply vanished from the windows. Even better, she was very patient with the girls, taking the edge off the long summer days that would ordinarily have had me begging for year-round schooling. Elise in particular had taken to the little fairy, and if she wasn't haunting the college's library or reading in her room, she could be found trailing Iris around the house like an oversized shadow.

Every day I felt I ought to be looking for a new job, but then I would remember where I was and laugh out loud at my nonexistent options. Having been let go by the college, what was there for me? The town didn't even have a grocery store.

After dinner we'd all go out to the back yard and watch the day's radiance give way to darkness. You could see stars blink on almost one-by-one, mirrored on earth by the creepy staccato blink of hundreds of fireflies. Warm nights were a relief after sweltering days, and Iris and I would sit on the verandah and sigh into our wineglass and toothpaste cap.

Iris fidgeted with her cap of wine, picking it up then setting it back down, then picking it up and passing it from one hand to the other. Without looking at me or at Kari and Elise, she asked, "Do you see what they're doing out there?"

"They're catching lightning bugs." Almost every night my girls were out in the tall grass trapping the luminous bugs in a jar.

"Maybe you can't see it from here," she said, peering into the dim yard. "Kari's catching them; Elise is doing something else."

I covered my eyes with my hand and squinted, but I could only see the shapes of my daughters hunched in the grass. They were just figures outlined against a backdrop of tiny green lights blinking on and off.

"Maybe you should go look," Iris said, still avoiding my gaze.

I pulled myself out of the low chair, feeling huge and ungainly and suddenly excluded, and stepped into knee-high yellow grass. It whispered as I waded through it, but I couldn't understand what it said.

I came up behind Elise without her noticing, she was so focused on something in front of her. She knelt so motionlessly that I almost worried about her; she looked like she'd been turned to stone. In front of her, fireflies blinked on and off and she watched them, intently.

I knelt behind her and watched what she watched. As my eyes adjusted to the dark, the lightning bugs came into better focus, and I could confirm visually what I knew intellectually: that even with their lighted butts extinguished, the bugs still existed, flying about as modestly as any fly in the dark. But then, two feet in front of my daughter, I saw one that didn't. The firefly's taillight went out, and with it the whole bug popped right out of existence. I blinked my eyes and shook my head, hoping to clear whatever distortion had produced the effect, but as soon as I opened them I saw it again. The light was snuffed and the bug was gone.

"Elise . . ." I said.

I said it calmly, but she jumped so high she almost fell over. She turned and looked at me with saucer eyes.

"Are you doing that?"

She nodded, a grin creeping onto her face.

I stood up, startled by a tug on the back of my shirt. Twirling around I saw Kari, lifting a jar high in front of her for my approval. "Look, Mom," she said.

In the jar were four lightning bugs, and I stared at them for a long time. When I was satisfied they weren't going anywhere, I looked back to my younger daughter, forcing a smile. "Good job, Kari," I said, backing toward the house. "You too, Elise. Good work."

Stumbling back onto the solid ground of the porch, I felt my heart racing. Iris was still sitting on the edge of an overturned ashtray that served as a bench, and when she looked up at me her tiny face was blank. "What else have you taught my kids?" I asked.

"It wasn't me," she said.

I laughed, bitterly. "Like hell it wasn't."

"Sit down, Deb."

"Don't tell me what to do," I said, weakly. I wavered between sitting and standing before dropping into my chair.

"Do you know what Elise's wish is?"

I looked at her, overcome by a sick feeling in my stomach. "I don't know," I said. "What? To become a witch?"

Iris shook her head, a sad smile on her face.

"Okay, what? I don't know."

"That's exactly the problem," she said, and with a sudden flap of her wings she lifted off the table, floating toward the yard.

"Wait," I said, wondering how we'd gotten so far off track. "I think you should leave." Even I could hear that my voice carried no conviction.

Iris just started laughing, bobbing up and down like a buoy. "You gonna make me?" she asked. "Your kids like me better than you, and we're more powerful than you are. I like you, Deb. So relax, and stop saying stupid things." She turned sharply and flew off into the yard, leaving me stunned and alone.

I grabbed my wine glass and went back into the kitchen to re-fill it. Damned uppity fairy, I thought. First Allan and now her. I thought of calling Allan, making him come back. I had the feeling it would fix everything that was broken, but something stopped me. Pride, maybe. Or something deeper. *It wouldn't fix everything*, my editor-brain corrected. *It would fix everything but you.*

I wandered around the house. Everything sparkled a little more than it used to; it seemed fresh and clean, but also unfamiliar and subtly menacing. I found myself standing in the doorway to Elise's room, looking into it as if for the first time. The room was a sea of lavender, her favorite color. Every surface was covered with either stuffed animals or books, and they all seemed to be watching me with dark accusing eyes. I stepped into the room and sat down on my daughter's neatly made bed.

Her bedside table and the floor in front of it were littered with library books. Setting my wineglass down I picked the top one up. *Magic, Applied* was the title, and the one under it was *Invocations, Spells & Charms*. They were all on similar topics. The topmost book on the floor, *The Magical Encyclopaedia: R–V*, had a rainbow-colored bookmark sticking out its top, festooned with a red yarn fringe. I picked up the book, opening it to that page. There were a number of entries in the two-page spread, but one of them was marked with a penciled-in star. "Summoning," the book said, "is the act of bringing an object or a person to the summoner by means of incantation or spell. The degree of difficulty — and danger — varies with the object being summoned, with even small inanimate objects requiring a moderate to high level of magic. The summoning of persons should not be attempted except by one well-trained in —"

"Snooping, huh?" The voice startled me, and I dropped the book. I whirled around to see Iris shaking her finger at me as if to say *shame on you.* Guiltily I picked up my glass and took a step toward the door, but as I got closer I saw that Iris was smiling. "It's okay," she said. "I snooped all the time when I had kids." She waved her arm in the air, brushing that topic away. "But that's beside the point. Have you figured out what your daughter's wish is yet?"

Iris hung in the middle of the doorway like the littlest gaol-keeper, and I couldn't bring myself to brush past her. Diminutive as she was, I was tinier still.

"No, I was just — " I paused, remembering the book. "Summoning? Is that it? What does she want to summon?"

"Hey, you're almost there," she said.

In her eyes I saw encouragement tempered with frustration and mockery. "It's not Allan, is it?" I asked.

"You got it!" she said, flying in a celebratory circle.

"But the book said—"

"That's right. That's why you should be worried." She flew closer, so close she was looking into my eyes one at a time. "You may actually have to talk to your daughter."

———

I re-filled my glass, then changed my mind and left it in the refrigerator. While it might've been easier for me to tell Elise about the danger of easy answers with a glass of wine in my hand, it definitely would've been harder for her to listen. Taking a deep breath I stepped onto the porch, where both girls were sitting on its edge.

The screen door slammed behind me and they looked up together. "Is it time for bed?" Kari asked.

"Yeah, Kari. Go brush your teeth, okay?" She ran into the house, letting the screen door bang closed again. I had to smile; at least she seemed unchanged. Elise started to follow her little sister. "Elise, can I have a minute?"

She shrugged. I sat in the place Kari had occupied, unsure how to begin. I looked up at the bright carpet of stars, but they were silent, inert. I decided to lie.

"Hey," I said, pointing up. "Shooting star! Make a wish."

Elise looked at me like I was a lightning bug she hoped would disappear. "I didn't see it. Can't make a wish if you don't see it."

I sighed, dropping the pretense. "Elise, what's up with you lately? You've been so quiet." She shrugged again, silent and inert as the stars. "Is it because Dad's gone?"

Nothing.

"You know, it's not like I don't miss him too," I said.

Elise snorted.

"I do miss him. But you can't force someone to be someplace if he doesn't want to be."

"I can," she said, and I saw a scary gleam in her eye. It was probably my imagination, but in that instant her brown eyes seemed to glow green.

"Okay," I said, hearing the quiver in my voice. "I know you've found a way that you think you can bring him back, but—"

"I don't *think*," she said. "I know I can. Even if you don't believe in me." She started toward the house.

"Elise," I said, almost begging, "please don't. What if you get hurt?"

She snorted again. "Like you care."

Shocked, I could think of nothing to say.

"I'm doing it," she said, in an eerie low whisper.

"Elise"—my voice was raising into a shout, the twang of my frustration clearly audible—"just listen to me!"

"No, you listen!" She towered over me, and I was actually afraid of her. "I'm bringing him back, and you can't stop me." She stalked into the house, letting the screen door fall. But this time it stopped before slamming, settling into its frame without a sound.

I sat there for a long minute, looking out into the prairie grass. Fucking Ohio, I thought. Fucking Allan, fucking college, fucking prairie grass. Fucking magic. Fucking fairies.

As if on cue, Iris flew out the door holding her toothpaste cap in one hand, preceded by my wineglass. "Didn't go well?" she asked, landing beside me on the porch.

I turned to her, panicked. "What could happen to my daughter if she tries this?"

"Bringing things back is the hardest thing in the world. Even I couldn't do what Elise wants to do."

"Okay," I said, my patience at its end. "But what will happen to her?"

"It's like ..." she seemed to search for an appropriate simile. "Electricity, right? The wires in your house can only handle so much, and if you try to pull more through them they ... blow a fuse?" She frowned. Maybe this wasn't the simile she was looking for. "Except there are no fuses for this kind of power."

"So what happens?"

"She'll be destroyed. And so will I, and probably you and Kari too."

"What do you mean, destroyed? What does that mean?"

Iris just shrugged, an almost imperceptibly small movement.

"Great," I said, jumping up from the porch. "Thanks! So what do I do, smarty? Clearly I can't talk to her, and apparently I can't stop her." Iris stood on the porch in the strange light-and-dark shadow of my wineglass, impassive. I felt like grabbing her, crushing her in one hand, crumpling her into a ball like a piece of winged junk-mail. "This is all your fault!" I yelled. "I wish you'd never come here!"

"Wishes, wishes, wishes," Iris said. She floated lazily up and toward the house. "Keep dreaming, sister."

I fumed at her for a moment, then went into the house. As soon as I did I could tell something wasn't right. The air seemed shimmery, unstable, and the hair on my arms stood on end. I ran through the hallway to Elise's door and tried the handle, but of course it was locked. Pressing my ear to the door, I thought I heard murmuring, though it might have been the reflected sound of blood pounding in my ears. Otherwise the house was as quiet as it had ever been, which added to the spookiness. Was she trying the summoning now? How would I know? Did magic have a sound?

I rapped on the door with my knuckles. Nothing. I knocked harder with the side of my fist. Stepping back from the door I examined the handle. Maybe if I got a paper clip or a bobby pin I could pick the lock.

My left hand felt heavy, and my ring warm on my finger. My wedding ring.

Not just warm, hot, and getting hotter all the time. I pulled the gold ring over my knuckle as it started to burn, and quickly dropped it onto the hardwood floor. It clattered to a stop, emitting a mild glow, then it wobbled once and slid purposefully under the gap in the door.

"Elise!" I yelled, pounding on the door with the heels of both hands. "Stop! Let me in!"

"Go away," she yelled back. "Why don't you drink some more wine?" The air seemed less agitated while she spoke, which I took as a good sign.

Ignoring her insult, I continued. "I'm not going away, Elise. You have to stop before you hurt yourself." Iris flew down the hallway, and even from a distance I could see that she was worried. "Before you hurt all of us."

"All you care about is yourself!"

The door next to Elise's opened, and Kari stumbled into the hallway in her oversized nightshirt. "I feel funny," she said, leaning against the wall.

"That's not true, Elise. How could you even think that?"

Iris paused in mid-air. "That's a good question," she said.

I blinked, and opening my eyes I saw the little naked fairy hovering over Kari. She was peering into her eyes and feeling her forehead with the back of her arm, as Kari smiled sleepily back at her. I thought of the books in Elise's room. Why hadn't I known what she was reading? How could I not have known her wish? I thought of the wine, and the secret smoking, the three of them all awake before me, making breakfast. My girls used to help me in the kitchen all the time. When was the last time we'd done that?

I shook my head, blinking in the increasingly fuzzy air. My head was starting to hurt, and I felt dizzy. I leaned against the wall for support. "Nevermind that, Elise," I said. "I know why you think it. I haven't been spending much time with you lately, have I? I've just been so ..." *How were you going to end that sentence?* my editor-mind asked. Selfish? Mopey? Pathetic?

"Distracted," I finished, and immediately thought better of the whole sentence. "But that's no excuse. I screwed up, and I'll do anything to fix it."

The voice coming through the door sounded hard, yet brittle, like it could shatter. "You're just trying to trick me into stopping."

I hung my head against the smooth-painted wood of Elise's door. Kari had slumped to the floor, and Iris was hovering with her palms against the girl's forehead.

"Elise," I said, sounding weary even to myself. "I'm not. I love—Ow, what the fu...?" Something sharp had hit me in the shoulder, bouncing off to land on the door in front of me. It was a picture frame, held picture-side-down to the vertical surface of the door by some force I couldn't begin to understand. Turning it around I saw that, of course, it was a picture of Allan. He was sitting on Elise's bed in the old house between our two grinning princesses, all three of them done up in my makeup. I remembered the day; he'd let them dress him up as their "fairy godmother," with a pink tutu over his jeans and a too-small conical princess hat strapped tight under his chin. The lavender wings from Elise's Halloween costume had barely fit over his shirt, bunching the fabric at the armpits in what looked like an uncomfortable way. But in the picture he smiled his goofy smile, holding a wand with silvery streamers in the air over Elise's head.

You couldn't see me in the photograph, standing behind the camera. But I knew how I looked: plain old Deb, plain old clothes, no fun at all. Like an evil stepmother.

My eyes were wet as I looked up from the picture, and the door looked blurry. "Please stop, honey," I said. "I'll give you anything you want, I promise. If you want—Daddy—then we'll get him back." I paused, sniffling. "But not like this, Elise. It's not the right way."

There was a pause, during which I almost thought things would be okay. But then I heard Elise's ice-cold voice. "You don't mean it," she said. "You don't love him."

I couldn't respond. It was at once too simple and too complicated an accusation.

"It's true!" she said, louder now. "You don't love him and you don't love me either!"

Of course I did. I shouted as much. I pounded on the door again, pulling on the handle. I looked around the hallway for something to break down the door with, but there was nothing. There was only Kari twitching on the floor, and Iris hovering over her. There was only me.

"Do something!" I hissed at Iris.

The fairy glared at me. Then she suddenly smiled, in a way that made me sick to my stomach. I will never forget that smile. "There is one thing I can do," she said.

"You're lying!" Elise screamed, and it was the longest, loudest sound I'd ever heard in my life. The glass in the picture frame shattered. I heard things move all over the house, falling and thumping and clattering like loose stones in an earthquake. Iris snapped her fingers, and at last my daughter's shrill scream broke off into unnatural silence.

Iris was gone. Kari was stirring on the hallway floor, murmuring like she did just before waking. I threw my shoulder into Elise's door again and again until the latch finally gave, and I tumbled into an empty room.

———

I'd like to say that I never saw Elise or Allan again. It would be simpler than the truth, and truer than it too.

After Elise and Iris vanished, I put Kari to sleep, then I picked up the phone and dialed Allan's number. It rang and rang and rang, and I wasn't surprised. I was starting to think he was way outside cell range. After that I called the police and filed missing persons reports on both Elise and Allan, though I knew it was a fool's errand.

And then I wept. For hours, for days.

There was a lot of talk in that small town, especially when the police investigated me for killing my husband and daughter. But they never found any bodies, and most people thought I'd simply been abandoned. Perhaps Allan had been cheating, they said. Wasn't our marriage on the rocks already?

Part of me still thought Allan would be back for the fall semester, but of course he wasn't. I started working as a freelancer, refusing to move from the farmhouse and the town that I had never loved and hated more and more all the time.

Kari grew up, as children do, and went off to college on the west coast. She married and had kids of her own, two boys, and then divorced while they were still in school.

I spent many years alone. I grew older than I ever thought I would, until I was so old that I became young and helpless again. Kari's boys were grown by then, and after I slipped on the steps and broke a hip she came home to live with me.

She told me, as many had, that I should move. But I couldn't.

One day I was woken from an afternoon nap by the sound of the front door swinging open on squeaky hinges. It was a small sound, barely audible to my elderly ears, but I'd been listening for it for almost fifty years. A young man and a little girl walked tentatively through the door, looking with shock and fear at the house they thought they knew. I didn't need to look at the pictures on the walls to recognize them; they hadn't changed at all.

I stirred on the sofa and made ahem noises, trying not to startle them, but it didn't work: they both jumped. "Who are you?" Allan asked. "What are you doing in my house?"

"It's my house too, sweetie," I said. "I'm glad you're home. I've been waiting for you for a long time."

Kari came in from the kitchen then, and dropped whatever she was carrying with a clatter and splash. "Daddy," she said, breathless, and sounded just like a girl again. "Elise." She ran to them and wrapped them in hugs while they stared dumbfounded, looking like memory made flesh.

Allan's horrified stare cut right through me. I knew I wasn't beautiful anymore; I was old enough to be his grandmother. I was nobody's princess. Still, he came over to me and held me in his arms. "I'm so sorry," he said, and when he pulled away, his eyes were wet.

My own tears spilled over my eyelids and ran down a wrinkled, unfamiliar face. "I know," I said. "I've always known."

It wasn't exactly a storybook ending, but it was as close as we were going to get.

STORY NOTES:

I pretty much wrote this for the naked fairy humor.

This is one of my oldest stories, one that confounded me for a long time. The first draft ended with Deb offering to call Allan before Elise even got around to magicking dangerously, ho hum. A middle draft, which I used as my application story to Clarion West, let Elise get pretty far and hurt her sister a bit, before Elise listened to reason and desisted. Better, but still unsatisfying. I am still learning this most basic writing lesson: always take your characters to the place they fear the most.

My Only Sunshine

LIEF THOUGHT the wrecked car was a boulder. One of those road-colored cars everybody seemed to drive, it was crumpled against the road's support pylon in such a way that all he saw as he hiked up the wash toward it was dull gray metal. It didn't occur to him that rocks in the desert were never that shade of gray; he thought of home.

The rain was to blame: without the sun reflecting off shiny surfaces, Lief was lost. It had been raining for three days already, almost since the beginning of Arielle's business trip.

It had started as a dull drizzle, which was surprising enough. The town of Sunlight, Nevada, almost never saw clouds, let alone actual *rain*.

But it was while Lief hiked through what passed for a river in those parts—a wash, really, dust-dry most of the year—that the rain had suddenly intensified, blinding him with more water than he'd seen in years. Not long after that, he came across the boulder-wreck.

Once Lief identified the car as a car, he could see the signs: tire tracks leading from the road down into the wide wash, and a pair of deep ruts and sand spray some distance from the pylon against which the car had squashed itself. And—was he crazy?—it seemed to Lief that there was a curtain of even more vigorous rain enveloping the car itself. He looked for other cars up on the road, but of course there were none. Rain was like a natural disaster for the natives of Sunlight, so they'd all be hunkered down in their homes, nervously listening to the foreign sound on their tin roofs.

The tracks in the sand were clearly stamped, fresh. Steam rose from the front end of the car. Lief ran the remaining yards to the car, stumbling in the loose rock and falling once, and splashing his bare legs with gritty mud.

The front end of the car had accordioned. The windshield's safety glass had shattered, but clung together in one wavy sheet. Shielding his eyes against the rain and the imagined horror, Lief peered through the passenger-side window. He thought the man was dead simply from his complexion; beyond pale, it had the bleached look of certain subterranean fish. Water poured into the car from the sunroof, washing his skin clean. Otherwise, Lief thought, there would have been blood. The man had been crushed by his engine.

Eyelids flickered open. Lief jumped, hitting his head on the window frame. "Shit," he said. "Are you hurt? I'll go get help."

"I just wanted to see the sun again," the man croaked. His rheumy eyes looked up into a dark, cloudy sky. And then closed.

It was like the sky opened up. Lief hadn't thought it could rain any harder, but it did. It seemed to follow him as he ran for help, waited while the paramedics pronounced the man dead, and finally walked back home, wading up the ankle-deep river.

It rained all night long.

———

In the dream, Lief was falling. The whole town of Sunlight spread out below him, a jumble of squat buildings with flat roofs. Beyond that, the mottled desert stretched to the horizon, broken only by the purposeful black line of the two-lane highway and the meandering line of the river wash. He fell quickly, loving the way the air streaked past him. As he fell lower, he saw the red rock formations, then the Joshua trees and the creosote bushes, then as he fell lower still he saw a pale man standing amidst the brush and cactus. The man looked up, and in the instant before Lief struck him, he recognized the face as his own. He braced for a crash, but the impact felt more like a splash. As Lief broke apart, bouncing into a ring of droplets, his only thought was *yay!*

The rain was still tapping on the roof like hundreds of tiny hands seeking entry. Lief rolled over in the bed, and was only a little startled to find it empty. The house felt hollow without Arielle, gloomy and dark. He was glad she'd be home later, so he could wake up tomorrow to her long blonde hair tickling his nose.

Lief got out of bed and went about his own business — thank god for telecommuting — but all day he thought about the rain, so after lunch he went for another hike. Fearing dead men, he avoided the river and hiked out into the desert in the general direction of the Sunlight Solar Plant. It was still raining, but lighter now, and as Lief weaved his way around jumping chollas and other spiky plants, he started to feel better. The rain intensified the creosote and sage smells, adding a little ozone to the mix. It occurred to Lief that he liked rain. He missed it. Growing up in the Northwest, Lief had taken rain for granted, even been irritated by it. But in Sunlight it was novel, and it was familiar, and it was warm enough to enjoy. It loved him.

Lief paused, looking up into the praying arms of an old Joshua tree. He shook his head, feeling water fling from the ends of his hair. He decided to go back to the house, clean up a bit, maybe stick a nice bottle of wine in the fridge for Arielle. *She loves me too*, he thought.

Around four in the afternoon the clouds started to lighten. Though it wasn't particularly windy on the ground, the clouds were moving across the sky as though they were being chased. Somehow, though, it kept raining. The clouds would be blown away, but then they would regroup. Shafts of pink-tinged light sliced through them like swords, sweeping the town like searchlights. Rainbows formed, dissolved, and formed again.

Finally, a beam of light struck Lief and Arielle's house, bouncing off puddles in the driveway and giving every surface a gilt edge of sun on water. The air around the house grew mystical with evaporation, even as the rain continued.

Arielle came home a few minutes later. Lief met her in the driveway, swinging her around in a wild embrace before she could even shut her car door. "Isn't this amazing?" he asked.

Arielle certainly looked amazed. She stared at the sky, open-mouthed like a turkey. She ran a hand through her hair, then looked at the hand like she'd never seen it before. "So this is rain," she said.

Lief laughed. "It's the best rain ever! How 'bout a dance?" He held out his hand, bowing slightly.

"You're a nut," she said, smiling. "But I'm going inside. It's wet out here." She grabbed her suitcase from the backseat and shut the car doors, then scurried toward the safety of the overhanging roof.

Lief and Arielle ate dinner out on the covered patio, sipping white wine, listening to raindrops, and recounting their days apart. Arielle told Lief about her meetings with potential Solar Plant investors — she was sure they'd have enough funding to start building the second collector array within months. Lief told Arielle about the dead man in the river, babbling on and on about his waxy skin until she shuddered and asked him to stop.

As the sun slid down the sky, it left the clouds behind and its light poured in under the patio roof. The rain grew stronger too, clouds covering the rest of the sky.

"This is nice," said Arielle.

The weather went on this way for almost two weeks. Sunlight residents went about with surprised looks on their faces, talking about the rain that just wouldn't let up, the battling clouds, the beams of godlike light, the rainbows. It was the most rain the town had seen in thirty years, and it gave no hint of stopping.

Lief found that he liked it more and more every day. He went for long walks, loving the feel of the rain dripping off his hair and running down under his collar. One day he walked two miles into the desert, and when he got home he found Arielle cursing as she hurried to bring laundry in from the line.

"Why were you hanging laundry in the rain?" he asked, laughing.

When Lief saw the look on his wife's face he regretted the laughter. "It was sunny the whole time you were gone," she said. Lief looked up to the sky, noting that it was sunny still, and only just drizzling. "It just started again."

Lief started gathering shirts off the line. "Sorry," he said. "I could leave again."

He meant it as a joke, but from the way Arielle glared at him he wasn't sure she took it that way. She muttered under her breath as she went into the house, "Fucking rain." Apparently she liked it less and less.

Lief waited until he was alone outside before laughing again. As far as he was concerned, she still hadn't experienced rain worthy of complaint.

Arielle left for another business trip the next day. Lief held her new umbrella for her as she loaded her suitcase into the car, looking past her to the mushrooms that had sprouted on the little patch of grass they called a lawn. It was morning, and a double-rainbow gleamed vividly against dark clouds in the west. The rainbows were so bright that Lief could even make out the indigo between the blue and the violet. He pointed them out to Arielle, who sighed and leaned against Lief's side.

"That really is beautiful," she said. "Aren't those supposed to be a promise of no more rain, though?"

"I think it's just a promise of not so much rain that it kills us."

Arielle laughed. "Well then it better stop soon."

"You're not gonna die, you big whiner."

"No?" She turned around to face Lief. "Maybe not. I'll miss you though."

They kissed goodbye, and when Arielle was safely in the car Lief folded up the umbrella, shaking water out of it. "You want this?" he asked, holding it up for her.

"I think you need it more," she said.

Sure enough, the rain got heavier as soon as she drove off. The beams of sun faded away until clouds filled the sky, and it rained like that for three days straight.

Lief dreamed of falling every night. He was a raindrop; he knew that now. He was exuberant with the joy of falling, of being rain, of the wind funneling him into shape, of seeking people and plants to nourish. He loved all the plants and animals and people that he fell on, but the one he loved the most, in his dreams, as a raindrop, was Lief. He would do anything to land on Lief.

On the third morning, Lief woke to a drip on the side of his face, and rolled over to peer up at a yellow stain on the ceiling.

He couldn't help but feel that the rain had done it on purpose, actively burrowing into his house.

He put a saucepan under the drip and called a roofer. And then —and this is how he knew he was losing it—he went for a long drive. In a diner fifty or so miles from Sunlight, he stared out the window into a sheet of rain. When he got home, he couldn't bring himself to ask anyone if it had rained while he was gone. He was certain it hadn't.

On the fourth day, Arielle came home, and the battle-of-the-clouds weather began again. It hadn't stopped raining for over three weeks. In that time, Sunlight had received four times its average yearly rainfall. On his hikes, Lief was starting to notice fungus and mold growing on the prickly pears; Joshua trees were beginning to wilt and droop, their bristly limbs taking on an attitude of despair. In Lief and Arielle's own xeriscaped yard, cactus and other succulents were growing soft with overwatering.

Lief had spoken to Arielle the night before, so he already knew her trip hadn't gone well. Investors were spooked by the sudden yet unrelenting rain and clouds over the Sunlight Solar Plant.

Arielle pulled into the driveway, and the clouds parted. It was still drizzling, but now the house was highlighted in gleaming sunshine, turning water to liquid gold. This time she stepped right out into the trickle of rain. She stood there for a moment before Lief noticed her and came out of the house. "Has it been doing this the whole time I was gone?" she asked, a look approaching fear on her face.

"Mostly it rained," he said. "It rained a hole in our roof."

"Oh my god." She shivered, though it wasn't cold. She turned around in the driveway like she was looking for a place to go.

Lief retrieved her suitcase from the backseat of her car. "You probably want to get inside, right? Or under the overhang, at least?"

Arielle nodded. "I guess I do." They walked to the house but only stood on the porch, looking out at water falling. Water dried on their skin, making their hairs prickle.

"I think I'm going crazy," Lief said after a while.

"Well I can see why," Arielle said. "All the rain. If I hadn't had some sun on this trip I think I'd have gone crazy too."

"It isn't that, exactly. I mean, I grew up in Oregon. I know about rain. But there's something ... different about this rain." Lief stared out into it like a man hypnotized.

"Is there?" Arielle turned to him. "You know, I'd never seen rain before this."

"Yeah, it hardly rains here."

"I don't think you understand," she said, looking into Lief's eyes until he tore away from the rain to look back at her. "I'd literally never seen it before. I'd hardly ever seen clouds."

The thought surprised Lief, but only for a moment. He wanted to be surprised for longer, to disbelieve the statement. He would have, a month ago. But the more he thought about it, he realized he couldn't remember a single rainstorm that he'd been in with Arielle. He couldn't remember one when she'd been in town, before this month. Or even a solidly overcast day.

Arielle shrugged. "The sun loves me."

He wanted to be surprised, but instead all Lief felt was a cold, watery feeling in his stomach. "I guess it does."

————

Lief only got as far as Las Vegas before sunset. He checked into the Treasure Island and called Arielle from his room. "Not a cloud in the sky," she answered, her voice hushed. "And there?"

"It's a real storm," he said. His window looked west into dark clouds against a background of darker clouds. Palm trees whipped side to side by the pool and huge raindrops battered his window. He could imagine their psychotic enthusiasm, seeking him out, and it frightened him a little.

He drove west through Death Valley. The rain did slow down some, but to Lief's growing unease, it didn't stop. He drove south through the Cajon pass and then turned east toward Palm Springs and Arizona beyond. Phoenix. Tucson. Las Cruces. North to Albuquerque. Farther north through the Canyonlands of Utah and as far as Salt Lake City. It rained. Lief pointed his car back toward Sunlight.

It had been a week when Lief pulled back into his driveway, roadweary, missing his wife and the sun. The clouds in Sunlight were the patchy pink he'd come to expect when he and Arielle were both there, rain and sun fighting for control of the sky. It had been sunny and clear all week.

Arielle met him in the doorway with a kiss, but Lief's attention was immediately drawn to the stack of cardboard boxes behind her. He pulled away. "What's this?" he asked.

Arielle's tan face flushed. "The Joshua trees look much better this week. The Plant's output is back to normal."

"That's nice," Lief said, "but what's all this?" He gestured to the boxes.

"Are you really going to make me say it?"

Lief said nothing. He was going to make her say it.

"Well, you have to go," she said, a false light note pushing her voice into a higher octave. "It's not good for the ecosystem or the economy of Sunlight."

Lief tried to smile, but only half of his mouth cooperated. "I know that," he said. "But I thought you could come with me. We'll travel around. We can have two houses. We don't have to spend all our time together—"

Arielle was smiling too now, but her smile was filled with more sadness than all the clouds could hold. "I can't," she said. "It isn't good for me either."

Lief felt like rain, liquid inside. He went back outside before the clouds in his eyes could burst. He walked and walked without knowing where he was going, but he wasn't surprised when he found himself at the river. A thread of water ran down the middle of the wide sandy wash, and he followed it until he reached the road where he'd first found the wrecked car and the dying man. The car was gone now, hauled up out of the wash and probably long-since recycled. The tire scars were gone too. All that was left was the rain; Lief carried that with him now, and he thought he always would.

STORY NOTES:
The final week of Clarion West in 2009 had the hottest few days in Seattle's recorded history, a record that, as I write this in August 2020, has still not been broken, despite climate change. As we eighteen students sweated in an un-air-conditioned sorority house, insane from cumulative sleep deprivation, we were led further into insanity (in a mostly good way) by our instructor Rudy Rucker. He taught us about transrealism, in which the writer twists their own circumstances into speculative fiction.

I did not see this story as transrealism at the time, but in retrospect it's not hard to see how this story was melted out of my brain by the heat. That summer was also the first time I'd spent more than a couple weeks in the city of my birth since leaving for college. At the time, I lived in a desert town in California. But unlike Lief, I do not love the rain.

Frænka Askja's Silly Old Story

"WELL, I DIDN'T WANT to taste that anyway," Whale Breath said petulantly, and dissipated into the dark sky. A scant half-kilometer away, the lights from the new electric plant cast an orange sheen on the already-dark afternoon, reflecting between snow and snow-laden sky.

Móðir didn't *need* me to come in. The animals were put away, and she'd probably forgotten dinner entirely, locked away doing whatever it was she did in her workshop these days. I was older than you are now, little ones. But since Magnús had run off with the submarine whaling fleet and faðir died, móðir thought I was alone too much and kept a closer watch over me. I was late.

But I wasn't alone.

I had a number of good and true friends of discarnate nature who lived at the hot spring. They wouldn't tell me their names, so I was forced to dub them with the most unappealing monikers I could manage — in hopes they'd hate them enough to reveal themselves. That was really the only flaw in our relationship.

"She'll be wanting you the instant she's done," Hairy Troll Bottom advised, a stretch to his steamy limbs that reminded me of squinting.

I sighed. "I'm going. See you tomorrow?"

"We'll be here," came a chorus of their wispy, chirpy, drippy voices. Even the ones I couldn't see at the moment chimed in, as usual, in the ritual goodbye. Of course they would be there tomorrow, and the day after that, and the day after that, for longer than I planned to live. They were made of steam. Where else but a hot spring could my steam friends survive an Íslensk winter?

———

Móðir had her face pressed to the window like a puppy when I came up the path, steam from my water-heated body curling off me into the dark night. I stepped out of my boots, leaving them in móðir's fancy wind-up drying rack. She held her hands by the bustle at her back, the hump in the silly imported dress she'd had to have. The look on her face was a sort of manic excitement that, since faðir's death, I'd come to fear even more than her cold somber silence.

She waited just long enough for me to hang my coat up over a radiator, mercifully not scolding me for being "late," before whipping the surprise out from behind her. It was... something I'd never seen. A collection of bolts and cogs and gears and strips of tin and copper sheet intricately welded into the shapes of limbs and body and massive sheet metal ears, hinged to flop this way and that. It was a type of animal, something I'd seen in drawings in teacher's big reference book. An elephant! One of the whale-large monsters that roamed Africa and other such places. But móðir must have made this one strictly from memory. Its chunky body was a mere wire skeleton cradling blocky copper and wires. Its trunk was long and lumpy, segmented and bendy looking, dropping down between two black marbles sunk into the thing's face to make soulless, lidless eyes.

It was a horror.

Móðir held it out to me, thrusting it toward me as if she wanted me to take the thing from her. I reached out carefully, afraid of sharp metal edges. She'd made me toys before, delicate wind-up birds and sheep and horses, but none of those had looked so menacing, and none of them had made her so obviously proud.

"Well, what do you think?"

The unexpected weight of the thing dropped my outstretched hand as she let go. The tip of its ear snagged in my wool sleeve. "It's heavy," I said, grateful for an honest comment.

Móðir flipped a switch obscenely near the elephant's tail— were elephant tails supposed to be this thick?—and it sprang to life. Its legs moved back and forth and its head shook and its ears tanged like cymbals. I quickly set the thing on the floor, and it scampered off down the hall toward the bedrooms, striking the wall and ricocheting off at an angle.

"What was that?" I asked.

"A gift for you," she said. "A playmate. It runs on battery, so you won't even have to wind it." And she still had the scary enthusiasm in her eyes, so I just mumbled a thanks and asked about dinner.

In the coming days and weeks, more of the animals appeared, all powered by batteries from the new Dreki Anda power station tapping our hot springs. It was indeed convenient not to have to wind the toys, or it would have been if I had wanted to play with them. You understand, I was too old for mechanical monkeys and giraffes and alligators, no matter how intricate their multi-metal scales or how well they clapped pattycake. I turned them on enough to please móðir, then let them run down their batteries until they slowed to a stop.

There were always more batteries, though. Grief-stricken móðir had proven a much more capable negotiator than the battery man assumed, and among other perks for leasing them the land, our farm would always have free power.

I didn't need her "playmates." I preferred the company of the sheep and horses, whose simple, sleepy needs were easily met. I preferred hunting among the rocks and lichen for the Hidden People. I preferred the company of my steam friends. A mechanical shark with thrashing tail and snapping jaws was no substitute, especially one that couldn't even swim. I ruined that one by letting it loose in the spring, where it sank to the bottom like a rock.

The toys frightened me. I was more than familiar with clockwork; móðir had tinkered with it for as long as I could remember. These were . . . different. They were bigger than most of her creations, for one, and . . . angrier. Not cuddly. Not comforting. I'd sliced myself on more than one occasion with a ragged edge of cold metal, and I'd swear some of them were trying to trip me.

But it was more than that. Their behavior wasn't right. I could see most of the gears and pistons that made them work, but even so, I couldn't figure out how they made some of their movements, which changed more than made sense. A mechanical elephant should just walk, endlessly, while the switch is on. Instead, sometimes it folded its legs to sit or raised its trunk to the air. Or fixed its bottomless-well eyes on me for so long that I thought it was either out of power or thinking very deeply.

And maybe I wasn't behaving right either, because sometimes I'd swear the things had intent, a spooky agency to the way their sightless eyes looked at me. I kept them turned off as much as possible.

One snowy day, in the waning light of a long late-winter afternoon, I made the trek to the hot springs only to find it empty.

Don't get me wrong; it had water in it, steamy hot as usual. Just as I always had, I slipped my toes and legs and body into the reservoir faðir had fashioned from carved stone, but the steam that rose from the surface of the pool held no voices, no shapes, no friendship. It was formless and random, mere gaseous water like móðir always said it was.

My friends were gone.

I didn't tarry long, and I didn't rush back the next day. Water alone couldn't take the chill of winter out of my bones.

———

On the third day after my steam friends disappeared, I ran back from the hot spring right past the Do Not Enter signs into móðir's workshop and stopped in my tracks, awed by what her madness had wrought. The place was filled from floor to ceiling with scraps of iron and wood and wires and the assorted parts that made her creations move. As it always was.

But in the center of the space was what had to be her master-piece: a metal horse, bigger than life-size. It looked ready to rear up and trample us both. It had no mouth and only sockets for eyes, but it somehow looked angry, like Dögun did before she threw her rider. The rest of its body was a bundled mass of metal rods and gears and pistons and gadgetry that resembled muscles and tendons. The creature's massive ribcage held dozens of bat-teries wired together by a veritable nest of coiled copper.

"Oh," I said, words failing.

"Isn't it marvelous?" móðir said, creeping out from around the animal's flank. If my calculations are correct, it'll do the work of six horses."

"Marvelous," I replied, slinking away.

Back in the house I sat on the floor of my room surrounded by a clanking and ticking chorus of the unnerving toys. They really were the only friends I had now.

"I miss Whale Breath," I said, watching a tin sheep headbutt the wall again and again while a quadruped that móðir claimed was a zebra traced an intricate pattern in a circle around me. Across the room, a raven turned its head so suddenly that I had to look, and was met with the stare of its black marble eye. It raised both wings and opened its mouth as if to squawk. Luckily, it had no voicebox. But still, the thing seemed agitated. After a minute or two it lowered its wings in a huff, then raised just one, pointing it toward the zebra that still zigged and zagged seemingly randomly around the room. Even the sheep stopped ramming the wall and looked toward the zebra.

The hairs started rising on the back of my neck. "Are you..." I swallowed, "trying to tell me something?"

The raven flapped its wings. The sheep jumped. A number of the other little monsters reacted in some way, each of which felt like a nod. Only the zebra kept doing its thing, tracing strange shapes around me. *Were* they random? By the time it made a circuit I couldn't remember the beginning of it.

When the zebra came 'round again I picked it up, minding the sharp edges as its legs kept working mindlessly in mid-air. I set it on its side while I wrapped a winter coat around me and stepped into boots, then went outside. The raven and elephant and sheep and a couple of others had followed me, alarmingly, and I held the door open for them as they stumbled into the snow.

There were a fresh few centimeters on the ground, windswept into drifts and bare icy patches, but overall still deep enough for footprints. I set the zebra into a clean patch and it took off again, slowly, etching its pattern into the snow. It encircled me, and I took a step back to view the outline as a whole. It had almost come around, and it looked like it had drawn a big-headed shark. Which was impressive, but puzzling. And then the zebra took off at a tangent from the shark's head, exploding upward in a spume of trampled snow, and—

"Whale Breath."

They couldn't talk, but I had my friends back. Sort of. Some of them obviously wanted to play, but others still seemed to want to trip me or cut me with their sharp bits.

I gathered up the friendlies one day, and we all made our slow way back to the hot springs.

The menagerie got all excited when we got there. The raven tried to jump right in, and would have if I hadn't grabbed it. "I'm sorry," I told it. "Water is no good for metalbirds." You see, I had learned from the shark's demise.

The various creatures were all emoting wildly at me. "I know," I said, "it's very exciting." I stripped and slid into the water like a seal.

And instantly regretted it. Hot! Heat! Beyond hot, a feeling like all my skin was exploding, like I was being shocked all over. Pain, unreasonable pain. I flailed my arms, but they were so heavy, those fire-arms, burning even under my fingernails. I opened my mouth to scream, but I slipped under the water and the water shocked down my throat like molten lava. It filled my eyes and nose and ears, and then it was over.

For a few days everything was okay. My old friends ringed all around, and though we still couldn't talk, I understood that they'd been trying to warn me about the spring. Oh well. Too late now. Móðir came 'round to the hot spring eventually, and screamed when she saw my body. It looked bad by then, shrunken and hairless and boiled red like a beet. But I didn't mind. I felt I'd come home.

It didn't last. I felt . . . sucked under. I dove into the hot spring and couldn't surface. Down under the rocks through cracks I'd only ever plumbed with my toes, into the earth I went. Things were dark.

And then I woke up to a jumble of scrap metal and wires and gadgets and gizmos, and a face before me that made no sense — *Magnús?* — and maybe all of it had been a dream and I was in some kind of mad scientist hospital. There was móðir's face next to Magnús's, and I opened my mouth to ask her what had happened, but my mouth wouldn't open, and I heard her tell Magnús, "Isn't it marvelous? If my calculations are correct — " And I screamed louder than I ever have in my life, but it made no sound.

I had no mouth. I was a mechanical horse.

I couldn't scream, but I could flail my strong limbs, which I did. They moved differently from what I was used to, but panic is panic. I knocked things over, hearing them clatter onto the workshop floor. Móðir and Magnús cursed as they jumped back from me, out of the way, and I wanted to hurt them. But they were my only hope, weren't they? If I was ever going to escape, I'd need them to figure it out. I stopped thrashing.

The sound of Magnús's laughter overwhelmed me, and for a moment, I dared to hope that he recognized me in there, somehow looked into the horse's dead eyes and knew his sister's soul, understood what would make a clockwork horse startle. "Yeah," he said to móðir, "this thing will clearly solve all our problems."

———

Móðir tried to turn me off, but I wouldn't let her near the switch. I broke out of the workshop and followed Magnús around as much as I could, which wasn't a lot. I could have busted into the house, but it felt wrong. It was still my home, after all. I overheard some things: Magnús's obvious struggle with wanting to help móðir without giving up a promising career as the hvali kafbátur's chief engineer; his intense hatred of the mechanical menagerie (including myself); my own funeral.

He cried. Big brother Magnús. Who would have thought?

Móðir kept making animals, even the toys that she'd said were for me. They seemed to know me, though I couldn't have said who any of them were. At least the new ones were friendly. The ones who'd been hostile before—the elephant and monkey and alligator, and a few others—seemed to be getting worse. They'd peck at Magnús and wind underfoot like naughty kittens and cause basically as much mischief as five-kilo critters can.

My one goal was to make Magnús see me for who I was. I tried to write him a letter in the snow, but I couldn't get my four feet to make anything but a mess at first, and then it didn't snow for what seemed a long time—spring was on the way, finally. I tried nuzzling him, but he reacted with fear. I was, after all, a monstrous metal horse. I couldn't even bring him things: I had no hands, no mouth.

One day I found him sitting in the small family graveyard. The earth over my body was still mounded, hard as winter. "I miss you, sis," he said. "Faðir was one thing, but you too?"

He started as he heard me behind him. I wasn't a graceful creature. "You again!" he shouted. "Get out of here, you awful thing. Get!" He picked up a stone and threw it at me, and I just barely ducked away. He picked up another. "I'm not kidding."

And I flashed on a memory, an old memory of winters gone by. We always had the most fun with snowball fights: stagey, almost scripted reenactments of Viking battles with all his friends and me, the pesky sister, tagging along, and I always had the same role. I always died first, hammily, hugely, falling and writhing into mounds of soft snow.

Magnús threw a rock at me, and I let it hit me. It didn't hurt any more than a snowball would have against thick layers of sweater and parka. Which is to say not at all — I was made of metal, after all! But I fell. My four legs didn't want to let me, but I made them. I toppled over, not caring if I'd ever get up; I thrashed my legs in the air and rolled and then, suddenly and intentionally, went still as a corpse. It was the best I could do with no mouth to moan with.

Magnús was silent for a long time. He approached carefully, looking at me. My lidless eyes watched him, but I didn't move a piston. Not until he was right on top of me, and then I twitched once more, scaring him so badly he tripped backward over a rock. Man, did I wish I could laugh.

He came up, eyes wide as saucers. "Askja?" And then I wished I could cry. I nodded and nodded my horsey head, and he hugged me despite my coldness, and maybe, I thought, it would be all right.

———

And it was, sort of.

Magnús and móðir worked together to engineer voiceboxes out of radio parts, and eventually all we monsters could talk again. Whale breath and the others still wouldn't tell us their real names or their history, only that they missed the hot springs. We tried sending some of them back into the angry, now-boiling cauldron. But while it did soothe them, the effect was never very long-lived. The power plant sucked them right back out of the earth, and then it was anyone's guess where they'd end up. We lost a few that way. I still miss them.

But the real tragedy was faðir.

It took us a long time to figure out why, but some of the toys — the earlier ones — just never came around. When Magnús and móðir gave them voices, they blabbered. They ranted and raved. They became even more murderous.

The only real clue was in snippets of things that felt like memories. The elephant would look at Magnús and say, "Proud of boating. Just like me." And then it would pounce like a cat and leap on its stumpy legs and gore with its pointy metal tusks. But faðir had been a fisherman in his day, and surely he *was* proud of his son's whaling.

The giraffe and the monkey would team up and use tools to trap us, but then they'd look at móðir and say, "just beautiful wedding day."

We think they all were faðir. It seems the spirit can only be fragmented so much before it goes insane.

It makes me wonder, sometimes, what I might have lost.

We returned all the suspect toys to the springs, hoping maybe he'd be back, but if he has, it was only to illuminate lightbulbs, and we never noticed his particular light.

Magnús went back to the whale submarine fleet for a while but returned while still young, married, and raised your parents. He said he was afraid to die out there under the big sea, afraid that no part of his spirit would make it home if he did.

When he died, your móðir really, really tried to stop Dreki Anda, to explain why that day's power could not be allowed out through the transmission lines to every house and shop in the town. But the plant's new owners were not "superstitious," they said, and the people needed electricity.

I am sorry that the metal bird will never fly.

You are left with me and my silly old stories, and I know it's not enough. At least móðir's tinkering left me a bit cuddlier than I once was. Yes, it's nice when you scratch my furry ears that way.

Yes, I will take you for a ride if you fetch your frænka Askja a fresh battery.

Where would you like to go?

STORY NOTES:

This was one of a shamefully small number of stories I was able to complete while working full-time as editor of a Norwegian newspaper. I was immersed from afar in Norwegian culture, but the story that came to me for the *Ghost in the Cogs* anthology just would not work without massive geothermal power. So it would have to be Iceland.

Iceland is a truly enchanting country that I've been fortunate to visit twice. On my second visit, I even went to Elf School! It's common knowledge in Iceland that other intelligences share the land with the island's human inhabitants. I haven't heard any Icelandic stories about steam ghosts, but if such things exist, that's where they are.

Apology for Fish-Dude

OKAY, SO THE Seizure Pox plague was bad. I mean, seriously. Whichever motherfuckers set that apocalypse loose deserved whatever the CIA and the FBI and the goddamn NSA or whoever could come up with. Homeland Security, maybe.

But there were only two words I could think of for the flying tigers and lions and shit: Fucking Hilarious. I wanted to *be* the genius who came up with that one.

You never really saw them in the city, except maybe flying so far overhead you could hardly tell what they were, but one time T-Rex showed me a vid on his wrist implant that had me laughing so hard I snorted water out my nose. You see through the window on one of the downtown monoliths onto the deck, and there's this dog out there, a beagle I think, and you can tell whoever's snapping the vid is messing with the dog because it's looking right at you and dancing around like it wants to come inside. Then a flash of orange-y fur and the dog is gone. Gone. But the best part is the sound the dog makes. It's like he doesn't even have time to bark, and he just goes "oorf!" as he's yanked up into the air.

Maybe it's because we were goofy on CyBeans, but T-Rex and Koan and me were laughing about that damned dog all the way down to the lake. Oorf!

Koan was the one who turned us on to catfish noodling. He came from somewhere south, where before the Pox they used to noodle for fun, apparently. I did it for food.

The spot we liked best was out by the old water cribs. Once, my mom had told me, the lake reached almost to the tops of the cribs. Water from the top would go down through them, into huge pipes under the lakebed, and to the city. Now they were useless and spooky, standing ridiculously tall out of the shallow water like a pair of crumbling fairy tale towers. Maybe the spookiness is why no one was ever out there by them. I couldn't figure any other reason, because there were almost always fish there.

As usual, T-Rex was the first one into the water, stomping in without even taking off his boots. "Here, fishy-fishy," he called, peering down into the water in the predatory way he now had. "Hey," he said, looking up at me and Koan still taking off our shoes and jackets, "who wants to bet I catch the biggest one?"

We just nodded, pretending we thought T-Rex was funny. I, for one, was so jealous of his new infrared/UV-enhanced eyes that I wanted to pry them out of his face.

So we spread out around the cribs looking for the lakebed holes where catfish lived. What you do is stick your hand into the hole until a catfish bites it. Then you pull the fucker out of the water and go to shore, and then you can maybe knock him off with something, or else their bites relax once they air-drown. I swear, it's the weirdest thing in the world, but it *worked*. So whatever.

Except it wasn't working for me that day. I saw psychedelic colors and geometric patterns in the water and the blue spring sky and written on my own skin, but I didn't see any fish. I could hardly even spot their holes. And even when I did find one, let me just add: nothing makes you feel like a 'tard faster than crouching in the garbage and muck of Lake Michigan with your fist in a hole waiting for a fish to fucking swallow it.

Koan had waded out farther to the north, using his other trick. He'd sit in the shallow water like he was meditating or something, and wait for a trout to come to him. I don't know why they did, if he had some secret bait or something. But then he'd tickle the trout's belly and the fish would sort of go to sleep and he'd just pluck it out of the water. Koan was a strange duck all right. He could've had any body mod he wanted, but all he got were some old-fashioned tattoos of Asian writing on his face and arms. They weren't even luminescent or chameleoskin.

Anyway, the sun hadn't even come close to the tops of the monoliths when T-Rex and Koan quit. Koan only had one trout in his bag, or else he probably would've shared with me. T-Rex had a whole bag of catfish, plus a salmon he'd snagged with one of his forearm spikes. It was more than he could eat by his stingy self, but I knew he'd sooner throw them to the flying kittens than share with me, so I was no way gonna ask him. They left me knee-deep in the greasy lake with my empty bag on the shore, T-Rex shouting "we are the champions!" as they went. Sometimes I hated him.

Another hour passed, or maybe two, and I'd gotten desperate enough to wade far out where I'd have to dive under the water to get to the holes. I'd never been so far out before. Finally, I found a spot with some boulders under the water and a little while after I got there I *finally* glimpsed a fucking fish. It was just hanging out next to a boulder, rather than in a hole, so I thought I'd try Koan's tickling trick. I snuck up on the fish, standing on the boulder above it, and slowly reached out and touched it by the tail. That was when I noticed it wasn't a trout or a catfish. It was some kind of pretty fish, like one of those fancy-finned Japanese goldfish people used to keep as pets, only big. It was as long as my arm, with shiny orange and yellow scales and long wavy fins. The fish didn't dart away when I touched its belly; it just flicked its flashy tail and stayed where it was. After a while I felt it go rigid, and as quick as I could I grabbed it and wrestled it out of the water.

So I was standing on a boulder, far out into Lake Michigan, soaked but feeling triumphant, almost legendary, hugging the fish to my chest.

And then the stupid thing had to go and talk to me.

"Hey kid," he said, and I was so startled I almost dropped him right back into the lake, end of story.

His voice was totally human. Maybe a little on the high side, but not, I dunno, fishy. "Put me back in the lake and I'll make it worth your while." His mouth opened round and wide when he talked, like an O.

I couldn't really think of what to say. I mean, I'd never talked to a fish before, no matter how many CyBeans or SuperX tabs I'd taken. But I was thinking that if someone had figured out how to stick furry wings on a lion and make it fly, a talking fish didn't seem so impossible.

"Yeah?" I asked. "Like how?"

The fish's long pectoral fins moved against my chest, pushing with surprising pressure. They were almost like little arms. "Like however you want," the goldfish said. "Whatever you wish for."

I thought for a minute about all the sweet body mods I couldn't afford on the money I made slinging for T-Rex. I thought about the monoliths, the sorts of people who lived in them. I thought about girls. I thought about the file under my bed: GED study guides, Northwestern and UIC-UC application forms, financial aid forms. Ultimately, though, I shrugged. How much could you ask of a goldfish? I set him down in the water in front of me, and he swam in a happy circle before looking back up at me with his spherical dark eyes.

"So what'll it be?"

"Naw," I said. "You go on with your life, little fish." I looked around at the flat lake in front of me and the sun setting behind the monoliths on shore. "I just wish I had something for Mom and me to eat for dinner."

"No worries, kid," he said. "Go on home to dinner. Catch you on the flip side." The fish raised a fin to me before he turned and swam out into the lake, leaving a rippling wake behind him.

———

The shanty town east of Lakeshore Drive had been officially closed down a few years back, after the Seizure Pox ran its course and the city's buildings sat half-empty. But they hadn't got around to bulldozing it yet, and so it still crouched there against Millennium Park and the rest of the city, between the monoliths and the shrunken lake.

Those days the only folks there were the homeless kids who ran away from the orphanages, a few tramps and squatters who poached from the allotments and farms, the Docs, drug dealers, and various other nogoodniks like myself. I was born down there, in the luggage compartment of a stripped Greyhound bus. I walked by the bus on my way home, patting the gray dog for luck. Mom used to tell me stories about that dog when she ran out of books to read me, heroic stories where the little Greyhound pup always grew up to achieve his dreams. I hadn't heard any of those in a while, though.

He was spotted orange like a rust Dalmatian now, but he still looked determined. If nothing else, this was one dog that wouldn't be eaten by a flying tiger.

Home now was on the third floor of what had once been a college dorm. The only positive to it was that there were books there, stacks of them, that had been just left behind when the school closed. When no one could see me I'd smuggle the books into my room and read them, though it took me forever to puzzle through all the words.

Usually the dorm smelled like feet, or worse, but that day as soon as I got into the ground floor lobby I smelled food I couldn't even describe. I mean, I don't think in my whole life I saw food like I did that day. The lobby was crowded with all the people who lived in the building, former shanty-dwellers like Mom and me. They'd pushed a bunch of folding tables from the dorm's student center together to hold a feast. Just offhand I saw three plates of roasted meat, fruit salad, deviled eggs, and what looked like pies — I wasn't sure, because I couldn't recall ever seeing one before. There was no fish.

I spotted Mom as she came out of the crowd toward me. She was holding a plate in one hand and a fork in the other, and — my favorite part — she was smiling. "You won't believe it," she said, hugging me without setting down either her plate or her fork. "The city came today and they finally installed our rooftop garden." She was ushering me toward the tables now, gesturing with the fork. "There's no veg, 'cause they have to grow. But all the trees are mature. So there's beef, pork, chicken, eggs . . . well, you see. It's like a miracle. They installed the wire cage and the water system too."

I nodded, looking at the spread. Our neighbors must have been cooking all evening. "Way to go, fish-dude," I said. I hadn't thought he could do it.

Mom looked at me funny then, her eyes narrowing and forehead wrinkling up like she was looking straight into my thoughts.

"Fish-dude?"

I laughed. "You wouldn't believe me if I told you."

"Wouldn't I?" She was serious then. Motherly. Her look was like a dare.

Still I tried to shrug it off, speaking as casually as I could. "I let a magic fish go today, and I guess this food is my reward."

Mom just nodded. I couldn't tell if she believed me or not, and I didn't know which thought worried me more.

I woke up to Mom sitting over my bed like a fucking gargoyle, and nearly shit myself. "Fuck," I said, rubbing sleep out of my eyes and sitting up against the wall. "What the hell, Mom?"

She was holding a cup of real coffee and smoking a factory-rolled cigarette. For real, something was up. I got really suspicious, though, when she handed both luxuries to me.

"I want you to go back to the fish."

"What?" I asked. Coffee and adrenaline aside, I really wasn't awake yet.

Mom looked at me with her firm teacher look. She'd been a teacher once, before the Pox. I'd been a student. When she spoke again she enunciated slowly and clearly. "I want you to go back to the fish, and ask for a better home for us."

I couldn't think of anything to say.

"Look," she said, "you saved the fish's life, right? And he offered you a reward. Now just because you didn't think of it at the time doesn't mean we should miss out on what we deserve." Mom fidgeted. I thought she was regretting handing me the cigarette. "Don't you want anything?" she asked, but she didn't wait to hear. "I want to live in one of the monoliths." She went to my window. I couldn't see out of it from where I sat, but I knew the view: alley and cinderblock wall. "In the penthouse."

"I dunno. That seems — "

"Don't you remember the stories I used to tell you? How if you worked hard you'd be rewarded?"

I nodded, but she was still turned to the window and couldn't see me. "Yes," I answered.

"And haven't we worked hard? Don't we deserve something nice?"

She turned back to me then, and it was with such a look of sadness and sternness covering a lurking threat that I didn't see that I had any choice. The fish would have to be asked.

What I did have were priorities that momentarily outweighed Mom's nagging. As soon as she went back to her own room I threw the previous day's clothes back on, still a little crunchy from dried lakewater. By then I was feeling clear enough to get out there and sling the seventeen CyBeans I had tucked into the seam of my vintage denim jacket. With the cash I'd been stowing in my hollow boot heels, if I sold these I'd just be able to afford a base-level body mod, like T-Rex's spikes or some horns or maybe luminescent hair, if I could haggle the Doc down. Any of these would be a hit with the other slingers and basically a must if I ever wanted to get a promotion from T-Rex. I was still nowhere near affording the plug-ins I really wanted, though, the ones that would make me smart enough for a real career.

In the daytime, people came out of their homes, and the marina and shantytown was almost a busy place. Even Grant Park had people in it that day, clean-looking people who walked dogs on leashes but were flanked by serious-looking men with rifles. I thought about flying tigers and giggled. Oorf! There was one kid about my age playing Frisbee with a Golden Retriever. His clothes looked like mine, denim with patches and shit, but I could tell he was a phony; the holes in his jeans had square edges.

So I sold him two CyBeans for a third over shanty price.

So I'd sold all the Beans by the time the sun was overhead, and I was feeling pretty good. I killed a little time in the shanty, putting off Mom's errand, but finally there was nothing for it but to go.

I walked all the way out to the water cribs before I realized I didn't know how to get ahold of the goldfish. I mean, it wasn't like he had a cell phone. "Hello, mister fish?" I called, feeling insecure about it. Thankfully, my voice didn't echo. "Fish-dude? Oh, mister magical fish?" It turns out there *was* a faster way to feel like a 'tard. I picked up a flat lake rock and skipped it out over the water. It bounced eight times before sinking into the small waves. Finally, in a quiet, questioning tone: "Here, fishy-fishy?"

He popped up out of the water right in front of me like he'd been there all along, waiting for the magic words.

"You're kidding," I said, but I'm not sure he heard me.

"What's up, bro?" the fish asked. He looked at me with his right eye, then adjusted in the water a little to use the left. Both seemed deep and dark.

I didn't know what to say, so I picked up another stone and flicked it underhand out past the goldfish. Ten skips. He ducked underwater and swam in a little circle before looking at me with the right eye again. "I'm sorry to bug you," I said.

I don't know if fish can shrug, but if they can that's what he did. He waved one pectoral fin at me dismissively.

"And thank you for the food. You totally outdid yourself. I mean, I only asked for dinner, and you gave us the whole garden. It's like that saying that if you give a man a fish . . . well, you know." The fish's eyes didn't have pupils, so it was hard for me to read his expressions. I tried to explain. "It's just a saying Mom always used to say, about — "

"I know the expression," said the fish.

"Okay, right, cool. Anyway, thanks a lot."

"No problem," he said. "No scales off my tail."

I picked up another stone and tried to skip it, but it just fell into the lake.

"What's wrong?" the fish asked. He swam a few yards out on his back, watching me select the next flat stone.

"It's my mom," I said, winding up. "She wants to live in a fancy apartment. A penthouse, she says. She wanted me to ask you." I looked the fish in the eye and let the stone fly. It skipped six times before the fish stopped it with his fin. I didn't see how he was holding it without any thumbs or anything, but that fish somehow managed to skip the stone right back to me. It landed at my feet on the shore.

"No worries, kid. Go on home — it's 1030 North State Street now, top floor. Your mom'll be there."

"For real?"

The sun glinted off the fish's golden scales as he bobbed in the water. "For real. Anything else?"

Again I thought of the colleges, the illegal college prep plug-in mod that I figured was the only way I'd get there. I'm still not sure why I didn't ask, but I know Mom's greyhound stories were on my mind, and not in the way she'd used them that morning. *He'd* never needed magic. "Naw," I said. "You've done enough, little fish. Thanks a billion."

Again he waved his fin at me and flipped away into the lake.

———

The penthouse was fucking boosted. I can categorically say that I'd never been in a home that big, never even thought they could exist. It was bigger than the elementary school I went to before the Pox, an entire floor of a monolith. We had our own kitchen, bigger than both our rooms in the dorm put together. We had a whole room stocked with food. We not only had our own bathroom, there were three of them, and they had bathtubs made from polished stone. There were two rooms for each of us. The floors were made of shiny strips of wood laced together in a pattern, and the ceiling was so high I couldn't touch it even with a running jump. There were windows on every wall, more window than wall, and they looked out so high above the city that it felt like no one else lived in it.

Mom was there when I got home, and she was dancing with joy. Literally. She had on a long black dress and some wobbly-looking shoes that tapped on the wood floor, and she held a tulip-shaped glass by its stem in one hand, and a factory-rolled cigarette in the other. I mean, the apartment had come stocked.

"Check it out," she said when I came in. She tripped over to a wall and flipped a switch, and the clusters of sconces hanging from the ceiling — which I'd taken for candleholders — lit up with warm, yellowish light. "Electric light."

I stared, feeling like a yokel for being so impressed. I mean, it wasn't like I'd never seen a lightbulb before. Of course we hadn't been wired in the Greyhound bus in the shanty town, but the dorm had a generator, and even used it on really special occasions.

"It works all the time," Mom said, a reverent hush in her voice. "And so does the elevator. The building's communal garden is right above us on the roof, and let me show you this." She stubbed her cigarette out in a green glass dish, still with a half inch of tobacco left, and pulled me by the wrist down the hall. The room we entered was full of books — books from floor to ceiling, so high that the room came with a wooden ladder that slid on a track. The room even smelled of books, dry and papery and just a little musty.

"So?" I said. "Like I care about books."

Mom looked up at me then with her eyes clear and seeing. "Yeah," she said. "Of course you don't."

So Mom was pretty happy for a while. We had all the food we wanted from the meat and fruit trees and the other communal plants on the roof, and Mom was really happy with the new neighbors. Sure, she still didn't have a job, and I was still slinging for T-Rex, but the other folks in the building didn't know that, and they treated us like we were just like them — business people and bio-designers and lawyers and doctors. Educated. Owners of things. Mom went to all their parties and drank wine and flirted with professional men. She dated some, but always decided that the man wasn't good enough. "Oh well," she'd say, tossing a string of pearls over her shoulder. "There are plenty of fish in the sea."

It was an expression, I knew, but it threw me off every time. I thought of one fish. I thought of a lake.

I didn't have to go noodling anymore, so I didn't. T-Rex and Koan went a few more times, but I guess it got old when they couldn't make me feel like a loser for not catching anything. I was glad when they stopped, because the thought of T-Rex snagging my fish with his spikes made me sick. I thought he might kill the fish, even if he was offered wishes. But on the other hand, I thought he might wish for something seriously messed up.

I kept checking the Docs' storefront, but the prices for plug-in mods stayed high: a high-school education plug was almost twenty grand, or another 3,461 sold CyBeans. And after that I'd still have to think about upgrades, synapse boosting, and of course tuition. And then maybe I still wouldn't be good enough to be a bio-engineer. It depressed me when I thought about it, so I mostly didn't.

Sometimes I thought about asking the goldfish for some money, but I always decided not to. When I really thought about getting mods my stomach twisted up like the time I drank lake-water.

Meanwhile, while Mom was out on dates I read books. Our library had a lot of things that I'd need for the GED, and it also had an Internet link. Sometimes I'd download vids on my phone to show T-Rex and Koan, though I never found anything quite as classic as the one of the dog getting eaten.

I thought living at the top of a monolith I'd finally see some flying tigers, but I never did. I did see lots of flying housecats, though. They'd come up to our windows and I could get them to chase my fingers. They'd hang on the mesh of our deck with their claws, mewling. I wanted to get a better look at them, so one time I brought one inside, a tabby, mottled wings flapping in my face. It scratched me and I let it go, and then I spent the rest of the day chasing the fucker around the apartment to get it out again. Mom was mad. Lots of the glass and ceramic what-nots the apartment had come with broke that day.

So things were good, but still I wasn't surprised when Mom told me to go back to the fish. "Ask him to give me a man," she said. She stood at the window looking out, I presumed, on the dark city beyond.

"I dunno if the fish can do that," I said.

"Of course he can." From way up where we were we could hardly see any light, save a few fires on the lakeshore and the occasional light in a monolith window. And of course the moon and stars.

"Well then, I don't know if it's right."

She didn't turn from the window, though I wasn't sure she could see anything in it but the reflection of us and our electric light. I could see her face reflected there, a look in her eyes that she used to have when she'd tell me about her and my dad back before I was born and everything went wrong. It was an expression as dark as the night outside. For a second I actually thought she might cry. But then her face hardened. "What the fuck do you know, anyway?" she said quietly.

I thought about that question for a while. One thing I sure as shit didn't know was how to answer it.

"Ask him for a man," she repeated.

"What's the matter?" I asked. "No more fish in the sea?"

———

The goldfish was waiting for me when I got to the cribs. "Yo," he said, "what's happenin'?"

I sat in the shade of one of the huge round towers, taking off my boots and socks and rolling up my trouser legs. It was still morning, but already hot and muggy. "I dunno. Not much, I guess. How are you?"

The goldfish wiggled in the water. "Can't complain." As I waded in he lifted a pectoral fin to me like he wanted a high five. I hesitated. "Don't leave me hanging," the fish said.

I touched his fin with my hand, and he swam in a little circle. He looked like he really enjoyed being a fish. I picked up a flat stone and gestured to the fish. "Go long."

We skipped stones to each other in silence for a while. Finally the fish swam back over to me. "Why don't you tell me what you want?"

"What *I* want?" I looked up at the sky, the towers of the cribs. "Mom wants you to give her a man."

"Oh," said the fish, and his mouth reflected the O perfectly. Fish always kinda look surprised, but right then he really did.

"Tell me you can't do it," I said.

"I can do it."

"Oh." I sat down in the water, suddenly unconcerned with getting my clothes wet.

"This makes you sad," he said, swimming close to my lap. I loved the way his tailfin moved, like flames in the water.

I shrugged. "I guess so."

"You really want me to do it?"

I thought for a while. The fish waited. "Yeah, I guess I do. Mom seems sad, you know?"

"Think this'll fix it?"

"What the fuck do I know?" I said. It was so quiet, I'm not sure the fish heard it. When I looked down, though, I saw that my hand rested on his flank, just in front of his dorsal fin.

"Okay then," he said, his mouth barely out of the water. "No worries, kid. Go on home and he'll be there."

I took a long walk home, wandering around Northwestern's Chicago campus for a long-ass time. It didn't look like much, especially since it was summer and classes were out. I sat on a bench in a plaza and looked up at the tall buildings — they were just like the monoliths, actually, but covered in ivy instead of the climbing supervines that strangled the low-end monoliths and the garden plants that hung from the posh ones. I stayed for hours.

I got back to the apartment as Mom was getting ready to leave. A man sat in the front room. He was tall and thin, but not in a starved way, and he wore glasses with wire rims. He stood when I came in, and offered me his hand.

"This is Lloyd," Mom said from another room. I could envision her putting on jewelry or make-up or something in her enormous closet-room. I still thought it was weird that this was something she did now, but I'd gotten used to it. She'd dated a lot of fish.

As they left, she smiled and whispered in my ear, "I've got a good feeling about this one."

"Me too," I said. But it wasn't true.

Of course they hit it off, and before long he'd moved into the apartment and they were talking about getting married. I was wicked pissed about it at first, but it turned out that Lloyd was, if nothing else, a totally smart dude. He caught me reading a bio-chem text one night, and I was all embarrassed, but he acted like it was totally normal. Turns out he was a bio-researcher and professor at UIC-UC, a real egghead, and he was as obsessed with plug-in mods as I was. He studied the plug-ins, and people with them, even though he could get fired from the college for it. He'd lean over my books in our library, helping me study for the GED test or just teaching me about things I always wanted to understand but never thought I could. Like he explained not only the mechanics of how the cats were able to fly, but how the retro-gene worked on their DNA and how the changes were passed along to their kittens. I just listened, most of it going over my head faster than a flying cheetah. I knew once I had my plug-ins everything he said would make sense. But the thing that got me was that he didn't have any mods at all. Not even a plug-in.

Actually, he really hated the plug-ins, and I think he even hated the people who had 'em. He said they were dangerous, and that only people who were selfish and lazy and — I had to look this one up — *callow* would use such a thing. I thought it was easy for him to say; he was smart without 'em.

He also hated drugs, especially the new ones like the ones I sold. One time, he went off on this lecture about drugs while I was *on* drugs, and it looked to me like his head was getting bigger and bigger as he talked, and I thought about him just floating up until he hit the ceiling, and it was the funniest thing ever at the time. So, you know, I never introduced him to my friends. But then, I wasn't seeing much of them anyway. I hadn't even told 'em about our new digs.

Mom smiled a lot, for a while. Over time, though, I could see that faraway look creeping into her expressions, and I knew it was only a matter of time before she came to me again.

When she did, I knew right away what she wanted. On the dining room table sat a glass box maybe three feet long by two wide by two tall. I'd only seen one once, at one of the posh monolith parties. It was an aquarium.

It was winter, and every time I lost my footing on an icy street I hoped I'd drop the tank and it would break and I'd be off the hook. I didn't though. And it was just as well; I knew she wouldn't let it rest at that anyway.

The lake was frozen in the shallows, so I walked out past the cribs, sliding the aquarium along the bumpy ice. It had been stormy when the water froze.

When I'd gotten as far as I dared, I called for the goldfish.

It took a really long time before he appeared, popping his head out of a hole in the ice off to my right. I wore a scarf and a hat, but no gloves, and my fingers were freezing. "Hey kid," he said. "Come to shoot the current?"

I smiled and walked over to where he'd surfaced. I knelt down to give him a high-five. The cold water on my hand made it feel even colder; for a moment I was worried my hand would freeze to his delicate fin like a tongue to a lamppost. "How's it going, fish-dude?"

"Okay," he said, then he saw the aquarium behind me on the ice. When he spoke again his voice was lower. "What does your mom want now?"

I glanced back at the tank too, and knew that the fun part of this meeting was over. "She wants you."

The fish ducked under the water quickly, then came back up. "What do you mean, 'she wants me'?"

It would have been easy to walk away then, to shrug it all off and go back to the penthouse. But I realized then that I didn't want to go home alone. So I lied. "She's so grateful for everything you've done for us that she wants you to live with us. You know, so you don't freeze out here."

"Is that all?" he asked. A cold wind gusted, shaking me as I crouched on the ice. The fish looked at me first with his left eye, then with his right, just like he'd done when we met.

"I'd like you to come too," I said. I could hear my voice shake, but I wasn't sure it was from the cold. "You're my best friend." It was true.

The goldfish disappeared under the ice, then surfaced in a different hole, nearer to the tank. When he returned, he asked, "And that's all you two want from me? Your motives — and your mother's — are pure?"

There was probably a part of my mom that felt the way I'd said. She *was* grateful, and sometimes even said so, praising the fish as the miracle that he was. But her motive for wanting him was about as pure as the snow on downtown streets.

It took me a while, but eventually I said, "Yes."

The fish looked at me for a long time, evaluating. "I thought you cared about me," he said. He dove down again, and when I saw him again he was much farther out into the lake.

I stood and shouted, "Come back! I do care!" I moved forward a few steps on the ice, terrified that I would fall through.

"No worries," the fish said bitterly. "Go back to your home. It'll be as you deserve." He jumped out of the water and made a gesture with his tail in the air that I was pretty sure I understood.

"Please!" I yelled.

The fish jumped again, and there was a shadow across the air, and a flash of orange that had nothing to do with shiny scales.

It wasn't quick, and it wasn't funny.

The flying tiger was a mass of orange and black fur, twitching and hungry and shockingly *physical*, wings cutting through the air powerfully yet almost silently. It pounced while the fish was still in the air, but instead of catching him cleanly and hoisting him into the air like the dog, the goldfish was knocked across the ice, skipping like a stone. I could see him flopping and thrashing, looking for a hole to get back underwater. I took two quick steps forward before I felt the ice cracking and stopped myself.

The tiger's paws barely touched the ice before it leapt, swatting the goldfish across the ice again, closer to shore and to me. Pale fish blood splattered and froze.

The goldfish was screaming, but if the tiger thought anything of it, I couldn't tell. Between the shrieks of terror were words, entreaties. "Please!" he yelled, "Let me go; I'll give you anything you want!"

But you can't reason with a tiger. The cat batted the goldfish around until the screams died down and I thought with relief that the fish had finally died. Then the tiger started to eat its prey, and the goldfish made a noise of such anguish that I will never stop hearing it. The wail echoed off the surface of the lake as if reluctant to leave. And then it was truly quiet, save the muted crunching of fish bones. When it was done, the tiger looked at me, pink tongue licking its face, and it was only then that I felt the freezing tears on my own face, and remembered to be afraid.

As I started to run, the tiger flew up into the air, and it was so fast that I knew it would catch me no matter what I did. So I turned around to see.

I watched the tiger alight as gently as a feather on the top of the nearer water crib, fold its wings down onto its back, and disappear inside the ancient tower.

———

I don't know why I carried the aquarium away from the lake with me. In fact, I didn't even really know I'd done it until I found myself on the street in front of the monolith we lived in, staring stupidly up at the towering building.

I hadn't expected the penthouse to be there when I got off the elevator. I thought I'd find somebody else's home, or an empty ruin. It was all I deserved.

I have the aquarium to this day; it's one of many similar tanks in my corner of the lab. But that one remains empty. I've learned much about the variations of DNA, in the phylum Chordata and elsewhere in the animal kingdom, much more than I ever thought my unplugged brain and its unboosted synapses could comprehend. I've tested the boundaries of a fish's brain and a fish's power. I've made goldfish that walked on land, goldfish that warbled like canaries, goldfish with knowing looks in their dark eyes.

But I have yet to make a goldfish who will understand my apology.

STORY NOTES:

This story was written during my second week at Clarion West (yes, that place again — it's incredible and I recommend it to all aspiring writers of speculative fiction). It remains one of my favorite stories.

It's a retelling of the folk tale, "The Magic Fish," with some very major differences. In the original fable both the fisherman and his greedy wife are punished for asking too much, a rather straightforward morality tale. I was planning to follow that storyline in my version, until I became stuck writing the ending. After sitting up most of the night fretting about my impending deadline, I decided to write a totally unfair ending, in which the one truly innocent character is punished. Interestingly, my protagonist learned a deeper lesson from his Pyrrhic victory than he ever could have from a just outcome.

The setting of this piece was inspired by my long-standing fascination with apocalypses large and small, my time at Roosevelt University in Chicago, and my desire for flying tigers and meat trees. Somebody needs to get cracking on those.

Acknowledgments

DEAR READER,

I'm writing this to you from mid-August 2020, and if you're reading these words, I guess the world hasn't ended yet. I've just looked at the calendar and realized that this book's birthday is one week after the USA's presidential election. I hope we aren't mid-Constitutional crisis or civil war by then! I hope we've kicked the coronavirus's ass and you are gathered with loved ones, remembering how to hug.

In no particular order, these are people I owe hugs to, people without whom you would not be reading this book:

• My friend and publisher, Patrick Swenson. Thank you for accepting my somewhat unhinged query, for taking the chance on this project, and for being so patient with my first-book nervousness.

• Tim Powers, who began as my creative writing professor at the University of Redlands and became a dear friend and mentor. Without your totally unreasonable support for my mediocre writing, I probably would have quit a long time ago. Thank you for making me see the speculative fiction light. I can't imagine how drab my writing life would have been without ghosts and aliens and flying tigers.

• Stephanie Taylor, mother-in-law extraordinaire. You once set an emotional whiplash speed record by making me cry before we even got home from the airport, then more than made up for it by sending me to the Kenyon Review Writers Workshop, my first real taste of what the writing life could be. At that workshop I wrote a story about you, and no one found your character believable. Maybe work on that.

• Jeremy Goodman, husbot, hater of cities. Thank you for insisting I apply to that fiction MFA even though it was in Chicago. You don't roll your eyes too much at my made-up science, and you never take offense at characters who maybe share a few of your traits, for better or worse. Thanks, babe!

• My Roosevelt University MFA program cohort – Michi Trota, Krys Buckenwolf, Emily Culella, Ron Estrada, Jim McCarthy, Lori Rader-Day, and all the others whose names I cannot remember and yet whose poetry and prose remain etched in my mind – you made that experience worthwhile.

• Everyone at Clarion West. Seriously, everyone. The workshop is life-changing not just because of the amazing instructors and students (though mine were fab!), but also because of the incredible community supporting it.

• Too many people to name have spent their precious time critiquing my drafts or providing much-needed writerly moral support: almost all of my CW '09 "siblings" but especially Randy Henderson, Persephone D'Shaun, and Jordan Lapp/Ellinger; "cousin" Liz Argall from Clarion '09 (sorry I made you cry the first time we met), Andy Romine, Lauren Dixon, Caren Gussoff, Cat Rambo, Rashida Smith, Micaiah "Huw" Evans, Tod McCoy, Tegan Moore, and the other rotating members of Horrific Miscue. Thank you all!

• Every story needs an editor! Special thanks to Sheila Williams at *Asimov's* and Scott H. Andrews at *Beneath Ceaseless Skies* for their significant and thoughtful editing of the stories of mine they published. Thank you for seeing the stories I meant to tell and helping me tell them.

• Mom. I won't be able to hug you even when the 'rona is under control, because you died last December. I wish you could've held this book in your hands, but I also can't help thinking you got out of here at the right time. You wouldn't believe what a shitshow this year has been.

Life is short, and as far as I know, all of the methods for cheating death presented in this book are pure fiction. And yet life goes on, for some of us. Seeing my first book become a reality is a dream come true even in this darkest timeline, and I'm grateful for it.

About the Author

EMILY C. SKAFTUN'S tales of flying tigers, space squids, and evil garden gnomes have appeared in *Clarkesworld*, *Beneath Ceaseless Skies*, *Asimov's*, *Daily Science Fiction*, *Strange Horizons*, and more. She holds an MFA in Creative Writing and attended the Clarion West Writers Workshop in 2009.

Emily lives just north of Seattle with a mad scientist and their Cat, Astrophe. She is the former editor of a Norwegian newspaper and practices bokmål by translating comic strips. She's cofounded two online magazines, edited a tie-in anthology, and judged a Scandinavian haiku contest (haikuff-da!).

An avid traveler, Emily has cuddled a crocodile in Cuba, attended Elf School in Reykjavík, frightened fish in a Yucatán cenote, and flown over an active volcano. She's spent a summer backpacking Europe, six months living in London squats, and nine months exploring all but five U.S. States while living in a VW Jetta.

Emily doesn't want to live forever, but wouldn't object to being reincarnated on a sunny, wise planet.

Publication History

"Melt With You" originally published in *Clarkesworld*, Issue 79, April 2013 | "Diary of a Pod Person" originally published in *Asimov's Science Fiction*, October 2014 | "Last of the Monsters" originally published in *Strange Horizons*, October 2010 | "Frozen Head #2,390" previously unpublished | "Ten Things to do in Los Angeles After You Die" originally published in *Every Day Fiction*, October 30, 2012 | "Only the Messenger" originally published in *Beneath Ceaseless Skies*, issue 299, March 2020 | "The Thing with the Helmets" originally published in *Clarkesworld*, Issue 150, March 2019 | "The Taking Tree" originally published in *Daily Science Fiction*, May 13, 2013 | "Oneirotoxicity" previously unpublished | "Dad's Christmas Presence" originally published in *Every Day Fiction*, December 29, 2015 | "No Alphabet Can Spell It" originally published in *Buzzy Mag*, May 2015 | "A Matter of Scale" originally published in *That Ain't Right: Historical Accounts of the Miskatonic Valley*, September 2014 | "Snow Angels" previously unpublished | "Down in the Woods Today" originally published in *Attic Toys*, March 2012 | "A Fairy Tale" originally published in *The Colored Lens*, Issue 6, Winter 2013 | "My Only Sunshine" originally published in *Flurb*, Issue 8, Fall/Winter 2009 | "Frænka Askja's Silly Old Story" originally published in *Ghost in the Cogs*, October 2015 | "Apology for Fish-Dude" originally published in *Ideomancer*, Volume 10 Issue 1, March 2011.